HIS WICKED LOVE

CUFFS AND SPURS BOOK 2

ANYA SUMMERS

BLUSHING BOOKS

Published by Blushing Books®,
a subsidiary of
ABCD Graphics and Design
977 Seminole Trail #233
Charlottesville, VA 22901
The trademark Blushing Books®
is registered in the US Patent and Trademark Office.

Anya Summers
His Wicked Love

EBook ISBN: 978-1-947132-14-6
Print ISBN: 978-1-947132-33-7

Cover Art by ABCD Graphics & Design

CHAPTER 1

LATE SEPTEMBER

*W*ell, if those numbers didn't just chafe his ass.

Mason checked and re-checked the account ledgers. He'd been over them more times than any sane person would, but he wanted—needed—to be certain they were correct. The loss they'd sustained three months ago had been substantial. With what was left, they'd be lucky if the Black Elkhorn Lodge and Resort didn't shut its doors by Christmas.

"Are you sure about the numbers?" Cole asked.

Mason glanced across the expanse of his mahogany wooden desk at his brother. There were lines of tension in his shoulders and tanned features that were so much like their dad's, including the dark chocolate shade of his hair that he wore past his shoulders and his brown eyes nearly the color of soot. Whereas Mason took more after their mom, with his lighter shade of brown hair and eye color—in a manly way, of course.

His gut twisted. Despair and dread seized him.

Mason detested himself for their current plight: the lodge was nearly bankrupt. And it was all his fault.

Before all this, Mason had prided himself on reading other people. He'd been cocky about it. As a Dom, he'd considered his ability to size up a person to be top notch. But their last chef had proven him wrong. His arrogance had cost them. Mason hadn't seen the fraud and deceit behind the chef's apron before the no-good piece of trash had embezzled nearly every penny the lodge had.

He could still remember when he'd discovered the theft. The disbelief, the anger. His normal fun-loving personality had vanished overnight. The lodge, the dream their parents had conceptualized and that he and Cole had actualized, had tail-spun out of control. They had gone from having excess capital with savings to spare, to barely limping along and teetering on the brink of collapse.

In the last three months, they'd had to liquidate their investment portfolio just to keep their noses above water. But the costs of running the lodge were considerable. It took capital to make this place run.

"I'm sure. We are well and truly fucked. If we make it until Christmas and are able to pack guests in, maybe we can string things along enough to begin rebuilding," Mason replied. But word had spread about their legal woes no matter how much damage control they'd tried to do. Without a functioning restaurant on the property, the Black Elkhorn Lodge and Resort had received cancellations in droves. The once prosperous getaway hemorrhaged funds daily.

"Well, with the restaurant currently closed, we're losing a stream of revenue right there," Cole said, telling Mason something he already knew. Still, he was glad they were both on the same page.

Frustrated, he slammed the account ledgers shut and irritably ran a hand over his face. The irritation was all self-directed. Mason couldn't remember the last time he'd genuinely smiled. In the three months since the bottom had been yanked out of their business and a person he'd trusted had robbed them blind, there hadn't been much reason to smile. When he observed himself in the mirror every morning, he no longer recognized the person in it. The haggard expression and grim line of his mouth. The permanent scowl and self-loathing.

Life, for Mason, had once been a bountiful banquet, and he'd never given it deeper thought than the fun to be had. Now, it was a steaming pile of horse manure. He replied, "I realize that. While you were leading the fishing expedition trip this past week, I contacted Le Cordon Bleu on the west coast for a recommendation. We need a chef running the restaurant if we have any hope of staving off further losses. I figured we need all the help we can get at this point. Not to mention, it could be a potential draw in our advertising to have a fully trained chef from such a reputable institution. As much as we adore her, Tibby can't handle the load or full responsibility. Not that she's not capable, but she balances her time here with her daughter's needs. I can't make a single mom give me more time than she's able. Our new chef should arrive today."

Mason could only hope that re-opening the restaurant would staunch the flow of cancellations. They'd attempted to keep it open with Tibby and Faith pulling extra shifts here and there. He'd had them pare down the menu to just the basics. And those two had nearly staged a coup—not that he blamed them one iota. The onus was on him, not his employees, to improve the situation at the lodge. They already gave the lodge one hundred and ten percent. The rest had to come from him.

Mason had made the executive decision to close the restaurant temporarily a month ago. He'd directed Tibby and Faith to prepare boxed lunches for sale, limiting their hours, with the promise that it was temporary so he didn't lose them.

Mason had made sure their paychecks didn't reflect the loss of hours. Since then, guests had cancelled their reservations in droves.

Mason didn't blame his guests one bit. The Black Elkhorn Lodge and Resort wasn't close to the downtown hub. Their lodge was about bringing people back to nature. That was one of the premier selling points. And normally, with a fully functioning restaurant on the property, the place tended to thrive. Except most people didn't want to have to drive forty minutes just to grab a bite to eat.

Each of the lodges had a small kitchen with a stovetop, as well as gas grills. But people on vacation liked to eat out. Many wanted to kick back and relax. Re-opening the restaurant would, he hoped, get customers to rebook their stays with them.

"Just like that?" Cole asked, his face filled with concern. Mason was just thankful that when the shit hit the fan, Cole never once pointed the finger at him. He would have deserved it. They both knew who was at fault for their dire situation, but instead of hanging Mason out to dry, his older brother had stood by him.

Mason sighed and said, "Her background check came back clean and, to be honest, we're in a pickle. Tibby and Faith have at least been able to supply boxed lunches for the hikers, but with closing the restaurant, they've been picking up more catering jobs. If we want the slightest chance of keeping the lodge from hemorrhaging even more money, we need the restaurant back open for guests this week. Billie informed me this morning that there were two more cancellations today due to the fact that the restaurant is closed."

"Shit. All right. If you're sure about this new chef..." Cole replied with a grimace. Mason knew Cole would rather be out at his private cabin, avoiding people and surrounded by nature than dealing with the running of the lodge. It's why their partnership had always worked—if not seamlessly, at least without too many blips. He ran the business side and catered to guests, while Cole was in charge of leading hiking, fishing, hunting, and sight-seeing expeditions, away from the bulk of civilization.

"I'm not," Mason admitted with a shrug in an attempt to ease the anxiety building up. "But the problem is we don't have much of a choice."

The only thing that would ease his mind, take him out of his current default state of tension, would be playing with a sub at Cuffs & Spurs. Being balls-deep inside a willing woman was the only cure, even if it was a temporary reprieve. Or, at least, it used to be. Problem was, he'd not had a chance to make it into town and the club since the top blew on his world.

"Any word on the legal proceedings against the culprit?" Cole asked, leaning back in his leather chair, avoiding use of the chef's name. They both had stopped using the thief's name. It was easier to use separation, make it feel a little less personal than it had been.

Mason wished that the legal matters had been concluded. Then he would have a definitive answer on when they would get paid for all their accounts. Some weren't willing to work with them at all and were demanding payment. With a shake of his head, he said, "No. Not yet. Other than they haven't found what they actually *did* with the stolen funds and that the money was all gone. The prosecutor has assured me that part of the sentencing will include restitution but that the court would most likely allow the defendant to make payments, which doesn't help us one bit."

Cole cursed under his breath, his face stern and lines of worry present in his normally calm demeanor. He asked, "When does the new chef arrive?"

"Today at some point, out of Los Angeles," Mason replied. He could only hope his instincts were better with this one than the last and that they were worth the recommendation. The lodge couldn't afford another fiasco or for his judgment to be off in the slightest. One wrong move at this point and everything he and Cole had built with their dad would go up in smoke.

Cole snorted. "You mean part of our plan to keep this place open rests on the shoulders of someone from the land of Hollywood? Brother, I hate to tell you, but the chances of someone from the west coast willingly trading in for life here is slim."

Mason understood that all too well. This new chef, an Emily Fox, just needed to stay long enough to get them back into the black. If she didn't work out after that, well, they'd cross that bridge when they came to it. "We just need someone for now. It doesn't have to be permanent. In fact, I mentioned in passing during my conversation with her that it was a temporary arrangement, with a trial run included."

And the rest of their exchanges had occurred via email. In what little communication they'd had, Miss Fox had been blunt and to the point. For the time being, that was what they needed.

Cole shrugged. "At least that gives us an out. I have a few expeditions to lead this week. Day trips, so I will be around at night to help out."

"Focus on the trips. I've got the lodge covered. And Alex's trail rides are busy this time of year. So that will help," Mason added. Their buddy, Alex, used the Black Elkhorn Lodge stables to run his trail riding company. It was profitable for both parties. While Alex had his own employees taking guests on trail rides, if there any spillover, he or Cole picked up the ride. Likewise, on the lodge, if Cole and Mason needed an extra hand, Alex filled in when he could.

Thankfully their previous chef's sticky fingers hadn't

extended to the stables. It didn't hurt that Hunt Trail Rides was a separate company, either.

Didn't mean there wasn't a good chance that they weren't royally fucked.

"Are you sure this new chef can cook?" Cole asked, a pensive expression creasing his brow.

Fuck if I know. "She comes highly recommended. Has been a sous chef for two years."

"Actually, it's four years, but who's counting, right?" said a sultry female voice from his office doorway.

Mason glanced up and was glad he was seated. Emily Fox's resume and background checks had provided him with a boatload of facts about his new hire. But they hadn't prepared him for the red-haired siren currently standing in the wooden door frame. The long waves of her hair reminded him of the sunset, the myriad hues of burnt orange and sienna hung over delicate shoulders and more than ample cleavage before ending above her trim waist. Her skin was smooth and the color of iridescent pearls, which only seemed to magnify the natural pale pink hue of her lips that were not overly plump but perfectly formed.

Yet it was her eyes that were the real killer. On top of a voluptuous form that made the Dom in Mason want to weep in thanks, her hazel eyes were large pools that sparkled with lively zest and were surrounded by a wealth of inky lashes. Intelligence flashed in her gaze. The electricity of it zapped through him.

"You must be Emily Fox," Mason said, finding his voice after nearly swallowing his tongue. Standing, now that he'd found his legs, he shoved away the unwanted and rather inconvenient lust she evoked in him.

"You'd be right about that," she said, with a hint of sarcasm that she softened with a grin as she placed her free hand on her denim clad hip. The other clutched the handle of a small leather satchel about the size of his goody bag. He must have been in a mood when they'd briefly talked on the phone because the sound hadn't affected him as it did now. The dulcet tones curled along his spine, into his gut, and made his dick twitch.

"I'm Mason Stewart. This is my brother and business partner, Cole," Mason informed her. His gaze roved over her form. While she was dressed casually, in a pair of well-worn blue jeans and fitted mint green Henley top that accentuated her curves, with a black jacket tied around her waist, Miss Fox was anything but casual. She was stunning—exotic, even. He couldn't help but wonder what she looked like naked.

Yet her demeanor didn't scream *Rodeo Drive*. That was good. It made her appear accessible and down to earth. As though, perhaps, if he and Cole played their cards right, she wouldn't mind trading in city life for country life in Wyoming.

"Pleasure." Emily smiled and nodded towards Cole, who tipped his hat in her direction in greeting. From the expression on Cole's face, Mason surmised he wasn't the only one a bit taken aback by her looks. It should make him feel better that he wasn't the only who'd been momentarily struck dumb, but it didn't. He couldn't afford to be attracted to the newest chef. The paradox of it, given their current situation, was not lost on him.

"I'm glad you made it early. Hopefully the drive wasn't too hard on you. If you like, I can have the front desk get your belongings to your cabin. Then I can show you the restaurant and where you will be working," Mason said as he emerged from behind his desk and walked toward her. He gestured with his hand outstretched to take the case from her and help her out. Miss Fox really was a small thing. While he was six one, he had to look down to meet her gaze. He hadn't known what to expect—certainly not the vision before him.

Yet instead of handing it over, she shifted the case behind

her back and held her other palm up, stalling his forward progression.

"Hold up, cowboy, no one touches my knives without losing body parts. I know I agreed to accept the position over the phone, but I need to see the kitchen first before we go any further," Emily said, her sultry voice making him think of sex. Long, languorous, Tantric style sex before a roaring fire. Sex that left a body boneless and too sated to move. Her voice was sex, plain and simple. And it made his dick hard in his jeans. Mason tempered the unexpected and rather unwanted desire she stirred within him. Or tried to.

Instead he settled on annoyance with a simmering underbelly of lust, which only served to piss him off. It had been way too long since he'd availed himself of the subs at Cuffs & Spurs. And his knee-jerk reaction to his new chef proved that. If Miss Fox was going to prove to be a mistake, he'd rather know now. And if her bossy attitude didn't end, he would toss her out on her ass. Contract or no.

"If you want to lug a heavy suitcase, be my guest, sweetheart. I think we need a demonstration, a sample of your skills, before we go any further. Don't you?" Mason challenged, letting his annoyance creep into his voice. She'd accepted the position without the clause of needing to see the kitchen first. So she thought she could toss in an extra demand, put a wrench in his plans to bring the lodge back from the brink, test who was in charge? It wasn't her. Miss Fox could try but she would fail. This was his place and he would fight like a rabid dog to save it, to protect it further from outside harm. He wouldn't ever allow the lodge or himself to be overrun by a pretty face.

She smiled. The air was charged between them, electrified, as she stared him down, then said, "Cowboy, once you've had my cooking, you will be my slave and beg me to stay."

An image of Emily, collared, naked, and on her knees

begging him to take her, flashed through his mind. The unbidden thought unleashed a windfall of lust and it roared through his bloodstream. Mason tensed, beating back the unsolicited desire. Compartmentalizing the unwanted, erotic images, he narrowed his gaze. "Doubtful. I could take my pick from twenty line cooks today from one of the restaurants in town."

She rolled her eyes in an exasperated fashion and asked, "Then why did you call me?"

"That's what I'm beginning to wonder," Mason retorted, not admitting that he wanted a chef at the top of their game. That he believed if they offered culinary delights not found at other resorts or restaurants, they would attract customers, and maintaining the current menu that was a crowd favorite was paramount.

She was their Hail Mary Pass, even though she didn't know it. Nor would he tell her that. She already had an overabundance of confidence.

Cole intervened, severing the electric livewire connection as he stepped between them. Mason finally inhaled a deep breath while Cole gave him a brief glance with his brows raised high enough they nearly disappeared beneath his Stetson, and a *what the hell?* expression. Then Cole shifted fully toward Miss Fox, his face calm with the pleasant smile he typically used to win over a sub, and said, "Emily, why don't I take you over to the restaurant and you can see if it's to your liking? We updated the kitchen two years ago and have all the latest equipment. Not that I have any idea what all those gadgets do."

It was the gamine grin, the spread of her pale pink lips exposing her straight, white teeth, and transforming her face into breathtaking. And it was directed at his brother. It shoved Mason toward caveman status. He wanted to snarl at Cole to back off, not to touch her, that she was his. Which was fucking asinine, and only fueled his internal engines to near record levels.

"That would be fabulous. Thank you. Is he always like this?" she asked Cole, indicating Mason with a jaunty tilt of her head. Her hair shifted, making it shimmer.

A half grin spread over Cole's face and he replied, "No. Sometimes he's worse."

Emily's full-bodied, sexy laugh sucker-punched Mason in the sternum. The sound skittered along his spine and pooled in his groin. The throaty, jazz singer sound made him wonder what she sounded like when she came. It made him yearn to discover whether she was a screamer or issued almost silent, throaty moans. There was a part of him that wanted to bend her over his desk and fuck her until his legs buckled.

"Good to know," Emily responded with another shake of her head which made the waterfall of red tresses shift and move like flames. The color was so vibrant, Mason ached to feel the strands in his hands. Would they be as soft as he imagined, or would they singe his flesh?

"It is; better to be armed and prepared. If you'll follow me," Cole murmured, diffusing the situation and ignoring Mason.

"Honey, I'd follow you anywhere," Emily flirted. With his brother. Jealousy gripped Mason, which was idiotic at best. He couldn't want Emily. Wouldn't allow himself to desire her. One, she was his employee and there were some roads that were better left untraveled. Two, he wasn't sure he liked her. She was brash and mouthy, and most likely as vanilla as they came.

But that didn't seem to matter to his dick, who liked the thought of playing boss and naughty secretary with her a little too much.

Except then Cole picked up the ball Emily had lobbed his way and responded, "Likewise, sweetheart. Mason, you coming?"

Almost.

And from a damn fantasy. He shook his head, attempting to distill the lust raging through his veins. He bit out, "I'll be right behind you two."

Mason watched Cole lead Emily from his office. His gaze, trained on her perfectly formed, heart-shaped ass, did nothing to detract from the fantasy. He adjusted himself and winced at the discomfort.

Breathing deeply, he called on his training, on the stalwart control that made him a Master, to corral his needs to a more manageable state. Using that control, he remembered the last time he'd allowed lust to guide his actions. It was akin to dousing himself with a bucket of ice water.

The absolute last thing Mason would do would be to allow his hormones to do his thinking for him. He'd done that once, and look where that had gotten them.

CHAPTER 2

*B*eefcake central, party of one.

Emily surveyed the Black Elkhorn Lodge and Resort as one might an alien planet. A testosterone-laden alien planet.

The scenery was gorgeous, both the outdoor and indoor variety. During her trip there, driving on highways through mountain ranges to reach Jackson Hole from Southern California, there had been moments of breathtaking beauty, along with mind-numbing terror at the sharp twists and turns. She was from Los Angeles and they had mountains aplenty. But the peaks in Wyoming made the ranges surrounding downtown Los Angeles seem like nothing more than baby mountains—foothills, really.

The beauty of Jackson Hole, Wyoming, the area surrounding the lodge, was postcard worthy. The sky was a pristine, vibrant blue with no hint of smog. The air even smelled different here. Clean, fresh, with a hint of wet earth, and pine. Thick forests of pine trees with deep emerald boughs blanketed the lower elevations of the surrounding mountains. Those were interspersed with rolling fields of tall grass and wildflowers. The first hints of autumn were upon the land, and the deciduous trees' foliage was in its final glory, sporting bright gold, deep maroon, and vibrant orange leaves.

The Black Elkhorn Lodge and Resort was billed as a retreat away from the hustle of city life, an oasis where a body could relax and ease their worries. She knew this because she'd fully researched the resort online when Mason Stewart first contacted her about the position five days ago. The land, the cabins, and the attractions were offered to appeal to the outdoorsy type—to someone who just wanted a quiet reprieve away from it all. She'd scoured reviews on various travel sites. Over and over again this place had been proclaimed as super friendly, a home away from home, the staff was excellent and just the nicest people one would ever meet.

And so far, the physical lodge was more beautiful than the pictures had captured. The structures on the property, from what she'd viewed when she parked by the main building, were woodsy; hickory colored log cabins with a rustic appeal. They blended in with the surrounding forests and fields as if they were a part of the land.

Emily surmised the guests' reviews about this place being friendly was because they'd never been introduced to the co-owner, Mason Stewart. Her instant dislike for him was most likely due to fatigue from her drive across country. And the fact that she hadn't eaten much more than fast food—chips, all things snack cakes—and had imbibed large enough quantities of coffee that her blood type had probably changed from O negative to classic roast. Emily's philosophy, considering both the making of and consuming of food were her life, was that when she went on a road trip, her snack supplies looked as if she were a ten-year-old left unsupervised with a hundred bucks. So she was fueled on Ho Hos, Ding Dongs, salt and vinegar potato chips, and slim jims. The road trip fuel of champions.

Which meant her knee-jerk internal reaction to her new boss was likely due to the over-caffeinated sugar high currently inhabiting her body, and not because she actually found the jerk attractive.

But she did. Devastatingly so.

From his trimmed golden walnut hair peeping from beneath his dark brown Stetson to his piercing, light brown gaze that made her think of melted caramel, his tan face was a contrast of hard planes and angles that, when put together, made him appear carnal and sinful. And yes, it had been a long, long time since Emily had looked up from her mixing bowls and pots to notice anyone.

But Mason Stewart, with his broad shoulders and rangy build clad in denim and plaid was without a doubt the most inherently alpha male she'd ever come across. Emily had nothing against the metrosexual movement. But, well, many of the men she'd come into contact with or had dated were soft. Not in the sense that they didn't work out, because hello, Los Angeles was the land of hard bodies and fitness gurus, the land where the kale movement began. But Mason was different. His confident aura saturated the space around him. He was raw and unapologetically male, as if he'd been hewn from the very mountains outside.

And then there was his brother and co-owner of the Black Elkhorn Lodge, Cole. Whereas Mason was clean-cut in his cowboy appearance, the brother... not so much. Cole was just as handsome, without a doubt. But he didn't spike Emily's blood like she'd been sitting in a broiler too long. She could see the resemblance between the brothers. The similar builds. Except, Cole's hair was shades darker and fell in thick waves an inch or so past his shoulders. Instead of a clean-shaven face, he sported a shadow beard with a few days' growth the same shade.

Mason's gaze had rankled the fabric of her being and heated

her insides up like a pressure cooker. Whereas Cole just made her feel comfortable, with his easy smile and languid gaze. Which was why she didn't mind harmlessly flirting with the cowboy mountain man in his jeans and navy flannel shirt.

The lodge itself was stunning. Glossy wooden pine floors, exposed beam ceilings, and all manner of stuffed animal heads on display on the walls. Emily would never understand the need to stuff and mount the head of some poor animal killed for sport. She understood the food chain and the need to feed people. But the idea of killing something for fun had never appealed to her.

The main lodge held the front desk that made her think of the O.K. Corral with its Western design, a great room with huge flat screen television, and a stone fireplace, surrounded by a plethora of sumptuous sofas. There was a bar in the corner of the great room that again sported the Western theme. She'd read that they hosted parties for weddings here and had a cocktail hour in the evenings. Beyond the great room, she spied a door that led to the indoor pool. The lodge offices were located on the opposite side of the building from the Elkhorn Restaurant.

The place she'd been hired to run. The place that would save her from needing to crawl back to her family a failure.

Emily strolled beside Cole, his long-legged gait in seemingly no hurry, down a long hall that sported doors for employees. At the end was a doorway made of tempered glass and wood with the name of the restaurant etched at eye level into the pane. The logo was a lone elk with its proud head raised, its stately horns bracketing the restaurant's name. Off in the right hand corner next to the door was a black hostess stand and small seating area with a wooden bench for waiting customers. Cole held the door open and ushered her inside the Elkhorn Restaurant.

"This is the restaurant, through here. There's also an

access door on the opposite side for guests coming in from the cabins," he explained, flipping on lights. Mason had explained over the phone that the restaurant had closed unexpectedly with the previous chef's departure three months ago. That the sous chef wasn't full time and couldn't handle the load.

Emily hadn't known what to expect when she'd packed her car in Los Angeles and struck out for a new adventure after subletting her apartment. She'd undertaken the journey partly because she had to and, in some respects, also because she needed the infusion of change in her life. She needed to prove that her choice of career was worthy of respect from her parents and siblings. Her dad had undercut her news of being named head chef with another dour outlook for her future and career. He couldn't even give her one moment, one victory that was hers.

She grimaced. The last thing she would do was allow him to spoil this for her. So what if her new boss was a bit of a jerk? She'd worked with far worse in the food industry. Not to mention, from the moment her little Mazda had crested the ridge overlooking the valley where the Black Elkhorn Lodge resided and driven the long, winding lane onto lodge property, she'd been impressed. Picturesque didn't even cut it.

They'd have to put her feet over flames to get her to admit that, at least to Mason. Yet, as she viewed the dining room, with Cole silently watching her reaction nearby, she realized the place exceeded her hopes. The rich, golden hued cedar walls created a warmth in the restaurant. The tables were decorated with crisp ivory linen cloths spread over them. The wooden chairs in a darker ebony complemented the color scheme. But it was the large bank of windows with a clear unobstructed view of the craggy mountaintops that was the true beauty behind the restaurant. It said: *Come, warm yourself by the stone fireplace. Enjoy a cocktail at the bar. Bask in the serenity of the scenic outdoors from the comfort and luxury of this fine dining establishment.*

Excitement hummed in her being. This was a place where she could carve a name for herself. It made the two-day drive across four states fueled by coffee and snack cakes, away from everyone and everything she knew, potentially worthwhile.

"It's lovely—the view, I mean," she said to Cole, watching fluffy white clouds scuttle past mountain peaks. A massive bald eagle swooped and danced gracefully on air currents before it dove beneath the tree line of evergreens to some unseen prey.

Cole stood beside her, a grin on his face as he looked out the window with her. "Yeah. It never gets old. And this is why I could never live anywhere else. The kitchen, which will be your domain, is back through that door."

He guided her through the tables toward their destination. Excitement, and possibly trace amounts of her sugar rush, riddled her form. What Emily spied in the Elkhorn Restaurant was possibilities. A good chef knew that not only did their edible creations need to be mouthwatering to make people clamor to come back for more, but the presentation itself was essential.

They passed through a wooden and glass door that swung on hinges and Emily barely contained her gasp.

The kitchen was a wet dream for a chef. Industrial, top of the line grade ranges with multiple gas burners, an entire griddle station, ovens, broilers, a multitude of deep fryers. A stainless steel center island prep arena. From what she could see, there was every tool she could possibly desire at her disposal. Granted, she'd want to rearrange a few items, make the work stations flow better, from chopping to prep to cooking, but overall, she loved what she saw. She peeked inside the deep freeze and the dry storage, already taking note of what they were lacking in stock. Mason had promised to have the restaurant resupplied for her arrival so she could re-open the place on day one—and he hadn't lied.

"Does it meet with your approval?"

Emily cursed under her breath and swiveled toward the speaker.

Mason.

He'd finally decided to join them. And she hated to admit that his attractiveness hadn't diminished. In fact, heaven help her, it had increased. In her experience, any man who inspired the desire to strip and beg him to screw her brains out was dangerous, and a recipe for disaster. Then there was his aura, his confidence, his alpha, domineering energy suffusing the kitchen and putting her on edge.

"It's manageable. Not what I'm used to, of course," she replied blandly, wanting to thunk her head against the wall. Unexpected sexual need combined with a sugar high were poor bedfellows.

Emily had to control herself better around Mason, regardless that he seemed to irk her merely by breathing. Or that his direct, forthright glare caused need to simmer low in her belly.

Focus.

She inhaled a shaky breath. She needed the job, not to act like a horny teenager without a lick of sense. After the epic way she'd quit her previous job as sous chef at La Vida almost a month prior, her options on the west coast were limited to chain restaurants. She knew that because she had looked and had doors slammed in her face. It didn't matter that her soufflés were out of this world or that she could whip up a batch of pumpernickel bread that made angels weep with pleasure. Until the furor of her departure had faded in people's minds, Los Angeles and restaurants in any other major city were out of her reach.

Temporarily. She'd make a comeback if it killed her.

In order to have the slightest chance, her testy behavior and sarcasm with Mason had to end if she wanted an attempt to make this place work. Otherwise, it was so long, dream of having her own kitchen, perhaps even owning her own place one day. Instead, it would be hello, Olive Garden—forever. And yes, that last infusion of sugared crème from that ding dong had been a bad idea. Regardless, she should watch her step. It would help, though, if the man didn't vex her, almost like he was doing it on purpose. At this point, she didn't know whether she wanted to smack him or kiss him. Nor did she want a definitive answer to that question.

She laid her case that carried her set of Yaxell Damascus knives on the center prepping island.

"You really carry knives with you?" Cole asked, running a hand over his shadow beard, contemplating her. She didn't miss the flicker of *hope this chick's not crazy* that flashed through his kind gaze.

She wanted—nay, needed—to put her new bosses at ease and make them like her. Perhaps if she won Cole over, Mason would follow suit.

Giving Cole her friendliest smile, she replied, "Yep. They're a bitch to get through TSA security when I fly, too. But it's not uncommon, we chefs tend to find knives that we like, that work well for us, and will guard them like they're our children. If you two want to give me an hour, tops, I can prepare a lunch for you as my test run."

She glanced between the two brothers. Big men; rough cowboys bred and forged by the land. And yet only one set her blood boiling and spilling over the ledge. It didn't bode well for her future here and she'd not been in town an hour yet.

"It better be worth the wait," Mason said and swiveled on his heel, stalking from the kitchen.

Her hand closed around the handle of her paring knife. It took everything inside her not to lob it at his back.

Yeah, that whole redheads have a temper thing? It was true. Every. Word.

And that man, as he strode out the door with the finest grade A prime buns she'd ever seen, lovingly cupped in denim, seemed capable of pushing every single one of her hot buttons and flipping the *all systems engaged* switch.

"Don't mind him. If you don't need anything, I'll be just outside prepping for the fishing trip I'm leading tomorrow," Cole said, his gaze missing nothing.

Blowing out a frustrated breath, Emily nodded and waved him off with her free hand. Cole departed with a tilt of his head before he retreated out the door. Staring around the space she hoped to call hers, the usual excitement she typically felt at the beginning of a new challenge was tempered by her unforeseen chemical response to Mason.

She had to overlook the rampant desire he engendered. Ignore the melting sensation in the pit of her stomach. Temper her body's response to him and infuse those unrequited emotions into her cooking. Nothing said *I'm sexually frustrated* quite like making her dishes mini-orgasms for the taste buds.

Shoving her thoughts of Mason under lock and key, Emily quickly familiarized herself with the kitchen. Did a quick cataloging of the dry food storage. Checked the spices on hand. She couldn't keep herself from running a hand over the countertop, claiming this space.

My kitchen.

Whatever she had to do, had to sacrifice, she wanted this place to be hers. Even if the Elkhorn proved to only be temporary and a stepping stone to get back into the big game.

Before she proceeded any further, Emily withdrew the spare ivory chef coat that buttoned up the front and fell past her hips, from her bag. The rest of her supply of chef attire was in her suitcases. Then she piled her hair up into a bun on top of her head to keep it out of the way. Usually, she'd cover it with one of her hats, but she'd apparently put them all in the rest of her luggage. For today's little test run, she wasn't worried about it. Then, with a dish in mind, she opened the fridge and withdrew ingredients, setting them on the center counter prepping station.

She enjoyed the routine as she started making her pizza dough. The blockhead wanted her to wow him. She would. This recipe was a party favorite among her friends. Not to mention, it was quick, and so routine she didn't need a recipe. Emily added the ingredients for the dough into the pastry blender. Once it was mixed, she covered it with a cloth to allow the quick rising yeast to do its job while she chopped, sliced and slid into her age-old rhythm.

From the time she had been a little girl, Emily had loved to cook. She wasn't really sure where it came from. It may have started with the easy bake oven she'd gotten in first grade. Or the first time her parents had taken her and her siblings to Hawaii on vacation and they'd stayed in one of those all-inclusive resorts. Everyone else remembered the waves, and the beach. She remembered it was the first time she'd had grilled pineapple with chicken. And she'd been sold. Cooking gave her a sense of purpose and joy. When she was in the midst of creating, nothing else mattered.

She loved the scents. The combinations. The ability to blend ingredients that one would think shouldn't fuse well together and in turn create a masterpiece that made your taste buds sing in praise. By the time lunch was prepared for Cole and Mason, her stomach was growling.

Emily found a wait staff tray, loaded it with their salads, prepped silverware rolled in linen napkins, and a bottle of sparkling water with two water goblets. If they wanted anything else to drink, they could help themselves. The water would help cleanse their palates between the salad and main course.

With the pizza finishing in the oven, she carried out the tray of goodies. The two cowboys sat at one of the tables near the window. She ignored the liquid pull of desire that spiked her blood. Any woman would be turned on when presented with such raw, untamed masculinity. Hell, she'd have to be dead not to feel her blood pressure rise exponentially in their presence. And, last she'd checked, she still had a pulse. The brothers spoke quietly in hushed tones.

When Mason's hard gaze noticed her, all talking ceased as she approached.

Emily had been working in restaurants as long as she could remember. And, ordinarily, balancing a serving tray was as ingrained in her as breathing, but under Mason's firm glare, her hands trembled. Refraining from dumping what she knew was a sumptuous salad in his lap, she set a plate before each man. As she placed the rolled utensils beside the plates, she explained the dish. "This is a salad made with spinach, arugula, beets, red onion, toasted chickpeas and toasted pecans with a warm balsamic vinaigrette. If you want to get started on these, I will be back out with the main course."

"Looks great," Cole said, digging in before she left the dining room.

Whereas Mason's movements were unhurried, almost baiting her, daring her to snap.

"Be right back," she replied with a forced smile, escaping before she gave in to the urge to bean Mason upside the head with the serving tray.

Inside what she already considered her kitchen, Emily drew in a deep breath, attempting to calm herself. Not that it worked, but at least she tried. The oven timer beeped and mobilized her into action. Slipping on silicone oven mitts, she withdrew the sizzling pizza. The aroma caused her mouth to water.

Once her little audition was at an end, she would whip up

some lunch for herself. As it was, the show must go on. Emily cut the pizza into triangles. Placing the pan on the serving tray with a trivet beneath it, she added plates and a pizza slice server. Then she hefted the tray once more and, with a deep breath, headed back into the dining area.

She felt like she was about to do battle with Goliath.

Emily bit back her grin when she saw Cole's salad nearly demolished. Likewise for the blockhead. Not like her cooking? Please.

She might fail in a lot of areas of her life: relationships, commitment, balancing her checkbook, but there was one thing she knew she was exceptional at, and that was cooking. It was both an art form and a passion for her.

She grabbed a tray stand on her way and erected it by their table. She set the tray down on top and then served each man two slices onto a plate before placing the dish on the table in front of them. Then she took a step back and said, "This is a made from scratch pizza with fig, prosciutto, goat cheese, and parmesan."

She didn't realize she had been holding her breath until Cole, an expression of bliss on his face, said around a bite, "You're hired. You can't leave. I won't let you."

Mason eyed her speculatively. Then, after taking a few bites, he said, "You'll do. You can have the rest of the day off and then start in the morning."

"Actually, if I could put my suitcases where I will be sleeping, I would prefer to acquaint myself with the kitchen and menu already in place. Perhaps cook a special dinner for the employees as a trial run this evening. I realize the rest of the kitchen staff won't be in until tomorrow, but I can manage." People were easier to win over when they were happy and had a full belly. In her humble opinion.

"Yes to dinner tonight. Let me finish this slice and I can

show you. Hey, dude—" Cole was cut off and glared daggers at Mason.

"I will show you where you will be staying. Follow me," Mason said, putting his linen napkin on the table as he stood.

Being this near him, Emily had to crane her neck to look him in the eyes. She wasn't short, but Mason made her feel every inch of her five-foot-four stature as he stared down at her. His gaze was shuttered and unreadable.

As she followed him out of the restaurant, she figured it was a toss-up as to whether they would survive being in the same space with each other. The man made her want to either commit serious acts of violence, or strip him and have her merry way with him.

She hadn't yet decided which was the better route to take.

CHAPTER 3

*M*ason escorted Emily out the front of the main lodge building. He always felt a measure of pride at surveying what belonged to him, what he and his brother had turned this place into. Even if that pride was a bit dented at present. He noticed the little blue Mazda hatchback Emily was ambling toward. If she was going to last here—not just at the lodge but in Wyoming—they needed to have a discussion about her choice of vehicle. That little matchbox toy on mountain roads, or any of the country roads around here, especially during winter, would be treacherous.

"Let me just get my suitcases from the trunk," Emily murmured, striding past him and giving him another glimpse of her spectacular ass. He nearly sawed his tongue off to clamp down on the groan in his throat. Logically, the last thing Mason could do was bed his new chef. Although logic didn't seem to matter; the Dom in him hungered to leave his mark on the firm globes. He yearned to see what they looked like red and covered with his handprints.

She opened the hatchback, leaned in, and hoisted a large,

bright purple suitcase from the trunk. Damn thing was half her size. Shaking his head, he strode over.

"Here, let me help before you hurt yourself," he grumbled.

He commandeered the first one from her hands and set it on the ground beside her vehicle. Nudging her out of the way, he lifted the second equally large suitcase from the back. There was a third, slightly smaller suitcase lying across the rear seat. When he didn't relent, she stomped around the side and opened the passenger side car door.

Shutting the trunk, Mason hefted her two suitcases as she yanked the third one out. The whipping fall wind blew escaped wisps of her hair around her entrancing face. The urge to wrap one around his fingers swamped him. But her movements, combined with the wind, caused an empty potato chip bag from the front seat to flutter out and fall to the ground outside her car door. At her short curse under her breath, he hid a smile. Emily jerked as she picked the bag up and shoved it back inside before slamming the door shut.

"Barbeque?" he asked, unable to keep the amusement from his voice.

She whirled around, her entrancing eyes wide, and asked, "What?"

"The chips." He nodded toward where she'd tossed the bag in the car.

"Salt and vinegar," she responded, her consternation clear as day across her expressive face. She'd never be good at poker. The woman wore what she was thinking crystal clear on her face. It was refreshing.

"Good choice. You'll want to clean anything like that out of your car before long or it may draw wildlife," he instructed. Last thing he needed was for her to draw bears or raccoons. They had enough of a difficult time keeping wildlife at bay.

"I will take that under advisement."

"Good. Your cabin is back this way. There's parking by the

cabins if you want to pull your car around later," he advised, lugging her two suitcases. They were heavy. Not that he struggled with them, but a woman her size would. What in the blasted hell did she bring with her? Transplanted palm trees?

Mason led her back through the cabins. The Black Elkhorn Lodge and Resort had been created cabin by cabin. He and his dad had constructed the majority of them ten years ago. Or had started it with his dad, at least. Mason and Cole had finished them, brought the lodge into fruition after their dad passed away. There were three circular drives with cabins spaced along them. In front of each cabin was parking for two vehicles. They were small and functional, since most of their visitors spent time hiking and enjoying the outdoors. And they were private, so guests were not right on top of one another.

Mason sensed Emily behind him as they walked. Hard not to, considering it felt like he'd plugged himself into a lightning strike in her presence. He'd put her in cabin G, about as far away from him as possible. As if distance would erect enough of a barrier to keep him from putting his hands on her. He took the two steps up onto the wooden porch to the cabin's front door and opened it with the set of keys he'd grabbed from the front desk.

Ushering her in, he watched her expression as she viewed her living space.

"It's not overly large, but it does have a kitchenette. On Wednesdays, employees have access to the laundry room in the main building."

"It's fine," she said, setting her suitcase on the floor.

"Are you certain you want to cook tonight and wouldn't rather get settled?" he asked, eyeing her luggage with a speculative glance.

"I can do that later this evening," she said and glanced his way. Then, "Spit it out, Mason. What aren't you saying?"

Pleasure washed over him at hearing his name uttered in

her sultry tone. Christ, it made him hard. And he wondered what it would do to him to hear her say *Sir* or *Master*. Considering the ferocity of his desire for her, it might make him get a load off without even touching her. He mentally shook the image from his mind.

"I will have the contract for you to sign tomorrow for a temporary thirty-day trial run. If we decide that we are a good fit for one another, then we will renegotiate the terms," he stated, his gaze fixed on her reaction.

Mason saw it, the flare of temper, before her eyes narrowed and she murmured, "That's if I decide to stay in Podunk, USA."

"Well, then it's good that we aren't entering into anything too long-term. You can find your way back to the main lodge. I have other things begging for my attention," he said, enjoying the way she stiffened and glared at him. He wished he could say that he was sorry for egging her on.

But he wasn't.

If she was angry and glaring daggers at him then he wouldn't be tempted to close the distance between them and sample her luscious lips. Discover if they tasted as sweet as they appeared. So he would continue to goad her, since currently, those same lips were pressed into a thin line. Not that it diminished her appeal in any way.

"I'll see you at dinner, Emily," he said, tipping his hat, then exited her cabin before he did something infinitely stupid. Like back her against the nearest wall and kiss her until she begged him to fuck her.

The sad fact was, Mason wouldn't need much prodding.

As he strode over the path to the main lodge, his phone rang in his back pocket. He slipped it out and grimaced when he spotted the number. It was the bank. Again. With a deep breath, he answered, "Mason Stewart."

The call shifted his focus back to where it belonged. His top priority was saving the Black Elkhorn Lodge. Not wondering how his newest chef would look bound to a St. Andrew's Cross.

Not that the distraction worked. Emily Fox had staked a claim in the back of his mind. One she didn't vacate as he dealt with accounts and the business of running the lodge.

CHAPTER 4

*B*y the time Emily trudged back to her cabin later that evening, she was ready to drop from her insanely long day—but also thrilled. Dinner had been a knockout hit. Well, for the most part. The only black mark that dulled the edges of her excitement and the evening was Mason. Emily didn't understand his grumpy attitude toward her. As if the very air she breathed offended him, judging by his stern glances and hooded gazes. Then again, it could be that was just the way the man was with everyone.

He was the one blight on her enthusiasm.

Emily stood in the doorway to her cabin and surveyed the landscape. The cabin sat on a small hill, a bit of a minor foothill, really, that overlooked a ginormous field of tall green grass dotted with forests filled with evergreen. Off in the distance, she spied a shimmering blue strand of a stream winding through the field like a garden snake.

And the craggy spires of slate that seemed to touch the heavens were bathed in the last golden rays of sunshine.

It took her breath away. The huge expanse of blue sky, deepening to indigo. The first few stars sparkled. She'd have to check once night had fallen completely, but she'd bet she would be able to see the Milky Way out here.

Even if Mason remained a surly jerk, she wanted to stay. At least until she determined whether this was the right place for her or not.

Since she'd driven half the day, she'd kept the dinner she'd cooked for the staff simple. A family style supper of lasagna, salad, and rolls, with a peach cobbler for dessert. Emily met the lodge staff, the registration clerks, the bartenders, her wait staff and bussers, the maids. They had all peered at her curiously but had been friendly, including Alexander Hunt, the owner of Hunt Trail Rides that operated out of the Black Elkhorn Lodge Stables. Alexander was just this side of gorgeous, ruggedly so, with a warm smile and broad shoulders. He'd called her ma'am with an easy smile and seemed to be a throwback to a different time.

Yet, as she had served the meal, between the three mouthwateringly hot cowboys, Mason still stood out. Even with Cole and Alexander teasingly proclaiming their undying love—for her cooking. Just like the rest of the staff she'd met that evening had. Except for Mason. He'd barely spoken to her. He had stared with his intense caramel gaze, studying her every move, and kept her on a razor's edge.

It was no wonder she was tired and her nerves were shot.

Her tiny cabin was charming. The exterior was rustic, fashioned with logs that were a burnished cinnamon. There was a small porch with two wooden chairs and a small table off to one side.

She could envision herself curling up on the porch with a hot cup of tea after a long day, looking out over the valley.

She shut the door and locked it. In all honesty, the cabin was about the size of her apartment in Los Angeles. Only here, she didn't have any neighbors she could hear through paper thin walls shouting at one another. Here, it was quiet. Blissfully so.

The interior was small, as Mason had pointed out earlier. But she liked it, the homey nature of it. Emily didn't need a lot of room. Maybe, if she ended up staying, and this became a permanent situation, she'd move into a larger space and adopt a dog. One she could hike the trails with in her spare time.

She smiled at the thought. If she was here past the trial run, she'd decorate the cabin a bit as well. Although, until then, maybe she could find a vase in town and put some flowers on the mantel above the fireplace to spruce up the utilitarian decorating. Inside on her left was a small eat-in kitchen. It held a miniature stove, minimal countertop, refrigerator that was a decent size for one person, and small pantry. There was an oak kitchenette table and two chairs.

Over on the right was a sitting area with a loveseat and matching chair in a navy blue pattern that made her dizzy if she stared at it too long, as well as an oak coffee table in the same golden cedar shade as the kitchen table and chairs. In the corner, next to a window that looked over the valley, was a decent sized flat screen television mounted on the wall. Finishing the room off was a fireplace that she could imagine would be downright cozy come winter.

The floors were hardwood. But she'd want to add a throw rug or two to help keep her feet from freezing.

Back through a doorway was the bedroom, where Mason had deposited her luggage earlier. There was a king-sized bed with a wrought-iron frame, a pair of nightstands and a dresser, all with that rustic feel. There wasn't much space to move around, but it was nice, clean, and the mattress looked inviting. She also had a closet that held extra pillows and was large enough to store her luggage and any clothing she needed to hang. The bathroom could be an issue. It was pint sized. Large enough for a commode, sink, and standup shower stall, but she would manage.

Emily unpacked her luggage and stored her suitcases away, then took a shower so she wouldn't have to first thing in the morning. By the time she climbed into bed, she would have bet she would drift right off, she was so tired.

Instead, she tossed and turned. Her brain must have short-wired on the long drive. Every time she closed her eyes, she imagined Mason, the hard set of his jaw, and firm line of his lips, moving over her skin. She pressed her thighs together at the low swirl of arousal pumping in her veins.

The man had not been nice in the slightest. And yet, here she was, imagining doing things with him. Naked, naughty, wicked things.

Why couldn't her body get all ooey gooey over his brother, Cole? He was hot and alpha too, and nice to boot. Or Alexander, whose easy smile should have made her feel something more than appreciation.

But no. Her ornery hormones chose the one not even remotely good for her.

Emily gave up the pretense of trying to sleep after an hour of envisioning her new boss screwing her brains out. She'd lost her mind. That was all she could surmise. It made no sense that she should want that one. Why couldn't her body get all quivery about Cole? Or, hell, the fellow ginger, Alexander, with golden amber eyes that made her think of a lion? And she'd heard that there were other men who worked at the stables under Alexander's employ. Perhaps there would be one or two of those cowboys who would get her motors running and she could stop this unholy obsession she had with Mason. Maybe that was what had happened to her. She'd crossed the Continental Divide and it had short-circuited her brain patterns. So now her wires-crossed brain was sending her body the wrong signals.

Instead of getting some much-needed shut eye, she sat on the couch, curled in a blanket, with sitcom reruns playing in the background while she made some minor adjustments to the menu. She liked what the Elkhorn had to offer already. But Emily planned to spice things up a bit. Bring some of her West Coast dishes to the ranch, so to speak.

Then she made a list of supplies she needed for her cabin, which meant she had to figure out where the nearest stores were located. She suspected they were in downtown Jackson Hole, but she'd ask the other staff. There might be a place the locals went where she wouldn't have to drive the forty minutes into town.

Emily worked until her eyes crossed and she drifted off to sleep.

THE FOLLOWING MORNING, Emily met her sous chef. Tibby was a tall, lanky blonde with goth inspired makeup surrounding her jade eyes and piercings in her nose and above one eyebrow. An inky tattoo made of vines and thorns circled her wrist, yet she wore blue jeans and a pair of cowboy boots. The woman was a study in contrasts. She had her own catering business on the side, as well as an eight-year-old daughter, Arianna, which was why she couldn't be full-time. Her schedule didn't bother Emily in the slightest because she was excellent in the kitchen. They hit it off well, with Tibby responding to her commands without question.

"There are a few items I want to change on the menu," she explained to Tibby, gauging her response.

She raised a brow in her direction and replied, "Have you cleared it with Mason?"

"Nope. But I'm the chef, he's not. If he wants to come in here and tell me how to run my kitchen, then he can go shove it as far as I'm concerned. My kitchen, my rules," Emily replied, drawing her line in the sand. Her sous chef had been here long enough that her reaction would help her determine, she hoped, Mason's response.

Tibby smile conspiratorially, rubbing her hands together. "I like the way you think."

"I figured you would. If you could start on prepping the usual dinner courses, I will work on the special for tonight. But first, I need to go see Mason in his office briefly," Emily said, not having any difficulty stepping into the command position in the kitchen. It was part of why she'd been forced to leave La Vida—well, that among other things. Like discovering that the head chef had stolen her recipes and slapped his name on them.

"Sure thing. Faith should be in shortly and I will get her working on chopping vegetables," Tibby replied.

"Sounds good. Be back shortly," Emily said and headed out of the restaurant. In her hands, she held the file with the menu changes she planned to make.

When she noticed her hands were trembling, she gripped the folder more tightly. Emily could not show weakness before Mason. Somehow she knew, even though he and his brother were partners in this place, it was Mason she needed approval from. And if she displayed fear or came across as wishy-washy, he would end up with the upper hand in their working relationship and would run roughshod over her dreams.

It was up to Emily to seize what she wanted for her life. A motto she'd adopted some years back from a pastry instructor: begin as you mean to go on. She'd done that all throughout her career.

Emily believed in the menu changes. This was her way of establishing a foothold and her position. It was her way of letting him know that she wouldn't be a wallflower for Mason to order about. He and the lodge might be paying her, but at the end of the day, she was the one doing the cooking. It was her reputation on the line.

The oak door to his office was open and she studied him for a minute without him being aware of her presence. His hat was absent. His hair stood up in golden brown tufted spikes like he'd been running his hand through it. Whatever he was studying on his desk had his full attention. His office was a good size. Not overly large or fancy, but Mason dominated the space. All the furniture, the mahogany desk and brown leather chairs, the matching book shelves behind his desk to the leather office chair he currently occupied, were merely accessories. He suffused the space around him. Made the room seem alive just because he was in it.

Handsome didn't begin to describe him. The man was like the land here. Rugged, stark, with the succinct ability to leave her breathless. All the fantasies she had about him last night came rushing back and a blush spread over her cheeks. She had to get a hold of herself.

She knocked on the door.

Mason's head snapped up at her interruption. His gaze zeroed in on her. Their eyes met and held. Thunder rolled, and lightning bolts of electricity flashed between them. Heat blossomed in her cheeks. Emily kept herself from fanning her face with the file, but just barely. His caramel gaze roamed her body from head to toe. And Emily felt her nipples perk up beneath her chef's jacket. She shouldn't be this attracted to him. And yet her body didn't seem to care one whit about her wishes.

"Emily, come in," Mason said, the command inherent. The low bass of his voice scuttled along her spine like a caress and made her toes curl.

She blew out a breath and approached, hyper aware that his gaze missed nothing. She sat in one of the leather chairs with his desk between them. She moistened her bottom lip and said,

"I wanted to make you aware of some changes I made to the menu."

She held the file out for Mason to take. When he reached for the manila folder, his long fingers brushed against hers. Shockwaves sparked through her system. She released the folder and yanked her hand away. Cursing herself, and her damn fool response to him, she smoothed her hand over her jeans. She stared at him as if nothing had happened. Daring him to comment. Mason's hard gaze studied her, dissecting her actions briefly before he flipped the file open.

The firm slash of his lips curved down as he perused the file. "Emily, I'm not sure these changes are going to fly with folks around here."

"But that's just the point. The folks who come here aren't from around here. I studied the area after our phone call. Many of the people who visit this area hail from Los Angeles, Manhattan, Boston, Chicago, and are fairly well to do. This is a menu that would appeal to them while keeping some tried and true favorites," Emily explained.

"I'm not sure it's the time for changes of this magnitude," Mason stated, his features set as he dug his heels in.

She knew he would be difficult to work with, but still. Exasperated and somewhat furious that he didn't want to give her the chance to prove herself, she asked, "Then why hire me? Seriously, Mason. If you want the original menu in place, you'd be better off with a local line cook you could pay much less than me."

"The terms of the contract I'm willing to offer is for thirty days, with the possibility of entering a long-term agreement. Making changes like this—"

"I realize this position might only be temporary. But you promised me autonomy on the phone. Or was that a lie? Because if it was, I'm out. If you won't deal with me fairly and honestly, there's no point to us continuing our verbal sparring matches." She clenched her hands into fists in her lap, mainly to refrain from launching herself across the desk and fastening them around his throat. The stubborn, mule-headed man was pushing her toward violence. He'd promised her free rein in the kitchen. It was one of the reasons she'd said yes and had completely moved her life up here so quickly.

"I don't lie," Mason snapped, standing. His eyes narrowed, and his jaw clenched so firmly she was surprised he didn't break a molar. Then he planted his big palms on his desk and leaned forward. The domineering stance was meant to intimidate her.

Nice try, buddy, but your threatening glare won't work on me.

Never one to cower, she stood and imitated his response. Emily slapped her palms on his desk, cocked an eyebrow and said, "Really? Because you're doing it right now."

This close, she could count the thick eyelashes framing his hard eyes. He'd forgotten to shave today, and there was a wealth of dark stubble on his jaw a shade or so deeper than his hair. It made him infinitely more dangerous, and more appealing. She caught his scent, a spicy, sensual male one that beckoned her closer and made her want to rub her face in his chest.

She swallowed a deep breath and licked her lips.

The light in Mason's eyes shifted. They darkened, filled with hunger. Became inherently more potent and much more devastating to her composure. They warmed. Emily felt an echoing liquid pull erupt in her body. Her gaze dropped to his lips. Up this close, they appeared fuller, more enticing. His stubble shrouded them and the thought of sucking on his lower lip, feeling the abrasion of his shadow beard upon her chin, caused tingles to flare along her spine. Heat swirled in lacerating waves. It drew her closer as if she were in a trance. He leaned forward.

Right before his lips brushed hers, he backpedaled and retreated.

Air exploded from her lungs and she rocked back on her heels. They glared at each other. Emily's skin felt tight and three sizes too small.

"Change the damn menu if you want, but I want numbers on the new dishes. What they are selling versus the items from the original menu. If I'm not seeing these new dishes catching guests' eyes and stomachs, then I will have you revert to the old menu. Understood?" he chewed out, putting distance between them.

Another shuddery breath expelled from her lungs. He planned to pretend nothing had happened. That they hadn't almost kissed. He'd tempered and extinguished every ounce of desire she'd witnessed moments before in his gaze.

Her nipples were still hard, beaded points and ached. Her pulse thrummed with need. But in this, Emily retreated. "Fine. Is that in the contract you drew up?"

It was the smart thing to do. Pretend like it never happened.

"No," he muttered, his jaw clenched.

"I want you to include that you agreed to give me autonomy in it. I won't sign the contract until then," she said, drawing her line in the sand.

The winds of winter were blowing between them for all the warmth present in his eyes. This man blew hot and cold to the point where she was developing whiplash.

"I will have it by day's end," Mason bit out, looking like he wanted to throttle her.

Well, the feeling is mutual, buddy.

"Good. You can bring it to the restaurant when it's ready. I have dinner to prepare," she said and swiveled on her heel, making her exit before he changed his mind.

At the doorway, his deep bass said, "Emily."

Not turning, she replied over her shoulder, "Yes?"

"Don't make me regret hiring you," he grumbled.

She stiffened and said, "Come have the special tonight and you will see that I'm right about the changes."

Then she escaped his office. Regret hiring her? Was he kidding? This was day two.

CHAPTER 5

*T*wo days and they were on the outs. It made her position precarious. Emily wasn't sure why Mason disliked her so immensely. It was odd. She hadn't done anything, at least, nothing she could think of off the top of her head that was offensive. Yes, she could be sarcastic, but that wasn't likely to change any time soon.

Yet she couldn't discount their almost kiss.

He couldn't think she was all that bad if he'd contemplated kissing her. The look in his eyes had been hungry, blazing with wicked heat. The most startling thing wasn't that Mason had nearly kissed her, but how disappointed she'd been that he didn't. In that split second, Emily had wanted him to override her common sense and close the remaining gap.

Perhaps this job wasn't the right one for her after all. Maybe she should just get in her car and go. And drive where exactly? It wasn't like she had another destination in mind. And sure, she had a little bit saved up but without a job, she'd go through that rather quickly. The last thing she would do, though, was return to Los Angeles a failure so that her father could gloat. Her siblings would look down their perfect noses at her and her mom would try to tempt her into becoming a realtor just like her.

No, the only way she would return home was victorious or not at all. She needed this job.

Rock, meet hard place. It was the story of Emily's life. It was for this very reason she was in the middle of Wyoming instead of cooking at a Los Angeles hotspot.

Emily entered the kitchen and her chest ached. A part of her wanted this place, wanted the chance to prove she could run her own kitchen. Maybe this job wouldn't be forever. She wanted, above all else, to find the place where she belonged. She loved her family, but they didn't exactly fit one another.

And she wanted to prove—not to them, but to herself—that she had the tenacity to carve out what she wanted for her life. It may not be something her family understood, but that didn't diminish that she needed to do this. Perhaps, if she succeeded here, she could make a comeback and re-enter the hotbed of culinary competition in Los Angeles.

Hopefully, given enough time, the scandal of her departure would die down. The fact that she'd told her boss, the famed Chef Ormond, in the crowded dining room at the exclusive La Vida, exactly what he could do with his damn truffles. There was video footage of it, too, that had been put on YouTube and other social media. She sighed. It was going to take a while for the furor of her latest foot in mouth disease moment to absolve itself.

Tibby and Faith were hard at work as she started preparing that night's special, chicken buddha bowls with a spicy peanut dressing. It was different than what they had on the menu, she knew that, but it was simple enough, and delicious. And Emily herself loved it because it was healthy, along with being power packed with flavor. There was the grilled chicken seasoned just right, roasted sweet potatoes, roasted red peppers, roasted carrots, spinach, and avocado over a bed of fluffy jasmine rice and drizzled with her signature spicy peanut sauce.

It was amazing.

Emily lost time as she cooked. It was a job hazard. Time always seemed to fly by in a blink because of her constant movement. And, apparently, word had gotten out in Jackson Hole that the Elkhorn Restaurant had a new chef. While the dining room wasn't stuffed to capacity, Emily knew once people started eating her cooking, they would come. It was that whole *build it and they will come thing* but, in this instance, she cooked, and they came with their forks ready.

The skeleton wait staff time and again put in orders for today's special, which made her giddy, in part because she enjoyed bringing her love of food to people, and creating a dish that was a big hit gave her a thrill. Although, she had to admit, it would be nice to make Mason eat his words.

Later that evening, Mason came to the Elkhorn and had dinner with Cole. She purposefully served them the special, hoping for a reaction from him. As she moved around the dining room, greeting guests, she could feel Mason's gaze following her. He ate the special, but his face didn't show pleasure or disgust. He was thoroughly unreadable. It unsettled her. It made her feel like she was under a microscope. It made her skin flame as if she'd been sitting inside a broiler, and she caught herself wanting to use her hand to fan her face.

Emily had worked in hot kitchens for the bulk of her existence, and she'd never been affected this way. So either there was something medically wrong with her—maybe because she was abstaining from her snack cake addiction, today at least, since she was out—or it was because of Mason.

She wasn't certain what to do with that bit of information. Even when she gave him the numbers near closing, with the special accounting for fifty percent of the meals sold, he just gave her a stoic nod and handed her the contract.

"I'll read it tonight and get it to you in the morning," she said, tucking the contract beneath her arm.

"Just sign the damn thing and we can move on," Mason said, exasperation lacing his voice.

"Honey, do you think I'm stupid? I don't care if you're Mother Theresa, I would still want to read through the entire thing before I sign it. Don't get your boxers twisted."

"My—never mind. Drop it off at the office tomorrow," Mason said and then stalked off.

She addressed Cole, "Was it something I said?"

Cole chuckled and shook his head. "No, he's just got a lot on his mind. Dinner was fabulous. I'm on your side with whatever you want to cook. Just try not to go to war with Mason."

"Even if he started it?"

Cole gave her a blasé glance and put a friendly hand on her shoulder, his gaze never wavering.

Emily caved and said, "All right, fine. I will be the grown up. Now, I'm going to go to my cabin, read this thing, and give myself a pedicure... if you don't mind locking up the restaurant behind you?"

Cole responded with a cock-eyed grin. "I can do that. Get on home. I bet they're real purdy, too."

"Oh honey, you can bet your ass they are," she retorted with a grin, then moved past him and headed for the door.

At Cole's deep chuckle, she left the restaurant with a smile. Cole liked her, at least. As did the rest of the restaurant crew. In two days, she had the budding hope of and start of friendships with everyone who worked at the Elkhorn—save one. The man who cut her paycheck.

The man who drove her crazy and tested her resolve to stay. Mason ignited feelings and desires that she had no business contemplating. Kitchens were always hotbeds of sexual relationships. And Emily had watched, time and again, as the woman got burned in the equation while the guy went on with his life as if nothing untoward had occurred. She didn't mix business with pleasure. It was a recipe for disaster.

She was sure she could chalk it up to frustrated hormones and that she needed a good boinking to get over it. Emily didn't necessarily care for one-night stands, but hell, in this equation if it made her stop looking at her boss like he was a piece of divinely cooked filet mignon and she was starving for a taste, then it wouldn't hurt. Tibby and Faith might know of a bar in town, could be a place where all the cowboys go to play, or any other place they might recommend.

Maybe it was just of a case of her needing some hanky panky and, for some asinine reason, her hormones wanted Mason. Surely she could find another cowboy in a local bar who would suit much better.

Because getting into bed with her boss would end in catastrophe.

CHAPTER 6

*M*ason spent the next few days holed up in his office, going over accounts, talking to creditors, to the bank, and to their vendors, getting them to extend their payment dates. He'd never been so thankful for having such a shit storm to deal with as he did presently. Because it kept him away from her. From Emily. It kept him from watching the way she walked into a room and seemed to light it up merely with her presence. It kept him from lusting after her. Or so he told himself.

When the reality was far from it. She'd been the star of his fantasies lately.

And her cooking was just about this side of heaven. The minute changes she'd made to the menu had made a difference. Receipts were up, as were end of day totals. As much as he had resisted her suggestions, partially on principle and, he had to admit, partially because he was being an ass because of his attraction for her, they'd been solid, positive changes.

The booked cabins had guests returning night after night to the restaurant and clamoring for her cooking. He didn't blame them one bit. She'd snuck in some comfort food favorites on her daily specials. Sneaky of her, to be sure. But just today for lunch he'd had her truffle macaroni and cheese with bacon and peas. It was without a doubt one of the best things he'd ever put in his mouth.

Not that he would tell her that.

Everywhere he went on lodge property, he saw her touches. Guests leaving the dining area content and happy. Guests carrying boxed lunches and to go orders back to their cabins. His employees raving about Chef Emily.

And the people loved her. She was warm and friendly. He watched her come out and greet guests in the dining room. And, Christ, he'd never considered a white tunic that hid more than it revealed to be sexy, but it was, decidedly so. Then again, it could have been the fantasy he'd had in his office after lunch where she'd appeared wearing what he knew now was her chef's jacket, and nothing else.

He was growing goddamn callouses. Because he couldn't touch her.

Even Cole, the traitor, was completely enamored by her. Then again, Cole was easy. More so than Mason, apparently. However, Cole hadn't been the one who'd put their dream at risk of collapsing. Mason had.

Which was why he had to maintain distance between himself and Emily. She called to him on a deep level that he didn't fully understand, even as a Dom. There'd never been a submissive who had incited this level of need inside him, only for him to deny himself the pleasure of her company.

Fuck, he wanted her. Wanted to see exactly what that sheet she wore in the kitchen was hiding underneath it. Wanted to hear her scream his name in ecstasy. Wanted to see how she'd react, bound and awaiting his touch.

It was a goddamn Greek tragedy. He could do none of that, even when he saw need reflected in her hazel eyes, her pupils dilated or her sweet pulse fluttering in her neck.

Mason was being tortured for his crimes, for the mistakes he had made.

Emily was his penance. As much as he craved her, he couldn't touch her. He scrubbed a hand over his face at his internal admission.

Glancing at the ledgers and the deficits in columns, Mason knew beyond any doubts, Emily was out of his reach.

Yet every time he gave her the cold shoulder or kept his distance, she would stare at him, hurt clouding her eyes. He realized she had no idea why he was being an ass where she was concerned. And the Dom in him wanted to comfort and soothe her. It was a damn sticky conundrum. Except, keeping his distance, erecting barriers and a line in the sand he couldn't cross with her, really was for the best—for everyone.

At the knock on his door, he looked up. His brother was leaning against the doorjamb.

"Alex needs us down at the stables," Cole said.

"Something wrong?"

"No. He just had some ideas he wanted to run by us for increasing the number of tours. Said it should help the lodge," Cole replied.

Mason grimaced. The last thing he wanted was for Alex to feel like he needed to help the lodge. "Shit, I don't want—"

Cole crossed his arms and stared him down, much like he'd done when they were kids and Mason was doing something foolish, before he said, "Mason, it's not just up to you. We're partners in this place. Which means I have just as much say as you do. And I say we need help from every quadrant. I still think we should ask Carter or Spencer for a loan. They know we're good for it."

And there it was, the proof that he had screwed them beyond measure. They would stand on their own and not go begging to have their woes fixed by their friends. Mason shook his head. "I'm not trying to be difficult here but I really don't want to borrow against this place. If I have to, I will go to the bank and see about a personal loan. Let's keep Carter and Spencer out of this. Carter has enough on his hands with his new bride and little boy. I won't take money from him, not even a loan. And I won't risk you or this place any further than I already have."

"It's not your fault, Mason."

"Actually, it is. And nothing you can say will make me think or believe otherwise. I put us in this position and I will get us out." Mason shoved his chair back as he stood. "Let's go talk to Alex. If he wants to add more trail rides to increase revenue for Hunt, he can. But we aren't taking a penny."

"Well, as your partner, I'm telling you that you have a month to figure it out. Otherwise, I will go to the boys and see who can help us out. Just because you're too damn stubborn and proud to accept a little help when it's warranted, doesn't mean I'm not. I won't lose this place over your hurt pride. Let's face it, Mason, you're more pissed that she fucked you and robbed us blind than you are upset about her. So get the fuck over it. You can't change what happened, and no amount of hurt pride is going to fix it."

"I just need a little more time" Mason growled. Cole was right. Hit the nail on the fucking head.

"Right about now it would be good to have a third partner as a tie breaker," Cole murmured, scraping a hand over his jaw.

"Never going to happen," Mason retorted firmly. Hell would indeed freeze over before he allowed anyone else in on their dream. They headed out the main entrance of the lodge and took the dirt trail down to the stables.

The stables were located back beyond the bend of a hill and a copse of trees not even a tenth of a mile from the main lodge. They had their own driveway access and parking for visitors from the highway, which helped ensure that the Black Elkhorn Lodge didn't have excess street traffic. Part of the attraction of the lodge—what they attempted to inspire—was for guests to get back to nature, to enjoy the outdoors. The place backed up to the Grand Teton National Forest, within hiking distance of Jackson Lake and the Snake River.

The lodge sat amidst the rolling foothills of the nearby mountains. The land was plush and untouched by manmade structures. Even the cabins had been built with the terrain in mind. Built not to detract from the land, but to be a part of it. There were twenty-five of them, of varying size. Plus a few extras had been built to accommodate employees.

He and Cole shared a house that was back beyond the main lodge, away from everyone and everything. Currently, the only employee living on the grounds was Emily.

Mason and Cole rounded the corner. The foliage dispersed, and he had a clear, unobstructed view of the paddock fences. As if thinking of her had conjured her up, he spotted Emily, wearing form-fitting blue jeans, currently bent over the rail of the wooden paddock. The view of her heart-shaped rear pointed in his direction ignited his hunger. She had one of the most succulent butts he'd had the good fortune to view.

Not wanting to startle her, they approached her quietly.

Her voice floated on the breeze. "Come here. I just want to pet you. I promise I'm nice."

Mason uttered beneath his breath, "Woman's a menace."

She wanted to pet a horse. Didn't she know anything about them? And then his heart nearly stopped. Her foot slipped. What the hell was she wearing, sneakers? Emily tried to catch herself. Her arms flailed. Her torso slid further down the opposite side of the rail. The nearby horses snorted and stomped their feet at her sharp yelp.

Mason didn't think, he just reacted. He was there before she fell all the way. He caught her around the waist and hefted her back over the rail. Turning her slightly in his hands to get a better grip and so he didn't drop her, he couldn't help but notice how her waist felt in his hands. Nor how her taut body felt pressed against his. Her hands scrabbled for purchase and clutched his shoulders. Their gazes clashed. Her hair, the wealth of burning russet sunset, was loose around her shoulders. Some of it brushed against his face and he inhaled her scent. Christ, she smelled like vanilla cookies. His mouth watered. His gut clenched. Mason felt her touch down into his soul. Her body slid against his as he lowered her until her feet touched the ground. There was a moment, when their gazes clashed and their breaths mingled, where time seemed to suspend itself. A hair's breadth separated their lips. All he had to do to finally discover what she tasted like was close the tiny distance. Emily's eyes widened and her pupils dilated.

Then one of the horses nickered and stomped. Mason released her like she'd burned him.

"What the hell were you doing?" he shouted, glaring down at her. Lust and fear for her safety combined into a turbulent sea of anger. He wanted to shake some sense into her. Wanted to take her over his knee and spank some sense into her. Wanted. Her.

He was so royally screwed.

"I just wanted to pet one. It's not like we have horses all over the place in Los Angeles," Emily said defensively, her chest heaving slightly, and he couldn't stop watching how it caused her ample cleavage to sway. His dick twitched at the innocent, innocuous motion.

"Don't go near the animals," he ordered. The last thing he needed was for her to get injured and file a claim against the lodge. Any hope for seeding life back into their place would be gone.

"Why not? I admit that might not have been the way to introduce myself to them, but I've never been around them. I didn't want to bother anyone, I just wanted to pet one. It's harmless—or should have been," Emily said and blew out a breath.

"You're here to cook, not to ride," Mason growled.

"And what about in my free time? I can't go for a ride or go anywhere on the lodge property?" She glared, her hands fisted at her sides, like she was trying to keep her hands off him.

"I didn't say that. Until you know your way around, just stay away from them. Last thing I need is you injuring yourself," Mason muttered and stormed past her. It was either that or go all Dom on her sweet ass. And he could see the lawsuits now, should he do something like spank an employee.

When he reached the door to the stables, she asked Cole, "Is he always this grumpy? Or is it just me he doesn't like?"

And Cole, the ass, replied, "Don't worry about Mason. When it comes to the lodge and protecting it, including the people on it, he can be overbearing."

"You mean he can be a jerk," Emily replied.

"Give him some space. And if you really want to learn to ride, either myself or Alex could teach you in our free time," Cole offered.

Mason knew that shouldn't rile him. He had no claim on Emily whatsoever. But the thought of his brother or his good friend touching her, even to help her learn to ride a horse, infuriated him.

"Thanks. I will think about. Especially if I'm here past the trial run. Later, Cole."

"Emily," Cole said.

At that, Mason turned back around and unabashedly watched Emily stroll up the bend to her cabin. Overbearing? He had kept her from breaking her damn fool neck. And she wanted to discuss methods?

If there was ever a woman who needed a bit of a firm hand, it was Emily. Too bad he'd forbidden himself from ever touching her.

CHAPTER 7

*I*t was finally Friday after one of the longest weeks in her life. Trying to impress Mason had taken on the intensity of an Olympic sport. Emily had worked in some of the finest restaurants in Los Angeles, and not one had challenged her the way this place did. It wasn't necessarily a bad thing. She'd been ready for the change. And having the chef she'd worked under steal her creations and call them his had been the shove she'd needed out the door.

She liked it here. Wonder of all wonders. The little cabin was comfortable. She could imagine sitting near the fireplace in the evenings, with a cup of hot cocoa or tea and a good book, once it snowed. If she made it past the trial period, she'd have to purchase a winter coat, hiking boots, snow boots, and who knew what else. The land was stunning. The slate mountains pierced the heavens. The evergreens blanketed the land. She'd seen eagles and hawks fly through the air. Last night, she'd spotted a small heard of elk in the distant field.

The lodge was comfortable and homey. She adored her sous chef, Tibby, and her line cook, Faith. And the wait staff was exceptional. Even her frustrating run ins with Mason were worth being here.

If she could just get past her obsession and the frankly unwelcome lust she felt for her boss, then everything would be perfect. Two days ago, she'd run into town and stocked her kitchen cupboard and refrigerator. She'd gone a teensy bit overboard on the Little Debbie and Hostess snack cakes.

And why had she done that? Because she'd seen Mason astride a horse. He was leading a trail ride and had a contingent of riders in line behind him. She'd spied him from the bank of windows inside the restaurant. His tall, firm body commanded the twelve-hundred-pound midnight black stallion with ease. Man and horse had worked in sinuous unity. A hunger unlike anything she'd felt before had set up camp. Her hormones blasted into overdrive. Emily had never been into country music. She'd never considered she would be panting after a man in jeans and a cowboy hat. But damn. Upon seeing Mason in his element, his focus and control evident, his confidence and pure alpha maleness on display as he sat astride the horse, all her girly bits had promptly swooned.

She'd watched him, unabashed, fanning herself with a menu, and then nearly fainted in truth when his head swiveled in her direction and he'd stared at her through the glass. Shadows from the wide brim of his Stetson had played with the angles of his handsome face. He'd not shaved again, and the patch of stubble lining his jaw made him appear more dangerous, more potent, just more everything. Their gazes held. The world around them could have been falling into disrepair, the Yellowstone super volcano could have been erupting and they wouldn't have known it, thanks to the supercharged kinetic currents flowing between them.

Even with the distance and the pane of glass between them, the connection was incontrovertible. She felt it and knew in that precise moment that he did as well. It shifted her paradigm. They were both fighting their attraction toward one another. The question was, why? What if she stopped fighting? Would the fire between them char them both until they were unrecognizable? Would they burn bright, only to have the flame extinguish in cataclysmic destruction?

Until Mason broke the sensual, intoxicating spell and tipped his hat at her. Then he turned away, man and horse moving as one, leading the group onto a trail and into the wild. She'd stood rooted to the spot until he and his group disappeared beyond a bend.

Emily had melted into a chair, staring out the window as she'd worked at containing the simmering lust pounding through her system.

During her town excursion the following day, Emily had stockpiled snack cakes as if the apocalypse were about to begin. Realistically, she understood deep down it was better that she soothe her sexual frustration with the chocolate and crème of a ding dong instead of propositioning Mason and doing what she really wanted, which was to affix her mouth to various parts of his body. However, that didn't mean she didn't have to be careful that she didn't overindulge, otherwise her jeans would no longer fit.

Tonight, she'd finished early in the restaurant, with Faith and Tibby promising to close up. Since many of the guests tended to head into downtown Jackson Hole to enjoy the nightlife on the weekends, the Elkhorn had been a little slower. Both Faith and Tibby had assured her it was normal. Sales for the restaurant had increased steadily day by day. That had to count as a feather in her cap.

But she wasn't going to celebrate just yet. She knew that often the newness of a restaurant or a chef could be a draw or attraction that would bring people in hordes initially, and then they would taper off once the sheen had evaporated. This first week had been good, the numbers solid. She had some ideas she wanted to run by Mason to help increase sales. And while she understood that the stubborn man would give her a hard time, she just needed to fine tune a few details. If she showed him what the potential bottom line could be, as in profits made, he might be a bit more amenable. Plus, it could solidify her position there enough that he would give her a contract extension past the thirty days.

With October a week away, she really wanted to host an Oktoberfest event at the Elkhorn, with beer, brats, handmade pretzels and Wiener schnitzel and the like. It would be challenging to pull off an event like that so quickly. But if they limited the number of tickets for the event, it could be manageable. And there was another, much more long-term idea she had—one she'd wanted to do at La Vida, but Chef Ormond didn't want plebian pedestrians in his kitchens. Perhaps, if she did one successfully, Mason would trust her with the other.

Instead of burrowing into her cabin that evening, she headed into downtown Jackson Hole. Emily wanted to get a lay of the land outside of life on the lodge. Not that she didn't find it utterly charming—she did, more than she'd believed she would. However, if she made it past the trial run, winter would descend shortly thereafter. She had an image of herself nearly hibernating at the lodge until spring. She was a Southern Cali girl, unused to the cold and the snow. The atmosphere of Jackson Hole was euphoric and catching.

It was eight on a Friday evening, and she strolled along the main drive. Store shop signs flashed and illuminated the darkening twilight. Emily window-shopped as she walked. Along the central hub of the town, most of the shops catered to tourists. But she got ideas for her restaurant when she spied fliers for different events around town.

Emily passed families, couples holding hands, and an elderly couple people watching on a bench outside the general store. A toddler cried at being denied a treat and a group of women excitedly chattered over their purchases. Emily sampled some out of this world ice cream from a local shop that apparently made their ice cream in shop. It was heavenly bliss in a waffle cone. She savored it, delight and pleasure filling her at the creamy, minty sugar rush, while she ambled along the sidewalk.

It struck her then that this could be a place where she would be happy. As much as she loved her family and her hometown, she'd never fit in there. But here, with the rhythm of the town, the pace of the lodge, the openness, the purity of the air, and even her attraction to her boss, she was comfortable. She didn't feel as out of her element as she'd worried she would feel in a new place. She'd barely been there a week, but she'd already wondered if she could make the Elkhorn hers. Become a partner in it at some point. Make it her place that food critics and foodies from around the world would travel to just to sample her cooking.

Those were big dreams. Some of it was ego, she understood that. When you've spent a lifetime having your family look at you with disappointment and confusion over your choice of career, there's a need to prove yourself. To be able to say, *See? I made it.*

And yet there was also a part of it that she'd been envisioning since she was a child. Her passion for cooking, for having her own place, was a lifelong dream that might actually be within her grasp. It was terrifying and thrilling all in the same breath. It was also another reason why she needed a saner head around Mason. As much as the man made her mouth water and her girly bits dance a two-step, giving in to her urges would be a death knell on her dreams.

There were restaurants she passed on her trek with aromas so intoxicatingly delicious, she knew she'd have to return and sample their food. Hence her need to walk tonight. While her job did make it so that she was on her feet and moving constantly, her love of food was not always conducive to her waistline. Out here, though, the mountain air tasted fresh and clean, and she was already making plans to purchase hiking boots and maybe a backpack. Perhaps Cole could take her on one of the trails and show her where to go. There was no smog to contend with, or traffic jams the length of a marathon.

Here, in this town, and this place, the possibilities were endless.

Then she spied the neon illuminated sign for the Teton Cowboy. She'd overheard Faith and Tibby discussing the bar the other day. When she had asked them about it, they'd said it was the place to visit in town if you were looking for a good time. Perhaps that was what she needed to turn her salacious intentions away from Mason. While she wasn't a huge fan of one-night stands, it certainly wouldn't be the worst idea she'd ever had. Especially if it helped dispel the lustful obsession she had with her boss. With a mission in mind to find a new cowboy to lust after and have rowdy, pulse-pounding sex with, she meandered in its direction.

And if she didn't find anyone appealing, she could come back tomorrow night, or the next night she had free, until she did locate a replacement.

Emily strode across the road with other tourists. The external building front had been constructed with slate gray stone that resembled the color of the nearby mountains. There was a dark cherry wooden trim porch and front overhang. At the street corner was a double door entry made of wood and glass. The club's symbol, a cowboy on a bucking bronco, was etched into the glass.

She entered the Teton Cowboy and grinned. This place was beyond cool and packed to the brim. Country music played over loud speakers. The din of conversations filled the air. The scent of fried food and distilled spirits tickled her senses. Emily was a sucker for bar food.

Her stomach grumbled. She shouldn't be that hungry. Granted, a mint chocolate chip waffle cone wasn't really a decent meal. But here she'd risk gravely adding to her calorie count with cheese fries or something equally damaging to her waistline.

Emily felt like she'd stepped into the Wild West with the décor. They had—she couldn't believe it—a stuffed black bear and a stuffed mountain lion on display. There was a wall bar that had to be a good fifty feet in length. She found an empty barstool, which was far and away the most unique feature in the bar, because the barstools were saddles. As in: giddy up, little doggy, fully fledged horse saddles, with stirrups for her feet. The bar was a lake of glossy golden wood with brass trim and fixtures. There were chandeliers made to look like wagon wheels with glass cylinders on top that resembled the old style kerosene lanterns. Even the bulbs inside were shaped like a flame.

In the crowded haze, she flagged one of the bartenders, who looked every inch a cowboy, from the top of his Stetson to the tip of his boots and everything in between. The blond stud, Jeremiah, flirted with her as he took her order. He was yummy, if a bit younger than she was looking for. She kept her order simple—a beer and, okay, she caved and got an order of cheese fries. But hey, if she was going to drink she needed something more substantial than ice cream. Otherwise, she'd never make it home.

Emily stuffed herself with the cheese fries. They were so good and hit every single one of her taste buds and pleasure sensors. She'd have to come back and sample some of the other menu items. The cowboy burger smothered in barbeque sauce with fried onion strings, in particular. Emily ordered a second beer, enjoying the comfortable warmth of a full belly. She paid her tab with every intention of leaving once she finished her second beer of the night.

She realized she was failing in her mission. But she could chalk tonight up to a bit of reconnaissance and could come back more prepared another night.

The two beers had mellowed her out. Sad, really, that what she wanted now was her pajamas and to cuddle in bed. She was such a party animal. It was barely ten and she was ready to turn in. Though, to be fair, she did have to be up at five in the morning to start on her pastries.

She swallowed a sip from her beer bottle and spied Cole walking through the room. She smiled and didn't swivel in her seat so much as dismount the thing. Taking her purse and beer bottle with her she followed him, winding through the crowd, enjoying the interested stares of some of the cowboys she passed. At least, she hoped it was interest and not because she had a smear of melted cheese somewhere on her person. Which, in her case, was totally feasible and a more likely outcome than not.

She hurried, trying to catch Cole as he walked through a door marked *private*. Curious, she caught the door before it closed and followed him down the stairs.

Whoa-ho-ho, what did we have down here? Another level? In the basement of this place?

She reached the bottom of the stairs and was about to call out Cole's name. It was on the tip of her tongue, but then she heard it. The moans. As in: plural. As if drawn on marionette strings, she entered a secondary bar.

The cowboy theme persisted, but that was where any similarity to the bar upstairs ended. There was another wall bar that was half the size of the one upstairs. The barstools were saddles like they had in the main bar area, but she spied silver loops in various positions that were puzzling. Areas were cordoned off with black velvet rope along the walls, with weird looking items of furniture behind them.

There was a seating area with brown leather couches and a smattering of gothic style furniture. The one that shocked her, and where some of the moans originated, was a mechanical bull in the center of the club. A woman was riding it. A very naked woman. Emily stared, not understanding why the women in here were in various stages of undress. The men had lost their shirts too. And she finally realized why the brunette riding the bull was moaning up a storm. There appeared to be a mechanical dildo she was riding as the bull moved.

With shaky hands, Emily set her beer down on a nearby table. Her face flamed with heat at the blatant, kinky scene.

She glanced around, not certain what to think or to feel. The buzz of alcohol and warmth pooled in her groin. Behind one of the velvet ropes, a blonde was restrained to a large wooden X and the man with her was—Emily blushed—actually screwing her out in the open.

What was this place? It was like a cornucopia for wicked deeds. She wished she could say she wasn't affected by it. But she was. And, dammit, she imagined it was Mason doing naughty things to her.

"What the hell are you doing here?" A rough hand closed around her bicep and jerked her around.

Speak of the devil and he appeared. She stared up into Mason's furious face.

"It's a free country. I followed Cole down here and—"

"You will leave now. This is a private club and you don't belong here," he snarled, his face an inch from hers. His caramel eyes blazed with an indescribable fury. His face was a harsh mask, his lips firmly compressed into a thin line.

Perhaps it was the liquid courage combined with startling need, but he pressed her hot buttons—and not in the right way.

"Make me," she dared, incensed at the way he was treating

her. Mason didn't own her just because she worked for him. She could go wherever she damn well pleased, and there was nothing he could say or do about it. It didn't help that being so near him, after what she'd witnessed in this lower level, made desire chug in her veins. Moans filled the air around them.

At her flippant response, his nostrils flared and his eyes narrowed to angry slits. And that was the only warning she received before he bent his torso, slung her over his shoulder, and carted her bodily from the club. Her face smacked into his back as he ascended the stairs. She screeched in fury while trying to hold her purse and not puke up her basket of cheese fries. It would serve him right if she did.

One of his big hands whacked against her rear at her struggles, and he snapped, "Settle the fuck down."

"Or you'll what? Unhand me, you freaking baboon," she swore. Patrons' laughter reached her ears, humiliating her further as they walked the main floor. She was going to give this man a piece of her mind the moment she was no longer upside-down and viewing the world from the wrong angle.

Blood rushed into her head. His strong shoulder pressed into her belly and made it difficult to draw in a breath. And through the thick tangle of her hair she had a prime view of his mighty fine behind. Muscular and firm, the jeans he wore defined the shape. It was a rear a woman could hold on to.

His hand was clamped around her thigh near her sex. Too near. As in, if she wriggled her hips the right way, his fingers would be pressed against her center. Emily stilled at the wicked sensations his touch ignited in her blood. Mason didn't stop his forward progression until they exited out onto the street. The sound of country music and murmur of voices dimmed. Night closed in around them.

"Which way is your car parked?" he demanded, his hand squeezing her thigh. None too gently, either.

Emily tensed at the unwelcome desire that scorched her

foundation at his intimate touch. Angry and humiliated at being hauled around like a sack of potatoes, she bit him on the back. Hard.

"Yeow! Fuck, Emily," Mason said, his fingers digging painfully into her thigh. And then her world was righted as he forcefully dropped her onto her feet. She wobbled, her center of gravity off from having her world turned upside down. His hands gripped her biceps to steady her.

"Back off," she seethed, glaring at him and wrenching her arms from his grasp. She was incensed at the way he'd manhandled her. Night had fallen and the temperature had chilled while she'd been inside. She crossed her arms in front of her chest to ward off the nippy air. Where the hell did he get off?

"I'm going to make sure you get in your car and leave. I won't allow you to go back into the club," he replied with a determined glint in his gaze.

Damn fool, pig-headed Neanderthal.

Emily gave him the stink-eye, not wavering from her stance. She wanted him to back the hell off. Wanted the desire currently hijacking her system to go away. Who the hell did Mason think he was, her overlord? With the Teton Cowboy's neon lights illuminating his gruff features, blocking out the swarms of pedestrians walking by them, realization settled in. He wasn't going to move, wasn't going to bend, and damn him, but that added fuel to her internal furnace belching out enough heat to melt the nearby glaciers.

Instead of allowing the stalemate from their little glaring contest to continue, because something told Emily they would be here all night, she finally relented. "Fine. This way."

She swiveled on her heel and stomped off. She'd only caved because, as a Southern California girl, she wasn't used to the cooler temperatures and was freezing. At least, that was the lie she told herself with Mason's firm, daunting presence behind her. He was near enough that she could feel his kinetic heat. The man thought he could run her life and she'd just follow along blindly, thanking him for his overbearing attitude. Don't go near the animals. Don't change the menu. Don't breathe around me. Don't go into this club.

"What the hell was that place, anyway?" she snapped as they rounded a corner to the parking lot where her car was parked. The club had piqued her interest, more than she wanted to admit. Then again, it wasn't every day that she found herself in a club with people having sex out in the open. After all, if there were a herd of giraffes stampeding down the main drag, she'd watch the spectacle.

Granted, the spectacle in the club had turned her on.

"It's a private club," Mason said after a minute, like he had carefully chosen his words and considered whether he was going to tell her or not.

At her car, she turned toward him and gave him a *well, duh* expression, then said, "I got that with your caveman skills back there. What I want to know is what type of club it is exactly?"

She stared, an eyebrow raised, in a defiant stance with her hands on her hips. She wasn't leaving until he answered the question. No more dodging from Mister Surly.

"It doesn't concern you," he responded, tension riddling his big, hunky body. A body she had imagined naked on more than one occasion.

She snorted and rolled her eyes at him. Did the man think she was missing half a brain? She retorted, "Yes, it does. If I'm going to be kicked out of someplace where people are having weird sex, I'd like to know why, Mason. Are y'all doing something illegal down there? Why was that woman restrained on the bull, or the one on the cross?"

Her words echoed in the parking lot. It was empty. But Mason's face hardened, his eyes narrowed, and he closed the distance. "Shush. It's private for a reason. As in: we don't parade our preferences or what happens in the club around town."

"So you are doing something illegal down there?"

Mason shook his head in the negative, consternation stamped across his face, and replied, "It's a BDSM club. Where those in the lifestyle are safe to practice their sexual tastes without censure."

"And you and your brother are members? Which makes you a what?"

"Yes, we are. Not that it is any of your business, but I'm a Master or a Dominant, if you don't know the terminology," he said. His gaze zeroed in on her response like a heat seeking missile guidance system.

Emily didn't so much as bat an eye, even as her blood heated. He made sense to her now. He hadn't before. With regards to his vaulted control when they were in each other's vicinity and how he held himself back, it wasn't that he didn't want her, but that he was rejecting his desire for her and controlling himself. She didn't know whether she should be offended or aroused. Who was she kidding? The idea of him being all controlling in the bedroom made her blood sing. She cleared her suddenly dry throat and asked, "So you like tying up women?"

Mason approached and took a step forward, placing his hands on her car. His large frame boxed her in against her vehicle. Liquid pulls of heat rushed through her system, her pulse thumped madly, and her nipples hardened into taut peaks at his nearness. Shadows played over his face as he stared down at her. Her gaze drifted to his mouth as he said, "That's not all, but some. I really like disciplining mouthy subs who can't take directions."

Was that what he was comparing her to? Emily should tell him to go to hell. Should shove him away and escape. He was her boss. He could crush her dreams of running her own restaurant into dust before they even had a chance to take root.

The air between them was hot enough to melt the Arctic tundra. Those liquid pulls of desire had manifested into a raging firestorm. Tossing her common sense into the gutter, Emily gripped the lapels of his shirt and, instead of retreating, drew her body up to his height and dared, "Is that what you were doing back there? Disciplining me?"

Her mouth was an inch from his. Their bodies were aligned from shoulders to hips. Going on instinct before he could form a response, allowing the desire only he seemed to ignite within her to guide her actions, she pressed her lips to his. Brushing his mouth with hers, she moaned deep in her throat. His stubble rasped against her lips. Spirals of heat lanced through her system.

Shock riddled Mason's form and he stood, frozen momentarily, before he crushed her within his arms. He surrounded her with his big body. Need exploded in all-consuming waves. Mason plastered his length against her. Her back was pressed against her car. Her hands slid around his neck, holding him in place. Emily couldn't get enough of his mouth. The man kissed like he did everything else, with a *take no prisoners* type of attitude.

It was devastating. Emily had never been kissed so thoroughly, so greedily. She wondered if she would erupt into flames.

Mason devoured her tiny mewls. She surrendered to the rising heat, plastering herself against his hard body. He slanted his mouth over hers, changed the angle of their kiss, and took it deeper. So much deeper. His tongue thrust inside to duel with hers.

She moaned.

Tongue, and lips, and teeth. It was hard and brutal. It was possessive and dominant. It was the most intimate, carnal, wicked kiss of her existence. A hunger for him unlike anything she'd experienced before had her climbing his rangy body like it was a tree. Emily wrapped her legs around his waist. She was certain the imprint of his belt buckle on her belly would be permanent, but she didn't care... as long as he kept kissing her.

His hands cupped her ass as he pressed his length against her. The ridge of his erection fitted against her cleft and she whimpered, greedy to feel him skin to skin. She wanted more. She wanted all of him. If this was what he called dominance, Emily had climbed aboard the Mason train.

Then he ground his pelvis against hers and Emily wondered if she would climax without doing the dirty, wicked deed with him. Lost in him, in the desire he created, she yearned to feel his naked flesh against hers.

"Get a room, you pervs!" a male voice shouted from somewhere nearby. It broke their carnal spell.

They sprang apart. Emily nearly landed on her butt, saved from an ignoble spill by clutching the door handle of her Mazda. They stared at one another, breathing in sharp pants, chests heaving from exertion. In the darkness, she couldn't see his eyes. But his shoulders were tense as he glared at her and his hands were fisted as his sides. He wanted her. It was in every line of his being.

Then Mason reached past her. His fingers brushed hers, sending electric currents through her as he opened her car door. He held it open and growled, "Go home, Emily."

She heard the undertone of command in his voice. It shivered along her spine. He'd just kissed her brainless and yet now he was dismissing her. The jerk. She wasn't the only who had been affected by their kiss, yet he acted as if it was nothing. As if she was nothing.

Damn him.

She wouldn't make more of a fool of herself than she already had. Emily jutted her chin, glowering at him before she turned away, hiding the fact that her hands trembled with need. That she was so wet between her thighs, she'd need new panties when she arrived back at the lodge. She climbed into the driver's seat.

When she was seated, he shut the car door, effectively shutting her out and cutting himself off from her. She had to know why. And she would find out the answer, but not right now. Now was not the time, on the public street, to have it out with him. One, her emotions. Her desire was too amped up and she feared she would cry. She tended to do that when she was supremely angry. Two, she couldn't guarantee that she wouldn't be loud. Her voice tended to carry. And in this instance, she knew if she pressed him here, he would shut down further and she'd never get her answer. Three, if she wanted a chance in hell at continuing to run the kitchen at Elkhorn, she had to be circumspect and approach him privately.

Like in his office, where they could play naughty secretary and sleazy boss. She kept herself from thunking her head against the steering wheel—but just barely.

Emily didn't look at him until she'd backed her car out of its space. With the pane of glass between them, they stared at one another to the point where her breath clogged in her chest. Mason broke the contact first. He tipped his hat and dismissed her. She idled in the car as he turned, his long strides putting distance between them as he headed back toward the club.

Shaking herself, she drove away and headed back to the lodge, replaying the events of the last hour. She could still taste him on her tongue; the whiskey on his breath combined with darker notes that were distinctly Mason. It had been the kiss to end all kisses. Emily had never been kissed so thoroughly in all her twenty-seven years. She wanted more. And she wondered how Mason could kiss her the way he had, as if she was all he had ever wanted, and then go back to a club to have sex with another woman.

And not just any type of sex—kinky, wicked sex. The kind she'd always pondered in her darkest fantasies, but had been too afraid of judgment to contemplate, let alone talk about with her friends.

The best thing she could do was ignore her desire for him, focus on her work in the restaurant, and go back to business as usual. Which meant Mason watching her every move with a hooded expression and making her skin feel too tight. Wanting him with every breath she took, but not touching him.

Could Emily pretend like their epic kiss had never happened?

CHAPTER 8

*M*ason had crossed a line of demarcation. One he never should have allowed. And one he needed to address.

The kiss that never should have happened. The one he had been up half the night replaying. The one that had made him turn down a submissive at the club and head home early. And why? Because the sub wasn't the one he wanted bound before him, begging for his touch.

It had belonged to the woman he'd hauled out of the club only to kiss against her vehicle. She'd tasted sweeter than he'd imagined. He hadn't thought she would close the distance. But she had. And, at that first brush, he'd lost his damn fool mind. Her vanilla cookie scent surrounded him. The feel of her supple ass gripped in his hands as he pressed intimately between her thighs... his dick twitched in remembrance. It made Mason wonder whether, had they not been interrupted, he would have stopped.

That he'd jacked off in the shower this morning to quell his raging lust and that it had been her image flashing in his mind as he'd come was telling. Her lips swollen from his kiss. Her eyes wide. The firm points of her nipples poking through the material of her top. Her breathing unsteady.

He squelched the need clawing at him as he walked into her kitchen. And yes, it was her kitchen. In the short amount of time she'd been here, she'd assimilated well. The staff loved her. She'd turned a steady profit in the first week, and people in town were booking dinner reservations as the news of the new chef in town spread.

She stood there, her hair piled on top of her head, hidden underneath her ivory chef's hat but a few tendrils had escaped. He knew what they felt like now. Pure, spun silk. His fingers clenched and he fought back the ever present desire whenever she was in range. The ivory chef's jacket she wore shouldn't be sexy. Hell, it was like she was wearing a sheet that ended mid-thigh and shielded all the good parts: her killer rack, slim waist, and ass that made his mouth water just thinking about it. But the fact that his hands had caressed her, knew what she felt like in his arms, and it was as if only he had the pleasure of knowing what her body was like beneath it, was heady. And he could envision taking her in her chef's jacket. In nothing but that as she throatily whimpered his name.

Emily was at the island chopping vegetables, likely for the beef stew she'd added to the menu for tonight.

"Emily," he said, maintaining enough distance between them that he wouldn't be tempted to do something marginally idiotic. Like haul her into his arms, screw her brains out and not let go until they were both spent.

"What can I do for you, Mason?" she replied, not even glancing his way.

"What happened last night, won't happen again. You need to understand that the club is off-limits to you," he said. *Just as you are off-limits to me*, he thought.

She laid her chopping knife down, braced her palms on the counter and shot him a look. She said, "You can't tell me where

I can and cannot go, Mason. It's a free country. And while you might be my boss, when I am off the clock, it's my time."

"Fair enough. I just want to clear the air." And erect as many impenetrable barriers as possible so that, even if he was tempted, he wouldn't be able to act on those wants.

Emily turned his way and crossed her arms in front of her chest. Then she retorted, "Pffft. Clear the air, my ass. You want to make sure your chef doesn't go running off or cause a scene. Let's get one thing straight, that little incident wouldn't have happened if I had not wanted it to. And let's call a spade a spade here, because you kissed me back. Those weren't my hands on my ass. So you'll forgive me if your attempt to do whatever the hell it is you're doing right now doesn't work on me. I'm not a piece of fluff and I know my own mind. You can take your self-righteous declaration and shove it. Now, if you will, I have work to do."

"You couldn't handle my world, Emily. I'm not vanilla in the slightest," he said, trying to explain and soften his words. Not to mention he wanted to avoid the minefield of having an intimate, physical relationship with an employee.

She looked at him then, her gaze livid, those incredible eyes of hers flashing with anger, and said, "How do you know what I can and cannot handle or what I like? You never even asked me, Mason. You pulled this *I'm a man and know better than you* bullshit. It's demeaning and it's wrong. At least own up and admit it—if not to me, to yourself—that you wanted me last night every bit as much as I wanted you. And as for whether I can handle your world or not, I guess we'll never know. If you don't mind." She waved a hand toward the door, shooing him out, dismissing him. She picked the knife up and resumed chopping the batch of carrots.

Emily wanted him.

Fuck.

He didn't know how to handle that bit of information. A

kiss in a darkened parking lot after a drink or two was one thing. But they were both stone cold sober now and her admission tested his resolve. Not trusting himself to speak after her revelation, fighting his sudden swift urge to throw his good sense into the nearby trash receptacle and take up exactly where they had left off last night, Mason swiveled on his heel. His only thought, escape. Otherwise, he would surrender to the lust pounding throughout his body, attempting to override his good intentions. He sauntered toward the door.

Except, before he could make good his escape, Emily said under her breath in that throaty voice, "Maybe it's more that *you* can't handle *me*. Ever think about that, oh wise one?"

Mason would have laughed if it wasn't so fucking tragic.

CHAPTER 9

*E*mily insinuated herself further into the lodge over the next few days, avoiding the blockhead at all costs. Hard to do when they worked so close together. But she treated the bulk of the main building as if it were the Grand Canyon. It was better this way. Simpler.

The one exception of her self-imposed avoidance was when she submitted her reports with the daily totals. Those she did on purpose. She could have relegated the chore to Tibby or Faith when they were present. Either one of them would think nothing of the task. Except Emily wanted Mason to know, to remind him, to show him she was the reason the restaurant's revenue continued to build profits. That it was thanks to the changes she'd enacted. And yes, she realized it was petty of her to gloat over the totals on the daily specials. Her specials, her recipes.

Granted, the stubborn caveman had commented on the YouTube video of her chastising her previous chef. She'd wanted him to be aware of potential fallout. Not that she thought there would be any—hell, it could be a potential draw. Although you wouldn't know that from his response, treating her like she'd committed murder. While she had killed her career, in a way, when she'd explained her side—that Chef Ormond had stolen her recipes and passed them off as his—the glittering anger in Mason's eyes had caused a lump to form in her chest. He'd been furious. For her.

No one had gone to bat for her. Not even her family or any of her friends.

They'd all treated her like she'd had a mental breakdown instead of the fact that someone she'd trusted had committed highway robbery. Except Mason, who'd nodded and said she wouldn't have to worry about anything like that happening here. He'd accepted her word as fact.

It made the gulf she'd erected seem petty.

They were grown-ups. Well, most of the time. And so they'd shared an incredible kiss. Maybe, if she softened her approach with him, he would show her the same courtesy. Perhaps they couldn't indulge in the wicked delights of each other's bodies, but maybe they could be friends.

If it weren't for her end of the day reports, she wouldn't see him at all. And it appeared Mason was avoiding her, as well. He stayed out of the restaurant entirely and had one of the registration clerks pick up his meals. He was treating her even more distantly, when he hadn't exactly been a bundle of warmth before. And now, the man likely had icicles hanging from his ding dong.

If Mason wanted to pretend that their kiss never happened, give her the cold shoulder as if they hadn't played tonsil hockey, fine. She could pretend, as well. But that didn't mean she wasn't trying to win him over. She just chose an indirect approach. Her food. When the orders for Mason came in, she tended to add a little something extra, like dessert. And she knew he ate every scrap because his plates were returned empty.

It was progress. Her plan to make him addicted to her cooking was working, one meal at a time.

The barriers he'd erected also gave Emily an excuse to bury herself in the restaurant, in her plans, tweaking the menu until even the standard fare they offered had her signature stamp on it. In the interim, she developed a solid routine with Tibby and Faith so that they operated together seamlessly. With her hand at the helm, she guided Tibby—who for all her brashness did not like assuming command—and the two of them rotated different shifts so that there was always coverage. But Tibby followed Emily's directions for the menu, and carried them out without fail.

"Okay, what gives, you two?" Emily asked Tibby and Faith. They had stopped talking when she'd walked in. The two of them had been casting her weird glances all morning long. Tibby had taken the morning breakfast shift today and Emily glanced between them.

"We overheard that you went into Cuffs & Spurs illegally on Friday night," Tibby said, giving her a *you're busted* smirk and wriggling her eye brows.

"And if I did?" Emily asked with a shrug, as if the incident had been no big deal. Never mind the epic kiss she'd shared with the boss afterwards. And that was something she wouldn't share with them or admit to, even if they threatened to melt her knives. Emily gathered together the ingredients on the counter for her pumpernickel bread. It had become such a big hit, they'd started serving fresh loaves by the basket with every dinner.

"Right on. You're such a rebel. I love it," Tibby said and laughed.

"I'd never have the courage to enter a place like that without permission," Faith added. But that was because Emily's cute line cook, with her blonde pixie cut and soft spoken manners, never did anything out of line. Faith was sweet and followed orders without question. Yet tell her to take command and she panicked.

Emily gave them a conspiratorial grin and replied, "Well, I've never been much for following the rules, especially someone else's. And who told you? I have no idea how you would even find out about it."

Tibby's eyes glittered as she replied, "My friend, Natalie. She was in the club that night. And your foray into the club has been the talk of members all week long. You and Nat would hit it off, by the way. We should have a girls' night one evening here soon so I can introduce you."

Pleasure spread throughout Emily's chest. Slowly but surely, she was being folded into the community here. The fact that Tibby felt comfortable enough to want to introduce her to her friend, include her, let Emily know she was building something here in the wilds of Wyoming. It made her feel welcome. She measured out her ingredients. Her foray had been the talk of members. Did that mean they were part of this club too? Her curiosity about the forbidden lower level piqued, she asked, "And you are all members of this Spurs club?"

"It's Cuffs & Spurs, but yes, we are members. We're both submissives. Why, you interested?" Tibby asked, a sly grin on her face. She hoisted a tray full of lasagna into one of the nearby ovens and set the timer.

"And if I was?" Emily asked, starting the industrial grade mixer.

Tibby performed a little booty shake move and said, "Woot! I knew it. Pay up, Faith. You owe me twenty."

"Wait, you bet each other?" Emily glanced between her sous chef and line cook. Was she that transparent in her interest? She had tried like mad not to think about what she'd witnessed that night, or the way it had made her feel. Or that, in the dead of night, she'd remembered those scenes, had dreamt about them... only she was the one experiencing untold wicked delights—with Mason.

Tibby snorted as Faith handed her a twenty and she shoved it into her pants pocket. She said, "Of course we did. So is it true that Mason carried you out of the club?"

"And if he did?" Emily asked, acting as nonchalant as possible when, in truth, the memory of his hands on her turned her insides into crème brûlée.

Faith's cornflower blue eyes grew wide at Emily's admission and she replied, "I would have melted into a puddle if he'd done that to me. Not to mention I wouldn't be able to show my face around here."

"But, my dear, sweet Faith, that's because you are the epitome of an obedient submissive. I have a feeling our Emily here is a bit more vocal and not as well-behaved," Tibby explained with a wink in her direction.

"And is that a bad thing?" Emily asked, uncertain about the unfamiliar terrain she found herself in. It begged the question: was she submissive? Or did she just like kinky sex?

Tibby shrugged. "Depends on if you like to be disciplined. I have a fondness for the cane and like provoking a Dom."

A part of Emily rebelled at the notion, made her think that perhaps she just wanted kinky sex and she asked, "But isn't that abuse?"

Shaking her head, Tibby replied, "Nope. Not when it's a properly trained Master or Dominant. And the level and tenor of a submissive's punishment is within a submissive's control as long as you are honest with a Dom about your limits. Not to mention, that's why there's a safeword. In case a scene or punishment gets too intense."

Tibby's explanation made sense. A properly trained Master. Wasn't that what Mason had said he was? That he enjoyed restraining a woman and disciplining—what had he said? Mouthy submissives? Except, Emily wasn't certain how she felt about that aspect. Especially since she was all tangled up with her desire for him, which conflicted so strongly with her need to prove herself as head chef and stay away from him. Did she want a man to hurt her during sex as a kind of foreplay?

Maybe. When Mason had smacked her butt cheek while he'd carried her, it had turned her on. Didn't mean she wasn't conflicted about it. Or that she wanted someone besides Mason to administer it, for that matter.

Faith sweetly asked Emily, "Are you a submissive?"

Wasn't that the question? Ever since her misguided kiss with Mason, Emily had imagined different scenarios with him. Not on purpose, but her blasted brain seemed intent on rousing her hormones into screaming idiots any time he was around, or while she was sleeping and unguarded. And in those visions, they were playing hide the pickle while she was restrained. Sometimes with a silk scarf in her bed, sometimes with a pair of handcuffs, and other times on the X contraption she'd seen at the club. And she enjoyed every minute of it. Just that morning she'd woken up, achy and needy—for Mason.

It infuriated her. It had been one blasted, misguided kiss.

"I'm not sure. Maybe," she admitted. "But it's not like I can figure that out. I'm not a member of the club."

"But you want to be?" Tibby asked while she helped Faith on the line, assembling burgers for a family of four in the dining room.

Would it hurt Emily to explore this path? Part of her adventure in moving here had been to shake up her stale existence and add some spice back into it. Among other things. Would she regret not taking a chance on herself and finding out if she really was a submissive? Or if she was just in an extreme desert wasteland of sexual frustration and anything—including the super kinky extreme—would do. Not showing a hint of her raging internal debate and uncertainty, she calmly said, "Perhaps. Why? Is there a way for me to join?"

"Spencer," they said in unison.

"Huh?" she asked, completely confused.

"Go see Spencer Collins. He owns the Teton Cowboy and runs the club for us," Tibby explained.

"I'll think about it," Emily replied. But then the lunch rush hit and there wasn't time for idle gossip. It gave her much-needed time to mull over her options.

What would Mason think if she became a member of his forbidden club?

CHAPTER 10

*O*n Thursday, Emily entered the double doors of the Teton Cowboy toward the end of the lunch rush. She hoped she'd timed this excursion properly. Her day had started before the sun crested the mountains. In the time since, she'd cooked breakfast for a packed dining room, prepped ingredients for lunch, and given instructions on the prep that needed to be done for the dinner rush that evening. Before she left, she'd handed in a proposal to Mason about hosting an Oktoberfest event at the lodge in two weeks' time.

She hoped he wasn't stubborn and refused. With him, she never knew whether she was coming or going.

In the midst of all the chaos, one answer had become startlingly clear. Emily wasn't going to sit on the sidelines of her new life but was going to jump in feet first and see where she landed. She hoped it landed her a membership to Cuffs & Spurs. One, because her curiosity was at an all-time high. Two, she had to satisfy her sexual cravings with something other than snack cakes or by this time next year, she'd be in a competition to become the next Goodyear blimp. Three, perhaps there would be another man at this club who would stoke her fires. That way she could stop lusting after Mason, stop fantasizing about him, and actually make a go of this place.

Emily approached the hostess stand. The short brunette woman behind it smiled warmly but she noticed the hint of exasperation in her jade gaze. Emily felt her pain. The end of a mealtime rush could leave a body frazzled beyond measure.

"Welcome to the Teton Cowboy. How many in your party, today? Just one?" she asked. Her nametag said her name was Paige.

"Actually, I'm here to speak with the owner, Spencer Collins," Emily replied, her nerves a bit on edge. While she'd made her decision and would stand firm with it, that didn't undermine the anxiety slithering through her system over that decision. Did she really want to join a kinky sex club and let some dude tie her up? Considering her brain flashed an explicit image of her with Mason, yes. Yes, she did.

"Did you have a meeting scheduled with him, because I don't see that he has any appointments scheduled," Paige asked politely with an edge of steel in her voice.

"No. But it's about Cuffs & Spurs," Emily explained. Her voice carried and she winced.

The hostess went stock still and the cheerful expression on her features dropped as she glanced around the restaurant, checking to see if anyone had overheard.

Then, with a steely nod, she said, "Follow me."

Emily trailed behind her. They wove around wooden tables and headed toward the back of the building. Paige guided Emily through a pair of double doors, past the kitchen that was still moving at a fast pace, even with the rush complete, to an open office door. Inside was a luxuriously furnished office, for a restaurant. Decorated with dark woods and burgundy walls, the richly appointed room seemed more like a personal at home office. Behind a stately lake of a desk sat a man whom

Emily assumed was Spencer Collins. The man was alpha, every line of him distinctly male. If not for the faint, jagged white scar that ran from his crown to his angular jawline, he would have been pretty. Too pretty. As in: Hollywood actor pretty. The scar gave him a dangerous air, with his thick black hair and trimmed beard. He wore a dress shirt rolled up to his elbows, and she spied the hint of tattoo ink where it was open at his neck.

"Excuse me, Sir?" Paige murmured with a knock on the wooden door.

He lifted his head up and said, "Yes, Paige. What can I do for you?"

"She would like to speak to you about our club," Paige replied.

His black gaze homed in on Emily in an assessing fashion. She'd left her hair down and had tried to appear casual in jeans and a layered top, but maybe she had been too casual. She typically didn't worry about the sort of tops she wore since they were usually hidden under her chef's jacket. The white tank top, layered with a pale blue Henley, the buttons open in the front, might not have been the best choice. They showed off her curves but maybe she should have worn something more revealing and low cut. What should you wear when you were trying to join a kinky sex club?

"Thank you, Paige, you may go. Come in, and have a seat, Miss—" he asked as he stood.

"Emily Fox. It's nice to meet you," she said as he approached and held out her hand.

He was tall, about Mason's height, a good solid six feet. His black slacks were molded to his thickly hewn legs. His long, blunt fingers closed around hers and he replied, "Spencer Collins, Miss Fox."

Then Spencer shut the office door before he returned to his

seat behind the desk. His black gaze studied her. "You're the new chef out at Black Elkhorn Lodge, aren't you?

"I am, but how did you know that?" she asked.

"The subs of Cuffs & Spurs have been all atwitter about your cooking," he explained. "I haven't had the chance to get out there yet but I hear nothing but good things."

"Thank you. You won't regret it once you do, I can assure you," she replied, and was proud of herself for sounding so calm when she felt like she was under a microscope.

Cocking his head a bit to the left, he asked, "Didn't you sneak into my club the other night?"

"I wouldn't call it sneaking so much as I saw an open door and wanted to see where it led." She didn't bat an eye or show that her internal systems blared code red at her obvious mistake. But this was her story and she was sticking to it. Emily wanted an in here.

"And you think you're submissive?" Spencer gave her a studious look, like he was attempting to divine her innermost secrets.

She shrugged. Emily had never been shy and figured honesty was the best policy. "Possibly, but only in a bedroom manner. I think I'm a little too independent for anything outside of that. It's a sort of conflict I'm having with myself. The thought of being dominated by a man in the bedroom is a complete turn-on yet, at the same time, if a man tells me what to do, I'd likely body slam him."

At Spencer's bark of laughter, she blushed.

Emily explained further, "I just want the chance to find out if I'm really submissive or if I just need some bedroom kink. Both Tibby and Faith mentioned that this club was a safe place to explore. Besides, I don't really know anyone here. I'm not used to being stuck at home. So it would be nice to belong to a community that I might fit in with."

"You have spirit, I will give you that. All right, Miss Fox, I will grant you a temporary membership. There are rules."

She snorted and rolled her eyes. Of course there were.

"Problem?" Spencer asked. His entire body had stilled. And Emily realized she might need to temper her sarcasm a wee bit around him.

"No, it just seems that everything in my life is temporary. My job here, the temporary insanity that made me accept the position at Black Elkhorn Lodge, coming here today..." She wondered if she would live to regret this decision.

"Sweetheart, life is temporary. Do what makes you happy and forget the rest. There's no time for anything else. Trust me," Spencer said, his stare haunted, almost as if he were saying the words to himself.

"And are you?" she asked, curious.

"What?"

"Happy? Are you happy?" Emily asked. Because she knew, deep down, she'd felt that there was a lack in her life. An emptiness that no amount of Ho Hos or Ding Dongs was going to fill. It was part of the reason why Ormond's betrayal had lacerated her so deeply. Before then, he'd been her biggest supporter, encouraging her to push her boundaries as a chef, and had showered her with praise when she succeeded. Chef Ormond had filled the lack that had always been present in her life. Her need for one person to acknowledge her and make her feel worthwhile.

Spencer observed her, his black gaze glimmering with respect, and then he replied, "In a roundabout way, yes."

"That's it? A maybe yes? No explanation?" she said, rather exasperated. She wanted him to tell her that yes he was, that being a member of this club was everything to him and made him deliriously happy. His non-answer deflated her a bit.

"I don't know you and you don't know me, so that's all you're getting," Spencer chided with a lopsided smirk, pulling paperwork out of his desk. It made him likeable instead of formidable.

"For now." She fluttered her lashes at him in a dramatic fashion with what she hoped was a winning smile.

He chortled at her antics, then said, "You'll do well here, I think. Fill all of these forms out with your limits and so forth. Then I will get your cuffs ready to pick up tomorrow if you want to attend."

Emily began filling out the forms to join, reading through everything. Making note of what she was going to need to research on the Internet because she had no idea what it was. And she was frankly too embarrassed to ask Spencer. He was a stranger, and a rather attractive man. There was no way she could ask him what medical play was without dying of embarrassment. She could feel the blush just from checking the box marked *restraints*. As she wrote, Spencer explained some of the rules that she would need to follow as a submissive. There was a submissive meeting she was required to attend once a month, as long as the weather cooperated.

By the time she had finished the application and all the paperwork required, her head was swimming with information.

Spencer gave her a packet of information to read through at home and then walked her out toward the front entrance. "I will have your cuffs for you tomorrow, if you decide to attend. Since you are new to the lifestyle, if you need any assistance, you are to let me know. That includes deciding to be with a Dom. I'd be happy to help in any way I can, including introducing you."

"Thank you, Spencer. I really do appreciate it," she said, grinning at his offer. He really was handsome, and she was certain, should he turn the charm on, he'd be a panty-melter. Maybe he could be the one to help turn her hormones away from Mason. When he lifted his face and looked past her shoulder, his face turned into granite.

"What are you doing here, Meghan?" Spencer bit out harshly.

Emily turned her head to discover who had earned the man's wrath, glad it wasn't her for once, and was shocked. The woman was stunning. Beauty pageant stunning. Glossy, long blonde hair that fell over one delicate shoulder in a thick braid. She wore a pair of skinny jeans and knee-high black boots with a formfitting pastel pink sweater.

"Well if it isn't Mister Grumpypants himself. Just here to pick up a to-go order before I head home," the blonde replied and rolled her eyes at Spencer.

"And you had to come to my place?" Spencer growled, his voice low and decidedly angry.

"First, I didn't know that you'd be here. Second, I like your wings. And third, I just finished watching my nephew all afternoon and all I want to do is eat and then collapse for the day."

"He's what, six months? How hard could it be?" Spencer said and gave the woman a patronizing look.

Meghan crossed her arms in front of her chest and dished out the attitude. Her voice dripped sarcasm. "Dude, he's also teething and trying to get into everything. You think you're so tough. I dare you to go watch him for an afternoon and get back to me on whether you feel like you've been hit by a train or not."

"You just don't have the stamina apparently, little brat," Spencer replied.

A waitress handed Meghan a to-go bag with the restaurant logo on it, stuffed with Styrofoam containers. And the scent of the hot wings made Emily's mouth water.

"And you like to overestimate your prowess, big guy. See you around," Meghan said and walked away without a backward glance. Spencer muttered something under his breath, his black gaze fixated on her retreating form.

"Well, Spencer, thank you for everything," Emily murmured.

Spencer's demeanor shifted and he glanced at her, but some of the previous warmth in his gaze was absent. She didn't know who Meghan was to Spencer, but they clearly had a history.

"Emily. I hope to see you tomorrow evening. If you'll excuse me, I have a meeting with a distributor in a few minutes."

"I'll get out of your hair. Make sure you come by the Elkhorn and have dinner. My treat as a thank you," she offered.

He nodded and replied, "Will do. See you around, Emily."

Emily left the Teton Cowboy resolute. She planned to head to the club tomorrow night. And then she would see what this forbidden club was all about. Mason didn't own her and couldn't tell her where she went or with whom.

He wanted to keep their relationship strictly business? Fine by her.

CHAPTER 11

*E*mily's hands trembled as she exited her vehicle and immediately smoothed her short skirt over her hips. Her incredibly teeny-tiny jean skirt that barely covered her bum. She couldn't sit in the darn thing without flashing everyone her wicked bits. And then there was the skin-tight leather vest Tibby had loaned her for tonight. It fit, but she was a bit bigger in the chest area than Tibby. The thing made her boobs look huge and pushed them up and out. They were just so out there.

At least her coat covered her up. Last night, the temperature had plummeted and she shivered at the cold. Her breath expelled in a shadowed plume as she walked toward the club. Maybe she'd have to rethink what she wore next time. If there was a next time. Back home, her club gear would have been fine in the warmer, milder temperatures.

Anxiety hummed in her veins and Emily wondered for the hundredth time in the last hour if attending the club was a good idea. She'd worn her hair down, and had added a few long loose curls so it fell in waves.

The heels of her black boots clicked over the pavement.

At the door to the Teton Cowboy, she inhaled a deep breath before she entered. This was it. And then she strode inside before she lost her nerve. It was Friday night and the Teton Cowboy was packed. She wound her way through patrons, noticing the admiring glances she received along her path. Even with their interest, she was too invested at this point to back down. She would go all the way and enter the forbidden club as a member or she'd go home and mainline Ding Dongs. There would be no half measures at this point. Tonight, at the private entrance, there was a man guarding the door. A very attractive man.

"Name?" he asked, his baritone smoky and decadent, like the caramelized layer of crème brûlée.

"Um, it's Emily. Emily Fox," she replied.

"The newbie? I'm Derrick. These are for you. Spencer said if you showed tonight to remind you no more than two drinks," he said holding out a set of cuffs.

"Is that all?" she asked, accepting the brown leather cuffs. She fastened them around her wrists with his help. The cowboy was cute with his soft blue eyes and winsome smirk. His fingers brushed against her wrist and she got nothing. No spike in her blood pressure. No sizzle. And that worried Emily.

"Just have fun. The ribbon here," he said, indicating the small red one, "means you're new to the club."

"Kind of like a scarlet letter, huh?" she said, trying to lighten her mood.

"In a roundabout way, I suppose. But it informs the Doms to go slowly with you," Derrick explained, his eyes kind.

"Good call. Anything else?" she asked.

"Nope. Just have fun. You can put your jacket and purse in a locker, they're located down the stairs and to the right," he said and opened the door for her.

She ambled past him and inside. When the door closed behind her with a solid thud, she blew out a shaky breath. It was normal to feel uneasy. A drink or two would calm her. It seemed like, after her little invasion the other night, Spencer had decided to post a guard at the entrance. Or he'd just taken a break and she'd gotten lucky the first time.

Ignoring the anxiety rising in her chest, Emily inhaled a few deep breaths and then descended into the belly of the beast. Clutching her small wristlet purse, she entered the private club. She glanced down the hallway on the right and noticed the doorways for the male and female locker rooms and a door beyond those. There was also a long line and row of hooks at eye-level along the wall outside the locker rooms that other patrons had already hung their coats upon. It was suspiciously warm down here. Warm enough that if she kept her coat on, she'd be sweltering before long. Probably had to do with the amount of flesh on display. She unbuttoned her coat and removed it, hanging it on one of the empty hooks near the stairs, but kept her small purse with her.

To her eyes, the club gave the impression that the night was just getting underway. The scene areas were unoccupied. But from what she'd read in the information Spencer had provided her yesterday, it wasn't unusual for the club to really kick into gear at around ten. Which was a hazard with her job, considering she didn't really get to sleep in.

Emily waltzed over to the bar, figuring it was as good a place to start as any. The gentleman behind it gave her a salacious smile as she sat down, which was hard to do in her itty bitty skirt. She sat sideways, with both legs on one side instead of how the saddle seat was intended to be used. No way was she sitting astride the thing. It wasn't the most comfortable position, but she wasn't prepared just yet to flash everyone her naughty bits. Hiding them was already difficult with the shortness of this skirt. No need to go lifting it higher yet. She was dipping her toes into the naughty pool tonight. After that, she would see.

The hunky bartender, his eyes the color of smoke in his tanned face, leaned forward and a blunt finger traced the red on her cuff. His midnight hair was trimmed short but she noticed some curl in it at the tips. He said, "I'm Matt. You'll see me behind the bar most nights down here. And I'm a stickler for ensuring subs don't drink past their limit. What can I get for you, darlin'?"

Again, his touch barely caused a blip on her radar. She gave him a soft smile and said. "It's Emily. Can I get a Guinness?"

"Good choice." He gave her a cock-eyed grin and moved around the bar, filling her order.

She felt someone slide onto the saddle seat beside her and glanced over. And found herself staring into some of the bluest eyes she'd ever seen. The broad-shouldered cowboy was melt-your-panties-off handsome. His chestnut hair was shaded with hints of deep auburn and the color extended to the trim beard he wore over his square jaw. But it was the gentleman's eyes, the sharp cobalt orbs reminding her of the sky at twilight and glittering with interest in their depths, that made him truly mesmerizing. Lines crinkled at the corners as he smiled at her.

"Evening," he murmured, his voice rich like melted dark chocolate. And his chest, his incredibly solid chest, liberally dusted with fine dark hair, was bare for all and sundry to behold.

Before she could respond, Matt returned with her Guinness. "Here you are, darlin'. Garrett, good to see you. I see you've met Emily, the newest sub to join our group."

Garrett replied, "That I have. We're old friends now, aren't we, Emily?"

"Um, sure," she said, uncertain how to proceed here, even with his gentle teasing.

"I can see you're not convinced. Garrett Brooks. I run the Indian Peak Ski Resort," he said and held his hand out for her to take. He had long, elegant, piano player fingers.

When she placed her hand in his and his larger one dwarfed hers, she was thrilled by the low hum in her blood. She replied, shifting toward him, giving him more than an eyeful of her cleavage, "Oh really, I've heard about that place but haven't had a chance to visit. Emily Fox, I'm the chef over at the Elkhorn Restaurant."

He held her hand in his, seeming unwilling to let her get away. A dark slash of brow raised inquisitively as he responded. "So beautiful and you can cook?"

She flushed. He was really cute. And maybe, even though it wasn't the flash bang grenade to her system like it was with Mason, Garrett did elicit a modicum of belly fluttering activity. It was enough. It had to be. He might be precisely what she needed to alleviate her frustration. So she flirted back. "And you seem to go after what you want."

"That I do. New in town and new to our club. What do you think?"

"Jackson is growing on me. I wasn't sure it would, since it's so different from Los Angeles, but I'm enjoying the changes. And just so you know, it's my first time ever in a club like this," she admitted, hoping it wouldn't be a turn off for him. Besides, one of the themes that had been repeated in her packet of information was honesty and communication between a Dom and submissive. So that was what Emily was doing.

"So you're a total newbie to the lifestyle?" Garrett's cobalt gaze simmered as it roved over her form.

"I am. And I will admit I'm a little nervous. I've never done anything like this before," she explained. Heat rushed into her cheeks and she took a sip of Guinness to wet her dry throat.

The lust-infused look he gave her, the way his eyes trailed over her form almost like a caress, caused goosebumps to erupt on her skin.

His voice low, he murmured, "Well, if you're amenable, I'd be happy to help ease your anxiety. Why don't you come have a seat with me on one of the couches, where it will be more comfortable and we can get to know each other?"

She chewed on her lip for a minute.

"Emily, no pressure. If you're not up for a scene tonight and need to work your way up, that's okay. We can just sit and talk," Garrett said, lifting the bottle of Corona the bartender had brought him.

She nodded and blew out a breath. "Sure. We can talk. Sorry, Sir Garrett, if I seem undecided."

"Just Sir will do for now. And you're doing fine. Let's go over there and we'll see what we can do about those jitters, eh?" Garrett gave her a lopsided grin. And she could only think, *oh, he's good. He's got that calm, bedside manner that could make a girl feel right at home.*

"Okay, I'm in. I'm all yours," she said and then flushed at the innuendo.

"I was hoping you'd say that," he replied with a sexy grin. Then he helped her off the saddle seat.

Emily picked up her beer. Garrett guided her over to a small leather loveseat. And it was small. Or, really, Garrett was just a big, tall cowboy and took up more than his fair share of space. He had an arm spread out behind her on the backrest and his outer thigh pressed up against hers.

"Do you have questions about the lifestyle?" he asked, searching her face.

"All of it." She gestured toward the scene areas. "I don't know what most of this stuff is. And then I'm not even sure I am submissive."

"Why do you think you might be?" he asked as one of his hands toyed with her hair.

Honesty was key to this, right? She explained, "I've always loved to please other people. It's part of the reason why I'm a chef. I cook and make people happy, euphoric even, by what I feed them. But when it comes to being intimate, I've always been bored with my partners."

"They couldn't have been that bad."

She said, "Nothing to write home about, that's for sure. And they were decent men. Good guys, but they always wanted me to take charge when we were physically intimate. Which for me was a snooze-fest. I'm in control of every aspect of my life, but it's the one area where, for whatever reason, I don't want to be in charge. Does that make sense? It's the one area where being in charge bores me to tears."

"And how do you feel about bondage?" Garrett asked. And from the light of desire in his gaze, she knew he wasn't deterred by her explanation.

She just wished she felt something more than mild excitement at his touch. "I'm not sure. The idea of it makes me..."

Her face flamed and she was sure she was beet red.

"Aroused?" Garrett pressed. His kindness and understanding were disarming.

It made her want to confess all her sins to him. She said, "Yes. Is that wrong? I mean, I know it's not, but I've never..."

Garrett cupped her chin. His piano player fingers were strong and calloused. The intimate gesture caused shivers to zing along her spine as he drew her gaze up to his. "No, it's not wrong to have desires that are different from the status quo. It's why we have this club in the first place. I tend to enjoy restraining a submissive and making her come undone from my touch before I fuck her. It's not wrong as long as both parties consent to the actions, the scene, beforehand. Understand?"

She swallowed the lump in her chest as some of her tension eased. The way he talked about his preferences, like it was how he liked his coffee, the certainty of it, the confidence behind it, made her want to lean into him. And yet, at the imagery he described, she had visions of just that—but it wasn't Garrett she was with. Guilt swamped her.

"Yes. Thank you. Now, what are all the different stations?" she asked, trying to get the ground back beneath her feet. She liked Garrett. His touch wasn't a bomb to her system like the man she had promised herself not to think about tonight. But it was warm, comfortable. And the slight stirrings of desire existed. It was enough. She would make it be enough.

He released her chin, reluctantly, and then proceeded to explain each of the stations. There was the sawhorse, the fuck bench, the St. Andrew's Cross, one with a suspension bar, a medical table, an upright stockade, there was a sex swing, and then a dungeon wall with chains. Garrett explained some of the different techniques, answering the questions she had, which were quite a number, but he wasn't annoyed with her for asking so many. Quite the opposite. His free hand lightly trailed over her leg pressed against his. His touch was hypnotic.

Emily could do this with Garrett. She could see the avid interest in his eyes.

"You're still a little worried. Why?" he asked, prodding her.

"I've never done it with an audience before. I'm worried that I would freeze and disappoint you," she said, watching his response.

"Well, if you really have a problem with a public scene, for your first entrance, I can get one of the private rooms for us in the back. If you're up for it. I like you, Emily, and I would enjoy indoctrinating you into the lifestyle. All you have to do is say yes," he said, his face serious as he studied her reaction.

What the hell. She needed to get her unholy obsession with Mason out of her bloodstream and Garrett was ready, willing, and able to fit the bill. Not to mention he was nice, handsome to boot, and something told her he would ensure she enjoyed every minute.

"Yes, Sir. I would like that," she replied.

His eyes crinkled at the corners as he grinned and said, "Stay here and I will check to see what's open."

She could only respond with a nod. Her throat was dry and her pulse fluttered in anticipation.

Emily rose and stood with Garrett, then waited at the nearby bar top table for him to return. A private room, she could do. It settled some of her anxiety so she could focus on what should be a fun and hopefully pleasurable night. While they'd been deep in conversation, the club had filled up quite a bit. The scene areas were no longer unoccupied. As she gazed around, she spied Cole. When his gaze connected with hers, she gave him a smile. Cole tipped his hat in her direction while he towed the hostess, Paige, whom she'd met the other day into one of the scene areas.

Emily liked the club. She felt like she'd made the right decision in applying for membership. Now that she knew what occurred here, the shock value wasn't as prominent. Not that she was one hundred percent comfortable watching Cole get it on with Paige in the sawhorse scene area because she wasn't.

In fact, it made her blush. That was all she'd seemed to do since she had walked into the club that night. But the woman with Cole was now unabashedly naked and he was restraining her against the sawhorse. It wasn't something Emily witnessed every day—or ever, really—and it was kinky as hell.

A low burn set up residence in her belly.

The way Cole moved in the scene area, his shirt absent, displaying a wealth of rangy chest muscles. But his movements relayed utter control and confidence. It was a mega-watt turn on. The dominance of it. She couldn't deny that the alpha maleness of the Doms aroused her like nothing else had before. She worried it aroused her a little too much and set her world on end. Perhaps this was why she'd never had a problem contenting herself in the kitchen and not worrying about dating. Not that she didn't enjoy sex, she did. It was pleasant.

But there had always been a lack. Emily had assumed the lack was with her. Now, she was reassessing her stance.

She spied Garrett, striding back her way with a big grin on his face. She knew it meant he'd gotten them a private room. Her stomach clenched. She was about to go have kinky sex with a virtual stranger.

"What the fuck are you doing here?" Mason growled from behind her. Her entire body tensed and kinetic lightning slashed at her resolve just as Garrett made it to her side.

Garrett glanced at Mason. "Easy, Mase."

"I'm a member," she replied and gave Mason a deadpan look when in reality her stomach was tied up in knots. "And I was getting to know Garrett here. He owns one of the ski resorts."

"Yes, I know that. But what I still can't wrap my brain around is the fact that you're here," Mason said, anger and something deeper, darker, and inherently more dangerous to her composure lacing his voice.

"Believe it. And Garrett here was going to take me into one of the private rooms tonight. He's being wonderful about my entry into the lifestyle. I'm ready when you are, Sir," she said to Garrett, giving him a gamine grin and threading her arm through his.

At her words, Garrett flashed a pleased, masculine grin, winked, and said, "And you won't regret it, sweet thing. Mason, good to see you."

Garrett's hand slid around her waist to lead her to the back of the club and the private room they would share. Her pulse pounded in her ears. She wasn't sure if it was from what she was about to do with Garrett or if it was because of Mason's presence. Damn him for interfering with her life this way.

"No," Mason growled and stepped in front of them, stalling their forward progression toward the private rooms.

"Mason, you need to back the hell off," Garrett warned and his arm around her waist noticeably tensed against her.

Mason leveled a gaze at Garrett, then said, "This one is not available. Not tonight, not any night."

What? He couldn't be serious!

Garrett and Mason had a wordless staring conversation. Emily really wished she understood what was happening. Why was Mason being such an ass? Of course she was available.

Then Garrett's hold on her slackened and he took a step away. Garrett backed off. She didn't know whether he saw the resolve in Mason or whatever their two-minute staring contest was, but he lowered his head and nodded. Then he glanced her way, regret swimming in his eyes. "Sorry, but I think you two have some issues that need to be worked out, Emily. Mason is one of my best friends and I won't poach."

"I. Just. Work. For. Him," she chewed out. Her blood pressure skyrocketed. She wanted to strangle Mason. Where did he get off?

Garrett's gaze hardened as he glanced at her and commanded, "That's enough. I've said my piece. But if you're going to be disrespectful, then I will take you over my knee."

It took everything inside Emily not to scream in frustration. Anger seethed in her veins. Mount St. Helen's had nothing on her. She was ready to blow a freaking gasket. But nice, sexy Garrett didn't deserve her wrath.

Mason did.

The bane of her existence. The man who kept her at arm's length and then told his club members that she was off-limits.

"Sorry, Master Garrett. I apologize for directing my anger your way," she said as demurely as possible, dismissing him. Emily had not really wanted him, but she'd chosen him for the night.

Then she rounded on the true culprit. The man who had destroyed her well laid plans. Who had no problem trying to control her. She glowered at Mason and said, with venom lacing her voice, "Are you happy? Do you get off on making me miserable? Is that your world that I can't handle? When in truth you're just an egotistical, controlling asshole? Well, chew on this, I fucking quit."

Then she strode around him. Fury dominated her steps and she danced out of arm's reach. The son of a bitch could rot in hell. She powerwalked to the door. Practically ripped her coat off the nearby hook. Took the steps two at a time and barreled out of the bar before Mason could stop her.

Emily was done attempting to please him. She was finished trying to scrape a measure of acceptance from him when it was clear as day to her now that he never would. And she couldn't live in a cage, begging for scraps.

Hadn't she done that most of her life? Seeking the approval from her family for the life she'd chosen for herself while they stared at her as if she were possessed?

Emily was moving out of the lodge tonight. She'd pack her stuff and go.

But go where? Hell if she knew. For tonight, she'd see if one of the nearby hotels had a spare room and then head out fresh in the morning. Maybe she could stay in Jackson. Surely there were enough tourists traps here that someone would hire her.

And as for Mason, the man could rot for all she cared.

CHAPTER 12

*E*mily drove back to the lodge like she was training for the Indy 500, a little surprised there wasn't steam pouring from her ears, she was so angry. The launch sequence of her internal combustion had been activated.

She parked by the door to the restaurant. She wanted her knives first. Good thing she'd left her case in the restaurant. Must have been a bit of foresight on her part. Emily hurried inside and stomped into the kitchen. Grabbing her bag from the dry storage, she hefted it over to the stainless steel countertop, where she'd stored her precious set.

She withdrew the specially made case for them and began packing her knives away. All she had to do was pack these. It shouldn't take her too long to box up her clothes in the cabin. She didn't have much. She could be in and out in a flash.

Anger boiled and brewed in her blood. She was surprised she wasn't foaming at the mouth, she was so pissed. Where did he get off? Did he dislike her that much?

She was gripping her chopping blade when the door to the kitchen slammed open. She didn't need to look to know who it was. She could feel him. The ever-present current saturated the kitchen.

"You can't quit. We agreed to a month," Mason growled with a finality that rankled the fabric of her being and pressed the all-systems-launch sequence.

Unwilling to ruin her knives, Emily slid the chopping blade in its case. And then she picked up a nearby empty metal mixing bowl. Swiveling, she lobbed it at his head. He ducked just before it connected with his cranium.

She shouted, "Screw you and your rules! I won't work for a tyrant."

Incensed that the bowl had missed, she fast pitched an orange at his head. Which he again ducked.

She continued her tirade, "If you don't want me, fine. But cock-blocking me like you did back there is fucking asinine. I don't belong to you. You had no right to do that to me. Fuck you and your self-righteous glares."

Mason advanced, his hooded gaze glittering knives as he approached. His jaw was clenched. The power of him, the overriding confidence as he prowled toward her, turned her insides liquid.

Emily didn't retreat even as tension gripped her, telling her to flee. She couldn't run. Not from him. Their present clash was nearly predestined from the moment they'd met. She wanted this fight with him, to finally have it out. She gave him a derisive snort. "Can't handle your world? Please."

He said nothing, his lips compressed as he advanced.

She tossed the salt canister at him and it bounced off his chest. The pepper grater followed. Nothing stopped him. Self-preservation finally made her backpedal. Mason stalked her through the kitchen.

Emily didn't realize until it was too late and she was cornered that they had been playing a game of cat and mouse. Only she was the mouse.

Her back hit the wall next to the dry storage. Emily wouldn't show fear. Not with him. She glared instead, ignoring that she was shaking. Her trembling hands were curled into fists at her sides.

Mason bracketed her body and placed his large palms on either side of her head. Her belly quivered at his nearness as his spicy scent washed over her.

"You can't quit," Mason snarled.

Then he pressed his full length against her, gripped her face in his hands, and slanted his mouth over hers.

At the first hard brush of his lips against hers, Emily moaned. It was hot. It was hungry. His kiss ignited the very fabric of her being. Emily knew she should push him away. But she couldn't keep fighting her attraction. She craved Mason the way dieters did sugar.

The way he kissed her. Hard. Brutal. Possessive.

And that was just a precursor. He told her with his kiss that he was staking his claim. Proving with this embrace that while she might have enjoyed a night in Garrett's arms, Mason was the one she wanted. The only one.

She lifted her fists to his chest. Her palms flattened against his pectorals. And she kissed Mason back with everything she was worth. He was the pinpoint of her need and her desires. His mouth moved against hers with confidence. She moaned as he changed the angle and kissed her impossibly deeper.

She dug her nails into his broad chest. Clung to him as he changed the orbit of her world until all she could feel and taste was Mason.

When he finally lifted his lips from hers, she whimpered at the loss. Her gaze felt heavy as she lifted her lids and sucked in a ragged breath. Hunger shrouded Mason's handsome features.

Emily found her voice and whispered, "Mason."

"If you don't want this, say so now," he ordered, his intense caramel gaze watching her reaction.

Not want him? She'd tried to stay away from him, but it was like trying to make her lungs go without air. She'd wanted him from the moment they'd met. And she was done fighting her attraction.

"I want this," she murmured.

No sooner had the words come out of her mouth than he was pulling her into the nearby dry storage closet and shutting the door behind them. He walked her backwards with his body until they ran out of room and her back was flush against the wall.

Mason's hands gathered her wrists. He drew them up over her head. Then he removed his belt and tossed it up over an exposed pipe jutting from the wall before looping it through the silver rings on her cuffs. She was restrained. Her breath backed up in her lungs. Emily had to rise up on her tiptoes. She worried some about the strain on her shoulders but knew Mason wouldn't let harm come to her.

"Your safeword is red," he ordered.

She nodded, her mouth suddenly dry.

Mason cupped her face again. The rough pad of his thumb rasped over her bottom lip before his mouth descended and claimed her once more. Emily hadn't realized she could feel so much. Want someone as much as she did Mason. She'd been kissed before. Plenty. But Mason's kiss was by far and away the most wicked of her existence.

It mimicked sex.

It was a pronouncement of what was to come. Now that he no longer held back or denied their potent connection, the full brunt of his lust and the carnal way his tongue thrust inside her mouth created a firestorm of desire inside her. She was wet between her thighs. The fact that she couldn't touch him, could only take what he was willing to give her, was half of the eroticism.

She had never been so aroused in her life. He invaded the

recesses of her mouth, plunging his tongue in rapid succession. When he pressed a thick, muscled thigh between her legs, she groaned against his lips.

Then realized she was rubbing her pelvis against his thigh and wondered if she would orgasm against his leg.

His hands undid the front of her leather vest, freeing her breasts. His hands cupped the globes, kneading the mounds. When he rubbed his thumb around a nipple, she moaned.

Mason lifted his head. She felt weightless and needy. He watched her reaction when he scraped his thumbs against her nipples. They hardened at his ministrations and she couldn't stop the mewl that escaped.

Then one of his big hands dropped down to her hip and drew her short skirt up until she was exposed to his gaze. At the groan Mason uttered, her belly tightened. He dropped to his knees before her. This big, proud man. When he reached the small swath of black lace covering her mound, he gripped it in his hands and tugged. The material snapped at the force.

And now Mason was staring at her pussy, lust covering his face. He spread her thighs and hissed, "Fuck, you're so wet."

Then he parted her slit with his thumbs, opening her up to his gaze. She watched, entranced, as he took her into his mouth. Mason ate her pussy. Ran his tongue along her slit, tasting her as if she were a delicacy. His tongue teased her clit, caressing under her hood, and then was plunging inside her pussy. He held her prisoner as he raised one of her legs up over his shoulder.

Emily was lost in a sea of need so startling and intense, she couldn't control it. She came. Hard. And loud. Her wails filled the dry storage locker.

Then Mason set her leg down and stood. He withdrew a foil packet from his back pocket and unzipped his jeans, shoving them to his thighs with his boxers. His cock sprang forth. He had one of the biggest dicks she'd ever seen. It was long and thick. Perfectly formed. She licked her lips as he rolled the condom down his length, protecting them both. And then he was lifting her legs up around his waist.

He used the wall for balance and guided his cock to her opening. When the crown pressed against her entrance, he ordered, "Look at me."

Emily hadn't realized she'd closed her eyes. She lifted her gaze and stared into his caramel depths. Then he thrust his hips and plunged deep inside until he was embedded inside her. She moaned. He was so big. He stretched her. And she—oh God, he felt so good.

"Give me everything. I want every sound, every cry. Don't hold back. Give yourself to me," Mason demanded.

She could only nod as he proceeded to move. His hands gripped her rear as he rocked his hips, plunging in a steady pace, bent on driving her crazy. She writhed against him, meeting his thrusts as he flexed his hips.

And she did as he asked. She wasn't quiet. She couldn't be if she tried. Mason pumped his big dick inside her in rapid succession and she saw stars. Her body clenched around him, wanting to draw him deeper.

The scent of their sex filled the small space. The slap of their flesh against one another competed with the cacophony of moans erupting from the back of her throat.

Emily's body coiled in on itself as Mason fucked her. She could feel the etchings of her orgasm like a runaway freight train from which there was no escape. His control began to slip and his pace became more frantic.

Through it all, he watched her, his gaze steady on hers. He jackhammered his thrusts. She rocked her hips. Keening now, she was in a heightened state where all she could see and feel was Mason. His scent, his body, his cock... as he fucked her brains right out.

"Come for me, Em," he growled.

When one of the hands clutching her ass pulled back and smacked her cheek as he thrust deep, Emily's body went over the ledge.

"Mason," she keened, straining as the orgasm ripped through her system. Her pussy spasmed and quaked around his pummeling cock. Teutonic plates shifted from the force of the tremors wracking her body.

Then Mason buried his face in her neck and his thrusts became impossibly faster. She barely came down from one orgasm before another ripped through her.

Then his cock jerked inside her folds. He slammed his cock home.

"Fuck, Em!" he roared. His hips pistoning inside her clenching heat set off another round of sparks in her pussy. He moved until his climax was spent.

And then he just held her close. Not moving. His face was buried in her neck. Her arms were tired from being restrained. But the rest of her was like molten molasses and twice as gooey. She could barely lift her eyelids. She liked that he held her. That he didn't pull away right away.

She sighed against his shoulder. Sex with Mason. Epic. There was no other word for it. And she was too sated to worry about the consequences.

When he finally lifted his head and looked at her, she inhaled a deep breath. The feeling, it seemed, was mutual.

CHAPTER 13

$\mathcal{M}$ ason released Emily's wrists from their restraints. Pulling her cuff loops off his belt, he rubbed her arms before setting her on her feet. He leaned her against the wall when she wobbled so he could collect himself and then take care of her. Disposing of the condom in a nearby trash can, he fixed his jeans and picked up his hat from where it had fallen to the floor in their earlier rush.

When he noticed her sliding down the wall and shivering, he took his flannel, and slid it over her arms. Then he scooped her up. She nestled her face at the base of his throat as he carried her. Her vanilla cookie scent surrounded him.

She really was a small thing. Much more delicate than he'd thought. A protectiveness he'd not felt with another invaded his chest. He strode with her out the back door of the main lodge, taking the short trail up the hill to his house. At the nip in the air, Emily murmured and snuggled against him more tightly.

An owl hooted nearby as he took the stairs up to the front door of the two-story Victorian style farmhouse. It was the house his parents had built when all the land around them had been nothing but wilderness and a dream. With his bundle cradled against his chest, Mason opened the front door single handedly, shutting it behind them with a booted heel.

Cole was still at the club and likely would be for a bit. Mason ascended the stairs and carried Emily to his bedroom. It sat at the tail end of the hall on the second floor. The same hallway he and Cole had built forts and had epic lightsaber battles in. There was a continuity he always felt at living here. Mason's room was the master suite. He had moved in there a few years after his dad had passed away.

He had added his furniture when he'd moved in. The four poster mahogany king-sized bed, for one, which he now laid Emily upon. The spill of her silken red hair against his pillows was a slash of color against the muted gray sheets. He hungered to feel those tresses surround him. He yearned to wrap her lengths around his hands as he buried himself inside her once more.

Fuck.

He never should have touched her. But tonight, seeing her in the sexy as hell short skirt, about to go with Garrett into one of the club's private rooms, had brought out a possessiveness he couldn't explain. It was as if the Master in him had already laid claim to her and considered Emily his.

Garrett, being Garrett, must have sensed that Mason would fight him over Emily. And Garrett, being the better of them, had conceded.

Mason wasn't sure if he would have been as gracious. In fact, he knew for damn sure he wouldn't have been.

And now that he had touched her, felt the silken clasp of her heat squeeze him, tasted her honeyed nectar, he craved more. Mason wanted to claim her in truth. Have her wear his cuffs. Show her just how good his world could be.

He stroked her cheek tenderly with the back of his knuckles, a final caress before he retreated. Because he wouldn't touch her again. He couldn't. He had to remain firm in his stance on this matter. The stability of the lodge depended on his ability to keep his dick in his pants.

He never should have touched her. Not with the lodge struggling. The previous chef had been embezzling funds from them. The absolute last thing he needed was to get involved with the new one.

Emily's eyes fluttered open. The heart-stopping smile she flashed his way caused his gut to clench. It was a mixture of satisfaction and unabashed invitation.

"Well, that was quite an introduction," she murmured, sliding her tiny hands over his chest. They scorched him as if they were a brand.

He felt her caress down to the balls of his feet. It rocked him. Shook him. Yet he persisted. "Em, look—"

She stilled. Those eyes of hers—fuck, they killed him, time and again—became a turbulent sea of disbelief and blistered him with a glance. She asked, "Are you giving me the brush off? Then why bring me here of all places?"

Yeah, why had he? Because a part of him had wanted her in his bed, craved to have her here. And tonight, seeing her in his bed, her lips still swollen from his kisses, her body enough to make him weep and give thanks, stirred him in more ways than one. Mason was having a singularly difficult time coming up with an excuse to walk away from her. Especially when every facet of his being looked at her in his bed and registered that it was where she belonged.

Walking away from his desire for her was the right thing to do. She was his employee. The lodge came first. It had to supersede his wants.

"This never should have happened tonight. You work for me. It's bad for business," Mason stated regretfully, glad that he sounded resolved in the matter when he was anything but. He stood, putting a foot of space between them. A small distance, but it erected a barrier.

"If you'll recall, I quit," Emily said.

"You're not quitting. I won't let you. If I have to tie you to that stove, I will," Mason swore.

She quirked an eyebrow and rose to a kneeling position. His flannel shirt dwarfed her and hung open down the front. It left her sensual body exposed. The hint of her ivory cleavage peeked through, taunting him with the fact that he hadn't tasted her there yet. Her skirt, what there was of it, was still rucked around her waist, leaving her pussy exposed, the creamy white skin bare. He could still taste her essence on his tongue and hungered to lap at her pretty pink folds once more.

She still wore her black, heeled boots. They'd never gotten around to taking them off. In her half-dressed state, her hair tousled around her shoulders, Emily looked like a wicked Greek goddess sent down to tempt him.

He was so fucking hard, his dick strained against his jeans.

Then she opened her mouth and said, "You don't own me, Mason. I can do what I want. And what I want, is this."

Then her hand slid beneath the waistband of his jeans and wrapped around his dick.

He growled. And then she squeezed him. Mason struggled to fight the waves of need as they crashed over him. Everything inside him clamored to claim her, put his mark on her. Demanded he prove to her once and for all that he was in charge.

"You. Are. Not. Leaving," he said through clenched teeth as she stroked him.

Her silken fingers gripped him and she cocked her head to the side. "You're not the boss of me."

"Yes. I. Am."

"Then prove it," she dared.

Emily's words were an incendiary tossed on his resolve.

Mason moved. Hauled Emily into his arms. He slanted his mouth over hers and reveled in her passionate whimpers against his mouth while she stroked him. She'd played with fire. Poked at him.

And now he wasn't fucking letting her go. Not tonight, at least.

As he kissed her, he stripped her. Mason wanted her nude this time. He yanked his shirt and her leather vest off. Then shoved her skirt down over her hips. He palmed the firm globes of her ass and growled against her lips.

Lifting his mouth, he shifted her body until her torso was bent over the side of his bed. He yanked the skirt off but left the heeled boots on. She looked so fucking hot. The plump globes beckoned him.

"Don't say I didn't warn you. This—" he swatted her rear, "—is for going to the club without my permission."

At her yelp, he gave her a series of hard swats. "Those were for tossing kitchen tools at me."

"And this," he swatted the flesh of her labia. The pink swollen lips were wet with her desire. "Is to show that I am very much the boss of you. And this belongs to me now. You won't fuck another while you are with me. Understood?"

Mason swished his fingers through her cunt, parting her, teasing her before he penetrated her with two fingers. Her musky scent invaded his nostrils. Her pussy gripped his digits as he plunged. He wanted her. Just like this.

"Oh god, Mason. Yes." She wailed. She canted her hips. Her hands gripped the mattress.

His balls tautened. Fuck, she was so open and receptive to his touch.

"In here, you will call me Sir or Master," Mason commanded. "Say it."

"Yes, Sir," she whimpered, tilting her hips up as he fingered her. Sawing his digits back and forth, a primitive, primal need swamped Mason. Hearing her utter those words caused his control to snap. He grabbed a condom from his nightstand and shoved his jeans down, freeing his erect shaft. He protected them both.

And then he buried his dick inside her dripping heat with a single, brutal thrust. He banded her arms behind her back. Pumping his hips, his dick glided through her grasping tissues. Mason didn't hold back. Her moans drove him wild. And the way she took him, accepted him. Even as his need to fuck, hard and brutal, overrode his common sense. But she was right there with him. Her throaty wails filled his room.

"God, yes, Sir. More!" She keened.

Repeatedly, he pounded. Her sheath clenched around him, pulling him deep as he pistoned inside. Then her pussy quaked and her body shuddered.

"Mason, Sir," she wailed.

He thrust. Sweat slicked his form. His balls drew taut. Pleasure arced along his spine as he exploded. He hammered inside her. Starbursts exploded in his field of vision. His knees nearly buckled and his hips slowed. He lay against her back, his breathing ragged, still embedded inside her. And knew, deep down, they weren't finished by a long shot.

She whimpered when he finally withdrew his softening shaft from her body. As he stood, her body began sliding toward the floor. Before she hit the ground, he lifted her, laid her back down on his bed, and finally removed her boots.

Then he took care of her. Shucking his jeans and boxers on the way to the bathroom, he disposed of the condom and cleaned his dick off before returning with a warm washcloth that he ran between her legs, cleaning any excess fluids from her body. She gave him a sleepy smile. He tossed the washcloth in the nearby hamper. When he tried to move away, Emily's small hand on his arm, tugging him into bed with her, stopped him.

He slid into bed beside her, where she wrapped her body around his like a pretzel. Mason wished he could say he didn't like it. That it didn't feel right. That she didn't feel right, in his arms, her glorious hair spread around him like a cocoon, her body snuggled up against him. But he'd be lying.

Instead of leaving to sleep on the couch, he held her and watched her sleep so trustingly against him, she made him ache. For things that would likely never be. Ache to keep her here beside him. Ache for a dream he hadn't realized he wanted. But with Emily, he could see it all. Crystal clear.

And he wanted it with a fierceness that shattered him. Mason had no idea what to do about it, about her. And about the fact that while he'd demanded she acknowledge him as her Sir, it was he who had been mastered tonight.

Instead of doing the right thing, leaving her to sleep alone in his bed while he slept on the couch downstairs, he held her tighter. And as he drifted off, he couldn't remember ever feeling as sated as he did with Emily beside him.

CHAPTER 14

*M*ason startled awake, wondering what the hell had woken him up so suddenly. In the blink of an eye, he recalled the events of the previous night. Emily had happened. His dick hardened at the memory of her flesh enveloping him, at gliding through her tight heat. He knew he shouldn't want her again. But he did. He shifted and encountered empty space. Glancing around his room, lit with the hazy, gray half-light just before dawn, he realized he was alone. Emily had been the one to leave.

Her scent was on his sheets, on his flesh. And he craved her. Disappointment barreled through him at finding himself alone in an empty bed. He was uncomfortable with just how upset he was that she wasn't still beside him.

Christ, he had it bad.

The aroma of her killer biscuits wafted into his room. His stomach growled, and he couldn't stop the stupid grin that spread over his face. She'd made him breakfast. He slipped out of bed and pulled on a pair of boxers. After a brief stop in the bathroom to relieve himself, he headed down the stairs.

Visions of taking her at the kitchen table before starting his day swam in his brain.

The wicked dream sputtered and died the moment he entered the kitchen. Instead of Emily's sexy as hell body standing at the stove, preferably naked, Cole reclined in one of the chairs at the table, plowing through freshly made biscuits and eggs.

"Morning," he said to Cole, watching his brother take another bite of what he knew were Emily's biscuits. Those flaky, buttery soft, melt in your mouth biscuits.

Mason snatched two from the pan before his brother finished them all. Fucker. These were his biscuits.

"You sure you know what you're doing?" Cole asked, staring him down with a pissy expression.

"It doesn't concern you," Mason said around a bite of pure doughy bliss, filling his coffee mug.

"Actually, when it comes to this place, as your partner, it does. We had agreed—anyone working here, even if they were members of the club, that we don't bring that shit here. There are boundaries we agreed wouldn't be crossed. And now, with the position we are in, you want to risk that? I sure as shit hope it's worth it," Cole replied, not hiding an ounce of his fury but blasting him with it. Cole shoved away from the table, the chair scraping against the tile floor as he shot Mason a disgusted glance.

Shame infiltrated his self-righteous and rather selfish stance. Emily's biscuits turned to sawdust in his mouth. This was the second time he'd crossed the line. How could he for one second have forgotten the blundering mess they were in because of him?

The lodge was teetering on the brink of destruction and all he could seem to think about was how much he wanted Emily back in his bed. How right she'd felt plastered around his body.

How much he yearned to hear her throaty moans as she came. How much he wanted to claim her, make her his submissive. But to what expense? All the torrid fantasies in the world wouldn't matter if they lost the lodge due to his blunder. He couldn't let his brother down again. He wouldn't. Even if it killed him.

"You're right. I wasn't thinking," Mason said, deflated. His heart ached at the loss. He'd held something perfect and incredible for a moment and been unprepared for the sudden loss of it; the potential for what could be shattered with the dawn. It cut him off at the knees because he wanted her, craved her still. Even after imbibing freely on her body last night, he yearned for more. He could still smell her on his flesh.

Cole put his empty plate and cup in the dishwasher. "At least not with the right head. I get it. She's a looker. I think she could do really well here as our new chef and she might help us stay above water."

"But?" Mason asked.

"What happens when you get tired of her? What impact will that have on the lodge? I know you well, Mase, you are not the settling down kind. And that one, she has permanence written all over her cute behind."

"People change," Mason said defensively.

"Not that much, they don't," Cole uttered, heading out past him and slamming the front door as he departed.

Mason stared after his brother for a minute and then took his coffee with him upstairs to shower. At one time, Mason might have been the love them and leave them type, the *call for a good time* type, with no desire to settle down or take anything seriously. Especially not getting so deeply involved with a woman that there was any hint of permanence to it. Then the bottom had been pulled out from beneath him. Somewhere, in the aftermath and fallout, he had changed. Mason wasn't that guy anymore. Nor did he want to be.

Mason grimaced as he stepped in the shower. Cole was

right though. They had agreed when beginning their partnership that they would never poach where they worked or bring it home with them. He'd broken those cardinal rules. Mason couldn't take back what had already occurred. And, in truth, he didn't regret surrendering to his desire for her. Except, knowing he couldn't be with Emily, couldn't continue whatever this was between them, would make the coming days and weeks being near her but unable to touch her, sheer utter torture. Because now he knew precisely how right she felt in his arms, knew the way she sounded when she came, and he craved more.

But he couldn't let Cole down more than he already had. Mason owed it to his brother and their parents to ensure their dream didn't disintegrate into dust over his poor choices.

And if his heart ached at the thought of never touching Emily again, he had no choice but to ignore it. The lodge was what mattered. Family mattered. His wants and desires came last.

CHAPTER 15

*E*mily started her day with a spring in her step. Who knew that multiple orgasms could turn her frown upside down? She cooked breakfast in her kitchen, humming as she did so, completely enamored with her new life.

Last night had changed things.

The way Mason had lost control, the way he'd dominated her, his hand on her sex, telling her that she belonged to him... her thighs trembled at the memory. It had been the most erotic, carnal night of her life. And her body heated like her broiler just thinking about it. Sex with Mason had been the best decision she'd ever made—next to moving here, of course.

All her naughty bits perked up and purred at the thought of being with him again.

She caught herself grinning. Cheesy grinning, too. The kind you don't even realize you're doing until someone points it out. Or you spy your reflection above the stove. She'd found her torn panties in the dry storage locker and had slipped them in her pocket.

She'd never look at the dry storage the same way again. It

made her wonder what scintillating sexcapade he had planned for tonight. And a low burn settled in her gut.

As the morning sped by, with guests filing in for breakfast and placing orders, Emily tried not to think about the night before, catching herself more than once nearly burning breakfast. Which she never did. It was all Mason and the fluttery, melty response in her system when she did think about him. Which was damn near all the time. She couldn't help it.

Thankfully, Faith was in helping her this morning, saving her from herself and the breakfast rush. The wait staff moved at a lightning pace. It was a beautiful fall day, and guests were heading out onto the trails or taking a horseback ride into the mountains.

After the breakfast rush, she went over the day's special menu with Faith. Then they began prepping for the lunch rush. Tibby strolled in at eleven just as they were finishing the mid-morning meal prep. Orders for boxed lunches were up.

By the time the lunch rush had ended, Emily had barely taken a break since she'd arrived that morning. Except one thing had become startlingly clear: Mason was avoiding her. He'd not come to the restaurant today to grab lunch, not even placed a to go order. It diminished the closeness she thought they had achieved last night, and it hurt.

Emily was not necessarily a woman men tended to want to keep. His absence in the restaurant resurrected some of her fears, that she was lacking an element that men found attractive and wanted to hold on to.

His avoidance of her smarted, more than she'd anticipated it would. She rubbed a hand over her chest to try and diffuse the ache setting up residence. They barely knew each other. She shouldn't be upset that he had dialed things back without so much as a *thanks for last night but we're done here*. Last night, he had acted as if he wanted more of her. Had pretended that she belonged to him. It made the brush off she was receiving today that much more pronounced.

Emily should just let it be. Worry about making this restaurant into her dream instead of the disappointment swimming in her chest. Chalk last night up to a climax filled extravaganza that was a once in a lifetime opportunity but was now over.

It would be a whole lot easier to do if she wasn't so drawn to Mason. The man only had to look at her and she got wet. The way he'd held her after the virulent storm of the lovemaking in the dry storage locker had made her believe, even if only for the moment, that he cared. It made the way he'd screwed her brains literally into her toes more profound.

Granted, everything she was feeling, that he'd made her feel for him, could just be due to hormones and the fact that the man was a walking sex on a stick.

Yet, she didn't think that was the reason. There was a potent connection between them. And it was much more than purely physical.

Although, judging by his complete and utter avoidance of her today, it appeared Mason preferred to maintain boundaries and keep their relationship strictly physical. That was fine by Emily. If that was what he wanted, she would roll the dice that way.

When Tibby took over the dinner rush, Emily headed home and showered quickly. She dressed casually in jeans and an easy to remove blouse. Then she trudged back over to the lodge in search of Mason. She wanted him. And she needed to prove to herself that she could make it just a physical relationship.

She knew he tended to sequester himself in his office. The door was open. And there he was, all big and broad-shouldered, hunched over paperwork. His hat was off. His hair looked like he ran his hand through it a hundred times today.

She liked his disheveled appearance. It made him more real and infinitely more likeable. It softened his normally gruff edges. She liked the way he looked, period. And the way he looked without his clothes on was enough to make her hormones sigh. The man took her breath away in his mocha flannel shirt. He'd rolled the sleeves up to his elbows, the sinewy muscles in his arms flexing as he worked.

Now that she had been with Mason, she couldn't go back to ignoring the fact that he seemed to know just the right temperature to bring her body to a boil. Just looking at him, she felt moisture between her thighs. Need hammered her veins. Her nipples hardened.

She shifted and his caramel gaze snapped up from whatever had him so engrossed at his desk.

His body was rigid, with lines of tension in his broad shoulders. His face was shuttered, his jaw clenched. Except his eyes gave him away—liquid pools of lust that darkened as she entered the office.

Her mind made up, Emily shut and locked the door behind her. Then she approached, noticing how his gaze flickered over her body. Heat pooled in her center. She put a little extra swagger into her hips, intending to draw his gaze. It worked. The man wanted her.

Mason cleared his throat and acted as if he was unfazed by her entrance. "What do you think you're doing, Emily?"

"What does it look like I'm doing?" Emily sauntered over and undressed with each step. She toed off the ballerina flats she'd slipped on. Unbuttoned her white blouse and let it flutter to the floor. Mason's gaze caressed her exposed flesh, stopping at the black lace bra barely covering her cleavage. She shimmied out of her jeans, but not before removing the foil packet she had placed in her back pocket.

Her blood thrummed in anticipation as she advanced until she stood before him in nothing but her black lace bra and panties. Mason didn't move to touch her. She watched his Adam's apple move as he swallowed. His lips were pressed into a thin line. His hands gripped the arm rests of his chair.

Desire—for her—was evident in every hard plane and angle in his rigid body.

If he wasn't going to take the initiative, then she would. Emily straddled his lap and hissed at finding him rock hard in his jeans. She rocked her hips against his groin and moaned in the back of her throat at the delicious, hot feel of him. She braced her hands on his firm shoulders and leaned forward, nipping his lower lip between her teeth.

"Emily. Fuck," Mason said as he caved, finally putting his hands on her. They caressed the slope of her spine until his big hands gripped her ass. His touch singed her to her toes.

"Yes, that's exactly what I want. I want to fuck, Mason. Let me, Sir," she said, panting. Need coursed through her system, overriding everything else. She needed him inside her. Needed to feel every solid inch of him. When her hands fumbled with the buttons of his shirt, she yanked at the material, ripping buttons off in her haste to feel his flesh beneath her palms.

She moaned when she traced the hard lines of his rock hard stomach down to his belt buckle.

She planted her lips over his when she freed his shaft from his jeans. Mason capitulated with a rough growl. Granted, it could be because now she had her hand around his cock. Men were fairly easy in that regard. But she loved the feel of him in her hands. That this was the first time she was free to touch him as she liked. She stroked his silky-smooth member with her hands, trailing her fingers over the velvety crest. She traced over the veins to the base of his shaft, where she surrounded his cock and squeezed him.

At his groan, she lifted her mouth from his and ripped open the foil packet. With his hot gaze following her movements, she rolled the condom over his length.

Then Mason's hands were at her pussy, shifting her panties to the side as she lifted her hips. He stroked through her labia. Pleasure simmered as he delved between her slick folds, and she mewled. At finding her drenched heat, he lifted her hips up as she fit the head of his cock at her entrance. Emily lifted her gaze and held his as she thrust down, enveloping his length.

She moaned.

Her hands dug into his muscled shoulders as she rocked her hips, setting the rhythm and pace. He was so huge. His shaft triggered every pleasure sensor in her sheath. She rolled her hips in a clockwise motion as she canted her hips. Mason let her have control for all of two glorious minutes. Then his hands clamped on her hips, fingers digging into his flesh, and he moved her over his cock.

He thrust and met her time and again until she was moaning his name like a litany, trying to remember to call him 'Sir' and failing.

One of his big hands drew back and smacked her across the butt. The slice of pain combined with the pleasure as she thrust down.

Emily came. Hard.

"Oh, Mason," she keened. Her head fell back as she rode him and the waves of her climax as it roiled through her body.

Mason pumped his fat cock inside her quaking heat over and over, setting off another round of tremors. His lips sucked and nipped at the sensitive hollow of her neck. Her hands threaded into his hair to hold him in place. Then he strained and mumbled a deep, masculine groan of satisfaction against her skin. His shaft jerked inside her sheath as he climaxed. His fingers dug into her buttocks, moving her until his tremors ceased.

When his hold slackened, before he could hold her close and make her feel things for him, she shifted in his lap. Mason tried to stop her as she climbed off him.

"Wait. Where are you going?" he asked, confusion and satiation clouding his face, along with banked lust at watching her boobs jiggle.

"Thanks for that. I have an early morning," she explained, dressing as quickly as possible. Hard to do when her legs were the consistency of jello, but she managed.

"But Emily," he said, reaching for her.

Yet she skedaddled out the door before he could stop her. Then she heard him cursing as she left the door to his office open as she exited. She didn't do it to be mean. She just didn't want him to follow her right now.

If he was going to make their relationship strictly about sex, then so could she.

∾

MASON WASN'T ENTIRELY sure what had just happened, other than the fact that Emily had just ridden him like a cowgirl. He shut his office door fast before anyone caught him in his state of undress.

He'd kept himself away from the kitchen on purpose. Because he knew deep down he was weak where she was concerned. He'd had a taste of her. Once wasn't enough. Twice wasn't enough. And now, he very much feared he would never have enough of her.

She'd been a vision. Her hair still up in a messy bun with tendrils escaping. He'd watched her striptease as she had sashayed toward him. They would have had to dynamite him out of his chair. Mason hadn't been able to move. He'd grown hard instantly. And then she'd straddled him and she had consumed him.

She'd rocked his world and then left so swiftly, he was surprised she hadn't left a trail of fire in her wake.

As he straightened himself up and disposed of the condom,

he wished he could say that it changed things. That he could give in. But there was too much at stake. That had to be the last time.

If he tasted her again, he didn't know that he'd be strong enough, unselfish enough, to let her go. Not when everything inside him roared that she belonged to him. That she was his submissive. That until now, he'd merely been biding his time until her advent into his life.

CHAPTER 16

In his office the following day, Mason and his brother had a meeting. One of the main rules they had established when they decided to go into business together some ten years ago, was that they keep the business side of things, the running of the lodge, out of their house as much as possible. Living together could be trying enough. Adding in the element of working with each other with their marginally different personalities, while it was an asset as it helped them offer more and gave the other someone to brainstorm ideas with, it could also spell disaster if they weren't careful.

Today, with the continuing theme of attempting to save the lodge from going under, they had the lodge accounts between them. Mason sipped his black coffee, which had gone cold. It didn't matter. He needed the infusion of caffeine.

Before the theft, he'd looked forward to balancing the accounts. He'd almost been cocky about it. And perhaps therein lay his arrogance and why he'd never seen the potential betrayal. In the first year he and Cole had opened this place, they'd managed to eke out a profit. Those profits had continued and grown each year. Had created a surplus beyond their wildest imaginings.

"If these numbers are correct, the daily totals in the restaurant have increased steadily since we re-opened by nearly fifty percent, with the specials accounting for more than half the revenue," Cole commented.

"They are. I've triple checked them to be certain. The changes Emily made to the menu have done well. I've had the front desk contacting the cancellations that came in due to the restaurant being shut down, offering a twenty percent off discount if they rebook with the explanation that the restaurant has been re-opened with a fabulous new chef."

"Any takers?" Cole asked.

"About half so far. It helps. We're making a comeback. And Billie is still working her way down the list," Mason said. It was a good, positive direction, even though they were nowhere near their typical operating capacity for this time of year. And they still had miles to go before he could relax. It wasn't turning over as swiftly as he would like. He still felt like his balls were in a pincer over their finances. Yet it was a start.

"If the trend continues, we might eke it out past Christmas."

Concern creased his forehead and, rubbing a pensive hand over his beard, Cole said, awareness in his eyes, "It's still not enough though. Not with the damage that's been done."

"No, it's not." And for that, the fault and the responsibility rested on Mason's shoulders. He realized he wasn't the one who had drained their savings. But he'd been the one to hire her. He'd been the one to trust her. His judgement, his skill for reading women, had been so far off with her as to be nonexistent.

"Well, it's a step in the right direction. I've been thinking of ways to help increase revenue. Why don't we offer a few packages that have free fishing expeditions tacked on, free guided hikes and the like? I don't need a paycheck for the foreseeable future. And I won't take one until this place is in the clear."

"You sure about that?" Mason asked. He already wasn't drawing a salary until their accounts were fixed, and to help supplement what he was paying Emily.

"As long as the employees are paid, yep. I have a nest egg I can draw from for things I need," Cole stated with a nonchalant shrug.

"I don't want you taking anything from your cabin fund, Cole." To hell with that. Mason wouldn't let Cole pay for his mistake.

But Cole being Cole, and much more level-headed of the two of them, replied, "So it will take me another year until I can have work on my place begin. All it means is that we'll have to live together a while longer. It works, as long as your panties aren't in a twist over something."

"Cole."

"Cut the shit, Mase. We're in dire straits here and you know it. As part owner, my word on these matters is just as final as yours. Just because I let you run the day to day operations of this place doesn't mean I can't put two and two together. If I don't draw a salary for the next six months, it will help out the bottom line. This is what we are going to do, period. And I won't take no for an answer. Now, I'm going to put together those packages we discussed and email all my previous clients. Even if twenty percent of them take the bait for a free day or two on the water, it will increase revenue." Cole finished his diatribe with a stubborn expression over his face, so like their father's. Mason knew the look. It meant Cole was digging his heels in and Mason would have an easier time of it moving one of the nearby mountains than he would his brother.

It was guilt more than anything that stopped Mason from getting angry or arguing with him. Cole was putting off his dream, his desire to build his own home on the land they owned away from the main lodge grounds, because of him.

"Fine. I'll agree to it, but mainly because I don't want to fight with you on this," Mason replied. Out of the corner of his gaze, he noticed something fluttering near the door. He glanced up. The door to his office was cracked open a sliver, doing a damn fine job of concealing who was eavesdropping on their conversation. Except the few fiery strands of red hair were unmistakable.

"Come in, Emily. Shut the door and have a seat," he commanded, making sure she understood from his tone that disobedience would not be tolerated.

She peeked in, her lower lip between her teeth, apprehension dotting her visage, holding a manila file folder in her hands. Mason indicated with a wave toward the unoccupied chair. If she so much as stepped a toe out of line, he would spank the fucking hell out of her. This was not the time for her to act out in any manner, or snoop on private conversations. If the confidential information she'd overheard got out, it could cause a panic among the staff. The gossip alone could be detrimental to the lodge's financial comeback.

He raked her form with his gaze, noting the stiff lines of tension. Her propensity for curiosity was absolutely the last type of problem he needed. Emily did as he asked her, for once, and slid gingerly onto the leather chair.

Her vibrant energy illuminated his office.

When she was settled, he pinned her with his gaze and asked, "How long have you been standing there?"

"Long enough. You didn't think to tell me that you could be out of business by the end of the year?" she said, not cowering or denying that she'd overheard their conversation about the lodge's troubles. At least she was honest. That had to count for something.

Mason controlled his expression and replied, "It's need to know only, and technically isn't our fault."

She rolled her eyes. "Yeah, right."

"Look, what I'm about to tell you stays here. If you breathe a word of it to anyone, I won't hesitate to give you the fucking spanking you'll deserve. The previous chef embezzled funds. The court and the police have not been able to track down what they did with the money they stole. If it looks like we can't keep this place open past the new year because of the situation, we will notify the staff and give everyone a nice severance package. Besides, didn't you tell me you were quitting?"

She snorted and rolled her eyes at him over his threat of discipline. Mason contained the smile her response evoked. Only Emily was so glib with him. And yet he noted the blush that spread across her cheeks, the slightly rosy hue that told him she wasn't as unaffected by his threat as she let on. His hands itched to tame her, touch the spark that was uniquely her.

Her eyes glittered with bemusement and she said, "*Now* you're going to remember that. Your secret is safe with me, for what it's worth. And maybe I can help."

"Honey, unless you have a wad of cash stored somewhere, I doubt it," Mason quipped, although the tightly wound ball of stress that had been lodged in his chest relaxed some. Emily wasn't anything like their previous chef, in temperament or design. And her desire to be of assistance made him like her more than he already did.

"Cooking classes," she replied confidently, an air of shimmering excitement emanating from her.

"Excuse me?" Mason asked. Cooking classes? Why would they want to offer those? It didn't make sense.

"Add it to the menu of activities offered to lodge guests for a nominal additional fee, just like you do with the various expeditions Cole leads. We charge a fee that covers the cost of supplies and my know how, plus some extra for the lodge. They're all the rage in the big cities. It doesn't even have to be what's on the menu, but basics and couples' cooking and stuff for kids. There would need to be insurance extended for potential injury but it's not much to add to the coverage likely already on this place. Plus, the possible income stream would make the profits outweigh the risk."

"And how much do you want for your fee?" Mason asked, looking at her through new eyes. It could work. He hadn't expected her to have such a head for business, which had been stupid and arrogant of him. Emily was intelligent and adventurous. She had a keen eye for what brought people into a restaurant. Extending that knowledge into other avenues associated with the restaurant was something he needed to start trusting. Her instincts thus far had been dead on. But what was her angle? What did she want in return?

"I would tack on twenty-five percent for the lodge, and then ten percent for myself above the costs of material. However, for the first year, I would let all the profits above the cost of materials go directly to the lodge in return for a stake in the restaurant," Emily stated.

"You want to own part of the Elkhorn?" he asked, stymied. She wanted to be a partner in the restaurant? Mason knew she'd been angling for something, but this wasn't what he'd expected. Cole's eyebrows shot up and disappeared under his hat at her pronouncement.

"Yes. And I'd want full control over the menu," she replied, and for once her expressive face was unreadable.

Her idea had some merit. Mason really wanted to know where she'd learned the business savvy skills she was displaying. It would require more conversation than he'd had with her so far. He already knew from watching her that she had a solid work ethic, that the kitchen and wait staff adored her, that guests were charmed by her. And he wanted to know more. That was a first for him. Typically, after the fun times with a sub were finished, he moved on to the next.

But not Emily. She called to him on a deeper level. It rankled. He couldn't want more with her. Mason tempered his desire and yearning for her. Maintaining his focus on the task at hand, he asked, "How much of a percentage are you talking?"

"Fifty," Emily stated, crossing her arms in front of her chest.

"Ten."

"Forty-five," she countered.

"Please, Emily. I'll give you twenty," Mason chided.

"Forty or I walk," she replied haughtily.

"Resorting to blackmail?" Mason asked, hiding his grin. She was something. Not afraid in the slightest to go after what she wanted. And it was making him question his sanity in staying away from her.

At his response, she settled back into her chair. "Nope. You need me and what I bring to the table to help keep this place afloat."

"I say we give it to her," Cole interjected.

Mason ignored his brother for the time being. "Thirty-five, and I want to see a full business plan first before we make it legal," he said, liking her idea. It could work and bring about enough of a bump in interest to help them continue to tread water, attract more business.

"Done," she said and held out her hand, the light of victory glittering in her gaze.

"Have it to me tomorrow," he commanded.

At that she quirked a brow and cocked her head to the side. "I'll see what I can do. Also, I think the Oktoberfest could be a big hit."

"I'm not sure about—"

Emily interrupted him. "Look, I know people when it comes

to food. We charge for admission, say twenty-five a person. Kids under five are free. That would include all the pretzels, hot dogs, brats, and other German fare I whip up. Then we charge for beer. Perhaps see if Spencer would be willing to donate a few kegs our way. Talk to Mister Hunt about offering pony rides for the kids—which we'll charge a nominal fee for. We could have balloons and games for the kids. Maybe a face painting station."

Fuck, her mind was fascinating. He liked the idea. Turned the numbers over in his brain. "And where would you get all these people to work it? We'd have to pay them."

"No we wouldn't," she said, entirely too pleased with herself, her expression superior, haughty, and controlled. Christ, it was such a turn on. Granted, everything she did turned him on. And now that he knew how wild and undone she became beneath his hands, he only had to look at her, smell her, and he was hard.

"How?" Cole asked, interjecting himself back into the conversation and sending Mason a frustrated glance for keeping him out of the negotiations. Mason would catch hell later. When Emily was around, everything and everyone else seemed to disappear into the background. Mason tended to heft most of the weight of the responsibility for the lodge on his shoulders. He knew he should ask Cole to shoulder more of the burden, but the way they operated had worked for them this far.

"By asking the club members to donate their time, of course. It would only be a day. Maybe see if the Teton Creamery and a few of the local shops would want a booth to sell their ice cream and tourist items. We can charge them a set amount for booth space."

Cole had a considering look on his face and said, "It's not a half bad idea. How soon could you put it together? October's next week."

"Give me two weeks. We can plan the event for the second Saturday in October," she stated.

"And if this is successful?" Mason asked.

"Then we look at expanding on it next year. Maybe make it a full weekend deal, or every Saturday in October. Perhaps look at doing other events here as well, throughout. I know that this place hosts weddings, and I wouldn't want to detract from the revenue the lodge makes off those. So there would be some coordination and planning involved but I think it could be beneficial all round."

"And you're fine with leaving LA behind permanently?" Cole asked.

She smiled at his brother and said, "The place has grown on me. Granted, I know I have yet to experience winter and I might be a popsicle come January, but I'm taking each day as it comes. I like seeing a herd of elk out my door instead of traffic jams along the four oh five."

Emily planned to stay in Jackson? She wanted to remain? It rocked Mason's world to think she was considering the lodge, being here long term. That she was looking at building a life here.

"Get me a proposal for them both and I will consider it. Isn't the lunch rush about to begin?" he asked with a raised brow.

"Yep. But I've got both Faith and Tibby trained well. The kitchen is safe in my hands, that I can promise you," Emily said and stood. "Oh, and you both should come for dinner tonight. I have a chicken pot pie as the special. It's to die for." And then she exited his office, shutting the door quietly behind her.

Mason stared after her. From the moment she'd entered his life, she had started slowly upending his tightly controlled world, day by day. And he had to admit, as much as it unsettled him, he was coming to look forward to his verbal sparring matches with her. Enjoyed trying to decipher the way her fascinating, intelligent brain worked.

"Both of her ideas have a lot of merit," Cole commented, bringing him back to the present.

"They do. How do you feel about making her a partner in the restaurant?" he asked.

"We could do worse. Besides, most days, she likes me more than you and would likely side with me if we needed a tie breaker."

"There is that," Mason said with a half grin. He'd been an ass toward Emily, for her protection, to keep her at arm's length. Even after their unexpected, soul shattering night together. He couldn't change what had already transpired. However, if she wasn't planning on leaving and hightailing it back to the city the first opportunity she had, a potential partnership could prove extremely lucrative for both parties.

"As long as you keep your dick out of it," Cole stated.

"I will. I fucked up, I know I did. But I won't go there again," Mason promised and hoped like hell it was a promise he could keep. He couldn't let Cole down.

"See that you do. I've never seen you willing to offer a stake in this place to anyone else. Why her, Mase? Is it because you have feelings for her?" Cole asked.

His question rocked him. His brother knew him too damn well. He didn't have feelings for Emily, did he? They'd only been together one night. And then that other time here at his desk, but who was counting?

It was finished. He wouldn't touch her again.

Resolved in his position to remain unaffected by her, Mason replied, "It has nothing to do with her. It's a business deal and is about keeping the lodge above water."

Cole leveled him with a glare, like he knew Mason was holding on to his resolve by a thread. A badly fraying thread that seemed liable to snap any moment. Cole shook his head at whatever he found in Mason's gaze, then left his office.

In the quiet stillness as he stared at the chair where Emily had sat, Mason knew, deep down, it had everything to do with her and his feelings toward her. It was a minefield littered with emotional debris that he had no idea how to navigate.

The idea of them agreeing to a partnership worried him. Not because he didn't think she could make it work, bring the lofty plans she had into action. No, it wasn't that at all. The more he was around her, the more he wanted her.

But he didn't know if he could continue to see her day by day and not cave. That his resolve to remain unaffected, to keep his distance, would crumble.

CHAPTER 17

*E*mily spent the better part of the previous night hammering her two proposals together.

Wired from a half pot of coffee and a package of Ho Hos, she trudged the short distance to Mason's house. Her breath plumed in frosty alabaster clouds. She shivered. In the early pre-dawn gloom, deep indigo receded on the horizon to the bright golden tangerine colored rays of sunlight streaking across the sky. She stifled a yawn. Even with the caffeine and sugar humming in her bloodstream, today was going to be a long day. One that was just getting started.

As it was, she was already tardy arriving at the kitchen. She should have been there half an hour ago and would have to fly through some of the breakfast prep. But it shouldn't take her too long. She had her system down pat for the biscuits and pastries, the pancake and waffle batter. She'd speed through it as best she could. There was nothing else for it. She'd not climbed into bed until three, and had gotten a full two hours of sleep. She had twenty minutes before the restaurant opened at six for the early birds. Plenty of time.

Emily had spent the better part of the night creating her

vision, her plans for the Oktoberfest event and the cooking classes. She wanted them. It had been a dream of hers to teach cooking classes. She'd done a few guest appearances at a local community college in Los Angeles a while back, and had loved it. Yet she wanted to expand on it. Make it fun and enjoyable, with perhaps a date night for couples where they could drink wine as they cooked. Do themes with children, like create a meal for superheroes or cupcakes for a princess tea party.

And Oktoberfest, well, she'd always enjoyed festivals surrounding food. She'd catered parties for each of her parents' businesses with success. This would just be a teensy bit larger than that. But she could do it. She knew she could.

In the short time she'd been in Jackson, the lodge had come to matter.

And she wanted a stake in the Elkhorn, to make it a place that belonged to her. While discovering that they were short on cash flow wasn't the ideal time for launching her bid for a piece of the pie, it was what she had to work with. If she succeeded and achieved the impossible with these events, she'd prove that this was where she belonged, demonstrate the value she brought to the Elkhorn.

She hadn't lied to Cole yesterday. This place had grown on her. She was falling for the lodge, more than she'd thought she would. Who could have known the sense of happiness she would feel at spying a herd of elk traipsing through distant fields? Emily had never considered herself an outdoorswoman or a nature girl.

When she'd first made the drive from Los Angeles she had worried that she would miss all the activity, all the people, and yet what she found was here was more than she'd expected. She was at peace here. She enjoyed the stillness on the air, like it was now. The indrawn inhalation before the day began.

There were no car horns blaring, no screaming neighbors. The drama that had always infused her life, from her family to the staff at whatever restaurant she worked at, was conspicuously absent. She thrilled at the fresh air that wasn't clogged with smog.

Even though being here meant she'd have to order things online and have them delivered if she needed new clothes or shoes or whatever else, in truth, Emily had never needed much. Oh sure, she liked clothes and shopping as much as the next woman. Yet she'd never been a fashionista, which was at odds with living in Los Angeles. She preferred jeans and cotton tops over heels that she couldn't balance in to save her life.

And, okay, there was the club too. Emily had dipped her toes in the water but there was so much more she yearned to explore. She'd loved it when Mason had taken command. Had never experienced such an endorphin high as she did when she was restrained. Emily still couldn't go into the dry storage closet in the Elkhorn without remembering her first time with Mason.

Whether she submerged herself in the deep end of the lifestyle with Mason or with another Dom, she knew she needed to explore more facets of herself. All those times she'd been intimate with a guy, and it had been just, well, yawn worthy. She'd thought it was just her, that maybe she just didn't get aroused and get the whole sex thing. Mason had proved her wrong. And yet, even as she considered or envisioned treading further into the lifestyle, in her mind it was Mason guiding her, showing her untold, wicked delights.

She climbed the wooden painted white steps up to the front porch and his navy front door. Mason and Cole lived in an antiquated, Victorian style farmhouse, very unlike the rest of the buildings on lodge property. This place looked almost out of sorts with its style and color, painted ivory with a deep navy blue trim and shutters. Emily wondered why the main house was so different from the rest.

It was one of those little mysteries she hoped to uncover.

She knocked on the front door. It was early but most days both Mason and Cole began at first light. Emily shivered in the cold as she waited. Someone was up because there was a light on inside.

The door opened. It was Cole, dressed in a forest green plaid flannel shirt and blue jeans, his hat conspicuously absent. A slash of dark brow lifted as he spied her. Emily hated to admit she was disappointed it wasn't Mason at the door. She had to push past her relentless need or she would get nothing accomplished around here.

"Emily, didn't expect you this morning. Come on in out of the cold," Cole said. He held the door open and then ushered her into the kitchen. She liked their kitchen; the dark cobalt walls with golden pine cabinetry and gray slate countertops. Against one of the walls was a dining table with bench seating along one side of it. The stove and fridge were stainless steel and a bit older but still worked well.

Cole picked up a coffee mug he'd left on the kitchen table and asked, "What brings you around so early?"

"I wanted to bring these by for you and Mason before I started my day. Included is a list of insurance companies with regards to adding liability coverage for the cooking classes. And, for the Oktoberfest Event, a list of prices—what we should charge versus expected operating costs, and potential revenue."

"You're that serious about this place?" Cole asked. His mocha gaze delved deep as he studied her. As much as she had come to like Cole, she'd never considered his role in the lodge as part owner. But that was mainly because his brother tended to dominate her thoughts and the very air whenever he was around. Cole might be a hunk of spectacular cowboy, but he wasn't a pushover. And his charming smile held a depth of knowledge he only seemed to let people see on occasion.

Interesting. Wonder what kind of woman it would take to truly turn his head?

Was she serious about the Elkhorn, about making it her place? "Yep. Absolutely certain."

"And is that because of Mason?" Cole prodded. She couldn't blame him for this question. If it was her and this was her place, she'd want to know the answer.

"No. These two proposals have nothing to do with him. I realize, after the other night, that you know about us. But it's not serious between us. Nor will I allow what happened between him and me to harm our business relationship in any way. Besides, I think whatever it was is done, now we've moved past it and we can both walk away. No harm, no foul," she explained, even though the sinking pit in her stomach declared her words a total lie. But Cole didn't need to know that.

And then the hair on the back of her neck prickled to attention.

Mason sauntered into the kitchen. His hair was damp, he hadn't bothered to shave, his feet were bare and he wore a pair of jeans. Only a pair of jeans, and without a belt they rode low on his muscular hips. Emily felt brain cells expire at the expanse of his finely hewn chest, the dark fur covering his pectorals and forming a single dark happy trail over his ripcord belly, only to disappear beneath the low-slung waistband of his jeans.

Her body electrified at his presence. Her nipples hardened. She pressed her thighs together.

"Emily? What can I do for you?" Mason gruffly asked, his voice reminding her of dark molten molasses. Yet his face was set in a stonewall. Mount Rushmore was infinitely more expressive than he was at the moment. Then she sucked in a ragged breath when the full brunt of his gaze met hers. The rest of him might not be showing any emotion, but his caramel eyes blazed, glittering with fury and desire as they took in her appearance.

Dammit. He had heard her conversation with Cole. But instead of acknowledging that, she side-stepped the potential minefield and said, "I have the proposal for you for the cooking classes and the Oktoberfest event. Both of them can be tweaked as needed."

"Leave them on the table and I will get to it when I can," Mason said, pouring himself a cup of coffee before he asked, "Shouldn't you be in the restaurant preparing for the breakfast rush?"

And that was how it was going to be between them. It was clear to Emily that the words he'd spoken the other night when they'd been intimate hadn't meant all that much. It had all just been the heat of the moment. While Mason might want to sleep with her, he didn't want anything outside the bedroom.

It hurt.

More than she was ready to admit. Emily was accustomed to men passing her over for other women. But there wasn't anyone waiting in the wings for Mason that she knew about. This was just him, showing her that theirs was a business arrangement only. That their night together was the abnormality.

That was what she wanted, right? To keep things strictly business between them. He was surly and rude. Emily's focus should be to make this place more than simply one where she worked but one where she built a life. And if there was a part of her that ached because she'd hope Mason would be a part of that life, she ignored it. Not that she thought about building a life with Mason—more that he would be in it, perhaps in an intimate capacity.

But he didn't feel the same, apparently.

It stung. She blinked back the sudden onslaught of moisture.

Firming her resolve and her shoulders, she masked her hurt behind a steely gaze and sarcastically replied, "Yes, Sir."

"Catch you around, Cole." She nodded.

Then Emily swiveled on her heel and stalked out the front door. Mason kept on tossing barriers between them. If he wanted nothing more than a business arrangement, even when she knew he wanted her, that was fine. The restaurant was what mattered. Her dream was what mattered.

That way she could show her family back home that she wasn't a screw up, that her dreams weren't unrealistic just because they didn't understand them.

And as for Mason, she'd ignore the ache in her chest and stop hoping for something more when there obviously wouldn't be.

She might have to stock up on more snack cakes though, if she was going to be around him all the time. Crave him but never be able to quench her hunger for him.

MASON SPENT the bulk of his morning on the phone with distributors, ordering supplies and paying on the accounts that they could. It was progress in bringing them back from the brink of collapse. And he combed through the two proposals Emily had left him.

The proposals were excellent. Thorough. And written in a way so he could easily visualize how things could be.

Not that he expected anything less than excellence from her. Emily was a fascinating dichotomy. All soft Suzy homemaker one minute, with culinary delights that would make angels weep, then, the next minute, she displayed a whip smart intelligence with a head for business. If Mason was honest with himself, she might even be smarter than he, a thought which both intimidated and aroused him beyond measure. And then, as if that were not enough, she swiveled on a dime into a seductress with soft lips and a wicked gleam glittering in her hazel depths. Her siren's call beckoning him to forget his duties to the lodge and indulge—in her.

He'd been harsh with her when she'd stopped by his house that morning. He realized that. Except, he had overheard her words to his brother. It had taken him by surprise, the vicious grip of pain that had lanced through his chest at her words. That she could walk away from the blistering, electric chemistry between them—as if she were changing a light bulb and could walk away—had left him spinning.

He'd been resolute about keeping his hands off her. Putting the lodge above his own wants and desires. At least, until she'd mentioned staying on at the lodge past the trial period and truly building a life here. Wheels had shuddered to life in his brain at the possibility. It had gotten him thinking long term. That, if she was going to be his partner and not his employee, it would change the dynamics of their working relationship. It gave her a stake in the productivity and leveled the playing field between them. Hell, all he'd been doing lately was re-evaluating the choices he had made in his life. Because the *here for a good time* Mason had withered and died in the aftermath of Claire's deception.

The way Claire had betrayed him and the lodge made him unable to trust what he felt for Emily. That his feelings for her were too fast, too quick for him to consider that he wanted more than just a night or two at the club. When he looked at Emily, he wanted more, wanted to hear her throaty laugh when he made it home in the evening. Wanted to wake up again with her cuddled at his side. Wanted to feel the tight clasp of her silken sheath milking him, drawing him deeper inside until all he could see was her.

Mason knew he'd promised Cole he wouldn't touch her again.

Yet he didn't know if it was a promise he could keep. Not when every fiber of his being proclaimed that Emily was the one for him. But he wouldn't say anything to Cole until he and Emily had discussed things.

Frustration dominated his footsteps as he marched the distance from his office to the restaurant. He and Emily needed to talk.

And not just about the proposals.

He'd blundered his way through their relationship. The overwhelming, nearly eviscerating need he felt for her had clouded his perception. Mason had done what he'd always warned other Doms against, he had acted out of fear because of the betrayal he'd experienced. Condemning Emily for another's actions. He'd been wrong in his treatment of her and he planned to apologize, for starters.

He wasn't necessarily comfortable with his feelings for Emily. He only knew that they ran deep, deeper than any he'd had before. Christ, he wanted more. He wanted all of her, every facet. Mason yearned to be the one to introduce her fully to the lifestyle, to train her, and show her the wicked delights of the flesh and rewards of being a submissive. His submissive, permanently.

She was open and responsive, calling forth a possessive streak he hadn't known he had inside him. Because until Emily, there'd never been a sub, a woman, he'd felt deep in the marrow of his bones belonged to him.

And he was to blame for his treatment of her. From day one, he'd been more than a bit of an ass. Emily hadn't deserved any of it. Hell, her proposals might just be the ticket the lodge needed to scrape back into the black.

The dining room was nearly empty when he entered. It was mid-afternoon, well after the heat of the lunch rush, and far too early yet for dinner guests.

He strode in through the kitchen door and was bombarded

by delicious aromas. They wafted over him. His mouth watered and his stomach growled, reminding him that he'd not stopped for lunch.

Christ, the woman could cook.

He'd expected to find her at a more sedate pace this time of day. However, Mason discovered Emily amidst a flurry of activity. There was a smear of flour across the bridge of her nose. She stood at the stainless steel counter, pounding an enormous ball of dough into complacency. He walked over to one of the pots simmering on a nearby stovetop and glanced inside. Cherries boiled with a hint of spices, cinnamon, and something else he couldn't name.

"Touch that pot and I will chop off your fingers with my fileting knife," Emily snarled.

His head whipped in her direction, his gaze narrowed to angry slits. A sub never addressed him in such a manner. He growled, "Excuse me?"

Emily shot him a frustrated glance, then rolled her eyes and said, "You heard me. Now, unless you want me to make good on my threat, I suggest you get out of my kitchen."

Her kitchen? It was all semantics, he knew, but she was pushing his buttons. It was like yanking on a tiger's tail. Eventually, the tiger got damn tired and decided to yank back. Mason crossed his arms over his chest and quirked a brow at her. "Your kitchen?"

"Damn straight it's mine—until it isn't. But until that time, get out," she ordered, nodding toward the door. The rhythmic kneading of her hands in the dough never faltered or slowed. Nor did the scowl on her pretty face fade.

"You'll pay for that," Mason replied quietly, unable to keep the lust from his voice at the thought of spanking her heart-shaped ass until it glowed ruby red.

"Pffft. You're all bark and no bite. You talk big about *this is mine* but your follow through is a bit on the flaccid side of things. I meant what I said. Out."

That did it. He could see he'd been rather derelict with her training and impressing on her the importance of respect towards a Dom. His tolerance for her mouth was at an end. If he had to haul her into the storage locker and give her the spanking she so richly deserved, he would.

Flaccid? Please. Whenever he was in her vicinity, his cock could saw through diamonds he was so hard. Mason prowled toward her. They were going to have it out. Now. No more beating around the bush, no more back and forth. Emily was his sub, and it was time she started acting like it.

Two steps before he reached Emily, Tibby barreled into the kitchen, shouting, "Yo, boss. Sorry I'm a bit late. Arianna's recital ran long."

Emily ignored him completely and said to Tibby, "Could you take care of the cherries? They should only have a few more minutes. I don't want them overcooked and I have my hands full with the dough for the tarts."

"Sure. Mason, I'm surprised you're in here. You rarely come to the kitchens," Tibby said, putting her apron on and sidling up to the stove and the vat of cherries.

"Just wanted to check and see if Emily needed anything," Mason replied to Tibby, then shot Emily a look and said, "We'll talk later tonight."

"Perhaps. We'll see how tired I am once my shift ends. Or I could just meet you in your office tomorrow," she said and gave him a defiant glare before turning her back on him and continuing her work as if he wasn't even in the room.

Like hell he would wait until tomorrow. The time for a reckoning between them had arrived. It was long overdue.

He'd give her the afternoon to believe she'd won this round. Because, by the end of the night, there would be no doubt in her mind that she belonged to him.

CHAPTER 18

*T*oday had been nearly endless. Emily stood under the hot spray in her shower, allowing the heat to soothe her tired muscles.

What with hardly getting any sleep last night, to Faith leaving early, to Tibby arriving late and the kerfuffle with Mason today, she was beat. It wasn't like her to run from a problem. And yet, Mason's demeanor in the kitchen today... his gaze had promised retribution. She wasn't in the mood. The man blew hot one minute, cold the next. His emotional pivots were giving her whiplash.

And she'd avoided going to see him because, in truth, as much as she told herself she could keep her emotions in check, that wasn't her. Emily couldn't touch him and not want more. Much more than he was willing to give.

She wasn't built that way. To use someone purely for the physical aspect—she might as well just use a vibrator. It was cold and devoid of emotion. Sure, it got the job done. But she wanted the closeness. She craved the way he'd held on to her that first night. Emily had not grown up in a warm household. Her parents and siblings loved her, in their own way. Yet their family didn't hug. They weren't touchy feely people.

And Emily had always needed it, always felt a lack because of it. At the end of the day, if she couldn't have the closeness with Mason, they were both better off just not continuing. It didn't matter that thinking of him made her blood sing. Or the fact that she knew he wouldn't turn her down if she marched over to his house at this time of night.

But it would be nothing more than two people using the other for sex. And that wasn't Emily, which was why, as soon as she finished her shower, she planned to feed her snack cake addiction. Nothing quelled sexual frustration like the finger licking yummy goodness of a Ho Ho.

Emily turned in the shower stall, rinsing the last bit of conditioner from her hair, and issued a blood-curdling scream. Mason was leaning against the doorframe between the bathroom and bedroom. His caramel eyes had darkened with covetousness, his brawny arms crossed in front of his upper body, looking dark and dangerous. Hazardous to her peace of mind and, if she were honest, her heart as well.

"What the hell, Mason?" she snapped, yanking a towel around her body as she shut the water off.

His patronizing stare chastised her for her attempt at modesty. She stepped out of the stall and said, "You shouldn't be here. You need to leave. This isn't funny anymore."

When she attempted to slip past him into her bedroom, Mason slid a hand around her waist and tugged her flush against him. She hissed at the salacious contact and her hands went to his chest to push him away. Her palms burned against him. Mason's free hand held her chin and lifted her gaze.

Her knees trembled at the heat, the sheer force of the arousal that shrouded his handsome face. His molten caramel eyes glowed in passion. Her defenses weak, her body melted against the hard planes and angles of his.

"I told you earlier today we needed to talk. But first, there's the matter of some much-needed discipline," he said, and carted her into the bedroom. Her feet had no choice but to follow. She stumbled and would have fallen if it weren't for Mason's arms around her.

He'd been busy while she had been in the shower. It made her wonder how long he had been in her cabin. He'd stripped the comforter and sheets to the foot of her bed and had attached lengths of nylon rope to each of the posts. There were leather cuffs attached to the end of each rope. On one of her pillows was a black satin blindfold.

Then she spied a black leather satchel next to the nearest nightstand. There were toys he'd lain out on the nightstand, along with a sleeve of condoms.

What was his game? Her belly quivered in delicious anticipation, her earlier exhaustion forgotten in place of a hyper awareness of him. She said, "You've been busy. What's this all about?"

Mason sat on the bed and then hauled her across his lap until she lay face down. She tried to push herself up. Her butt was positioned over his rock-hard thighs. Then he tugged at the towel.

"Mason? What the hell are you doing?" She jerked, scrambling to hold on to the plush material covering her. But she was no match for his unparalleled strength. He whisked the towel from her form.

His jeans rubbed against her stomach. He leaned a forearm across her lower back. No matter how much she squirmed and kicked—which she did—she couldn't get free.

"This is what being a submissive is about, Emily. You were way the fuck out of line today. And for that, you will be disciplined," he said, his voice controlled as ever.

"I'm not a fucking child, Mason!" she shouted, her anger

rising, along with a healthy dose of fear and self-preservation. What did he plan to *do* to her?

His palm cracked against her naked rear. The sting reverberated through her being. She yelped, "Ow! Stop it."

"No. You want to see what the lifestyle is about? This is it. It's not all about sex. It's about you willingly following a Dominant's directives even when they aren't in line with what you want." His hand fell against her butt, harder this time. Hard enough that moisture entered her field of vision.

She jerked in his arms at the next swat. She couldn't believe he was spanking her.

"This is for calling me flaccid." He peppered her behind. His hand fell at a rapid pace. Her butt burned. And yet, as his palm cracked against her bottom, a liquid fire stoked inside her core and her sex pulsed in desire.

Through tears of pain blinding her vision, she choked out, "Shoe fits. Damn you, Mason, you're the one who put up walls. Not me."

"I know I did. I'm sorry for that. And we will discuss more after I'm finished with your discipline. This is for threatening me today with bodily harm."

His hand whacked against her bottom. Her body burned from his touch. As his swats peppered her behind, the sharp pain morphed. As it did, Emily moaned and began leaning into his fervent touch. She'd never imagined a spanking could arouse her. But it did. Her system veered toward climax as he smacked her bum ardently.

Then his hand smoothed over her rear, massaging the enflamed globes. Emily mewled deep in the back of her throat. When his fingers swiped through her crease, pleasure speared through her. She gripped the mattress as two of his fingers penetrated her sheath. Her eyes nearly rolled back in her head as he breached her.

He stroked her. Emily canted her hips in open invitation, and then she shattered. She climaxed. Hard. Pleasure flooded her body. She shook. Her pussy clenched at his thrusting fingers.

And then he withdrew his hand from her folds. Before he could stop her, Emily scrambled off his lap until the headboard was at her back. She winced at the dull throbbing ache in her bum, and attempted to cover herself with her arms.

"Mason, why are you doing this to me? I can't keep up with your moods. One minute you want me and the next, you hold me at arm's length. If this is the way it's going to be, I'm sorry but I can't be with you."

He shifted and stood, then started unbuttoning his flannel, revealing his chiseled torso. "I know. And I'm sorry for that. I do want you, Emily. More than I should."

When he tossed his shirt and hat onto the nearby chair, she clenched her hands into fists. He was so damn beautiful, he made her ache with longing. "At least tell me why?"

Mason continued undressing, stepped out of his boots and said, "Well, first and foremost, you do work for me. It's bad form to fuck your employees."

She gestured with a wave of her hand. "And that's all this is, a quick fuck?"

His gaze never wavered as he unhooked his belt buckle, his voice husky. "No, it's not for me. Which is part of the problem. My job is to make sure that this place runs effectively. That I don't show favoritism, or risk losing this place, because I want you."

"And you think I would cause you to lose this place?" She slid off the bed, unmindful of her nudity, and jabbed a finger into his chest. "Do you think so little of me, Mason? That you think I don't know what this place means to you? I've seen you. You treat the lodge like it's a freaking temple to the gods. I would never want to take this away from you."

"I'm coming to see that," he murmured and shucked his

jeans until he stood in nothing but boxer briefs that displayed exactly how much he wanted her.

"And did it ever occur to your Neanderthal brain that I might want this place to succeed for purely selfish reasons of my own?" Emily's blood pressure boiled and mixed with arousal. She had to fight that she wanted nothing more than to lean forward and taste his skin. To kiss the flat disks of his nipples. To follow the dark, narrow happy trail south with her tongue.

"Not until I read your proposals today, it didn't."

"Oh really? But why? Other than my tendency toward sarcasm, I've done nothing but work my ass off for this place. That should speak volumes," Emily replied, exasperated beyond measure. Then Mason shoved his boxer briefs down his legs, freeing the thick shaft of his manhood. It jutted from his groin. Her mouth went dry at the thought of taking him between her lips.

"Because the previous chef pretended the same thing and robbed this place blind when I wasn't paying attention. I know I've been hard on you and I'm sorry for that. You didn't deserve it. I was more pissed at myself than anything," he said, pulling her close. Their bodies touched, aligned from shoulder to hip. His engorged cock pressed into her belly. Her breasts were smooshed against his incredibly firm chest. The man was hard everywhere. He'd barely touched her and already her nipples ached. Her pussy fluttered in heady anticipation. She hissed at the feel of his naked form against hers as it scorched her very foundation.

"Why? Why did wanting me make you angry?" she asked, and knew that she couldn't push him away. This wasn't just physical. She yearned to make him smile. Wanted to ease the strain between his brows. And, dammit, she just wanted him, more than any man she'd ever come across. It was chemical and elemental.

"Because I couldn't believe how much I wanted you and worried that my need for you would ruin this place. And then I read your proposal this morning."

"And?" she asked, sighing as his hands caressed over her back. Everywhere he touched, pleasurable tingles followed. Her hands pressed against his torso. Unable to stop herself, she lightly grazed his nipples with her thumbs.

"You've fallen in love—with the lodge, with Wyoming, with the restaurant," he murmured, his voice huskier, infused with desire.

As she gazed at him, she worried that those weren't the only things she was falling for. "And if I have?"

"Then I want the chance to truly explore what's between us. I want to be the one to train you in the lifestyle. I want to be your Dominant." His big hands palmed her rear. In his caramel eyes, his emotions were on display. The desire for her, the need, and the naked, unabashed truth of his words. It was all there. Everything he'd held back from her, all the hesitation she'd sensed was conspicuously absent. Mason did want her. It altered her center of gravity. *He* altered it.

"And what happens should we grow tired of each other? What happens if or when you decide you don't want me anymore?" she asked in a ragged whisper while his hands plumped and squeezed her ass, his fingers teasing the edges of her slit and igniting a fever in blood.

His gaze shuttered, he replied, "If that happens, we agree here and now that we will be civil and retreat to partners. What have we got to lose?"

Only everything.

"And if I agree to your terms? What then?" she asked. Because the truth was that she didn't know if she was strong enough to walk away. Not when it took everything inside her not to toss caution to the wind and beg him to take her where they stood. He was too damn potent. A simple touch from him and he blotted out the rest of the world. Turned her focal point to him and the desire that raged between them.

"Then we start tonight," he replied, studying every flicker of movement. Emily already felt her body yielding. At his words, desire curled like delicious flicks against her skin. Sex had never been this way for her, so intense that her need for a man outweighed all else. That she craved him, wanted to spend hours, days even, doing nothing but him.

The choice to accept what he was offering was a risk. An enormous one. Should a relationship between them blow up in their faces, she would be the one without a damn pot to piss in. Even if she was made partner in the restaurant thanks to her proposal, life here, the one she was building, could become unbearable at best. And the worst didn't bear consideration because the fiery pits of hell would be more agreeable.

With everything she'd learned about him, even with his surly attitude, his actions had always spoken so much louder. The way he watched her. The way he worked on this place. He wasn't a cold executive, sitting back in a stuffy office, but in the thick of things, day in and day out. It counted—that he'd fought his attraction to her out of responsibility and a duty to the lodge.

Denying any longer that she wanted to be with him would be a lie. Emily craved him in a way that defied all her superb reasoning skills and attempts to stymie the swell of desire that suffused her whenever he was near. Deep down she understood with clarity that she would regret not knowing him. Even if they burned so bright that they sputtered out in a flame of glory.

His palm cupped her cheek. The pad of his calloused thumb swept over her bottom lip. He had working man's hands. There wasn't an ounce of softness or weakness in his form. He was pure, undiluted alpha. And he was confident enough to admit he wanted her. That he'd been a jerk. For now, that was enough.

Wild horses couldn't drag her away from him. She slid her hands up his chest, humming in the back of her throat. Her palms burned where she touched him. She slid her hands up to his neck, drew herself up on her toes and said, "Yes."

The light of victory shimmered in his gaze. He stroked his thumb over her cheek and lowered his mouth, gently brushing his lips over hers. After all the fury of their previous entanglements, the tenderness, the sweet seduction, was unexpected.

It knocked her off her axis as he moved his mouth against hers. His kiss took her out of her mind. He pressed his thumb to the corner of her lips, opening her mouth up further for his illicit invasion. Her toes curled as his tongue traced hers. She yielded against him. With each stroke of his tongue, he seduced her further. His kiss was carnal. Desire rushed like a waterfall in her veins. She moaned into his mouth. Mason kissed her and the world around them ceased. They could have been in a hut in Timbuktu. It didn't matter when he kissed her.

There was a reason she couldn't turn away from him. She kissed him back, caught up in a fever that had taken hold. It was unmistakable how much she wanted him. That his touch, feeling him pressed against her form aligned from hips to shoulders, was scorching her from the inside out.

And then Mason hoisted her into his arms, breaking their kiss as he laid her on the bed.

When she went to reach for him, he caught her wrists. The desire in his eyes caused tendrils of need to curl in her belly. He said, "This is lesson number one. If at any time something hurts, is uncomfortable, or you're afraid, I want you to use the safeword 'red.' All right?"

She nodded, her tongue stuck to the roof of her mouth as he slid the soft leather around each of her wrists. Then he shifted, spread her legs apart, and fastened her ankles into leather cuffs. When he'd finished restraining her, she was spread-eagle on the mattress. Need combined with tiny flickers of apprehension at losing her freedom. Mason checked the restraints until he'd determined they were fastened correctly.

He murmured, "One of the biggest parts of a relationship between a Dominant and submissive is trust. That's what tonight is about. You putting yourself into my hands and trusting me, which is why we will use the blindfold. I want you to give yourself to me, yield to me, surrender to me, and trust me. Trust that my only mission tonight is to give you pleasure beyond your wildest imaginings. All that's required of you is placing yourself in my hands, my care, and trusting that I will take care of you."

Her eyes on his, she shivered, but not in fear, in anticipation. She whispered, "I do trust you."

Mason's gaze heated. His knuckles tenderly grazed her cheek before he slid the black blindfold over her eyes. Darkness covered her vision, blinding her. He moved her hair, gathered it for her so that it didn't catch. And suddenly, with her eyesight removed, her ability to touch him removed, Emily felt incredibly vulnerable. She shivered, testing the bonds around her wrists.

An unexpected panic clawed up her throat until the mattress depressed beside her. "Easy, Em." Mason fit himself between her thighs. She gasped at the erotic sensation. His cock pressed against her folds. Already she hungered to feel him move, feel him thrust inside her. Instead, his hands cupped her face. His mouth whispered over her lips, planting butterfly kisses. He kissed her tenderly, stroking his tongue over her lips. Nibbled at the corners of her mouth. Sucked her lower lip before taking the kiss inherently deeper.

Mason kissed her and the world spun deliciously.

His mouth left hers and whispered over her skin with

feather-light caresses. He added his fingers, lightly trailing them over her collarbone. They traced the shape of her breasts, gliding over the mounds but not touching her sensitive peaks. He nipped at her flesh, flicking his tongue against the sensitive hollow of her neck. Tasted her shoulders and the space between her breasts.

By the time his fingers caressed the hard points of her nipples, Emily's body was on fire. With every touch, Mason was incinerating her. The pad of his thumb stroked against a rigid peak and the rough callous sent pleasure whirling inside her chest. Even though she was blindfolded, a wealth of colors, like starbursts, shone beneath her eyelids.

And then his mouth... his wonderful, wicked, hot mouth... closed around a turgid bud.

"Mason." She moaned a breathy sigh. Emily strained, attempting to feed him more of her cleavage.

When Mason had said 'BDSM' that first night at the club, the night of their first kiss, she'd imagined something far different. She figured he'd tie her up and screw her brains out. But not this slow, tender lovemaking where pleasure stoked her internal furnace. A slow burn with every flick of his tongue or gentle glide of his fingers against her flesh. She wanted more, wanted the flash bang grenade of their previous interludes.

Yet, she had no control. She'd given it all to Mason when she agreed to be with him.

She couldn't anticipate his next move, which only added to the flames. And she understood, with a clarity she hadn't before, what he'd meant when he'd asked her to trust him. She'd handed him her free will knowing she could trust him not to hurt her. That he was going to show her with more than words what it meant to submit to him and, more, that he cared.

When his teeth clamped down on her swollen bud, she cried out. Pleasure lashed from his bite all the way into her center and made her pussy throb in sweet expectation. He did it a second time and then a third, sucking the beaded point deep into his mouth and laving his tongue against it. Then he released her nipple with a slight pop before he surrounded the nub with something that felt like metal.

"Ow, Mason, Sir," she said at the pain lacerating her breast.

"Deep breaths, Em. I'm just going to try some nipple clamps on you tonight. Nothing more," he murmured huskily and massaged the mound around her clamped nipple. It eased the pressure some. He flicked his tongue over the constricted bud.

"Oh my God," she moaned. Intense pleasure arced from her tit directly to her pussy.

"That's it, Em," Mason said darkly, lust clouding his voice. Then he switched his attention to her other breast, giving it the same delicious, wicked treatment. By the time he placed the second clamp on, Emily was straining with need.

Then he trailed open-mouthed kisses down her torso. Nipped at her hip bones. Swirled his tongue in her belly button. Then went lower. She trembled at the hot puffs of air from his mouth against her inner thighs and over her mons. Tendrils of desire pulsed in her veins as she waited. She could feel him hovering.

And then his hand slicked through her wet folds. At his guttural, needy groan, she shivered.

"You're so fucking wet, Em. Come as many times as you need to. Give me all of you," he commanded, his hoarse bass thick with lust.

Then his wicked thumbs parted her folds. The callouses scraped against her clitoris. Her back arched from the carnal sensations. Her breath clogged in her lungs as she waited. Then his tongue stroked over her clit and she nearly came up off the mattress. She would have, too, if not for the restraints. His tongue caressed her nub in circles. Stroked beneath her hood, swiped through her folds and dipped inside her pussy entrance before returning to her sensitive bud.

Emily was on fire. Torrents of need battered her. Her body coiled in on itself with every kiss, every nip, and every lap of his tongue against her.

Mason held her hips steady with his hands, immobilizing her feeble attempts at gaining more friction and putting her completely at his mercy. His mouth latched around her tiny nub and his wicked tongue flicked and licked at her core. He ate her pussy like a man possessed, tasting every nook and cranny. He slurped and nipped at her clit.

Emily's body shattered when he thrust his tongue inside her pussy. Her sheath clenched and quaked around his tongue as pleasure bombarded her. Her back arched as much as the restraints would allow.

But Mason didn't stop his sensual ministrations. He sucked at her clit, penetrated her sheath with a series of torrid thrusts and then tweaked and licked at her clit like it was his own private playground. He drove her body up a glistening peak of ecstasy so sharp and intense that when her climax hit, it was like glass shattering into a million pieces. His mouth against her most intimate flesh combined with the clamps squeezing her nipples. It was so powerful, it left her trembling and shaking. Her moans filled the small cabin.

Never in a million years did she think sex would be like this. That it could be like this. Mason growled against her pussy but, instead of stopping, gripped her thighs and ravished her further. There was no other word for it.

He turned her into a quivering, moaning mass of need. He plundered her pussy with his tongue, eating at her flesh with relish. Her thighs shook from the force of another climax.

She ached in her core, needing more than just his mouth on her. But she wasn't in control here. And for the first time in her life, she was fine with it. More than fine. She wanted it all from

Mason. His strength, his control, and the way he took her out of body with his lovemaking.

He was reshaping her, molding her being. Then two of his fingers penetrated her quaking sheath.

She strained. "Oh my god, Mason. Sir," she cried at the swath of pleasure sweeping through her system.

His fingers plunged and thrust, pumping inside her clenching tissues. She wanted more, she needed his cock inside her. But he was torturing her with pleasure so intense, she didn't know if she could hold on any longer.

When he added a third digit, stretching her, and sucked on her clit, she came. Hard. And long... until she whimpered and just let go.

She opened herself up to him, no longer fighting the pleasure but becoming one with it until she was floating on a cloud of ecstasy so profound, she didn't think she'd ever come down.

When Mason moved, lifting his head from her pussy, and withdrew his fingers from her sheath, she whimpered in frustration. But then she heard it. The rendering tear of foil.

"Sir?" she moaned, desperate to have him fill her, to feel him in her swollen folds.

"You've done beautifully, Em. Now let me fuck you," he said, and the head of his cock rubbed over her swollen tissues.

"Please let me see you, Mason. Sir. Please, I—"

And the blindfold was lifted.

Lust darkened his features. Moisture coated his chin. He was on his knees between her thighs, gripping his erect cock with one hand. With his other, he lifted her hips up slightly. "I want you to watch as I take you. Watch as I fuck your pussy," he growled.

Her gaze was fixed on his hand as he guided his engorged shaft to her entrance. Then, with a roll of his hips, he penetrated her, his cock disappearing inside her sheath. He gripped her hips and pumped his shaft inside her. Over and over, she watched, fascinated, as his thick width disappeared in her pussy.

He stroked inside, the pressure building as her tissues gripped him. His gaze was nearly black with hunger. Mason drove her body up a staggering ledge. The eroticism, the way he mastered her body, made it conform as he elicited pleasure from her, drove Emily mad with lust and need.

His name became a chant on her lips. She wasn't prepared for the explosion, for the earth-shattering effect another orgasm would have on her composure. It seemed to rip apart the very fabric of her being. He released one of the clamps and pleasure bursts enflamed her climax, taking her higher still. She was mindless in her need of him. When the second clamp was removed, she wailed, "Mason!" not even remembering to call him Sir anymore.

Then he moved, lowered her hips and leaned forward. His thrusts rocked and kept a torrid pace. But the new angle brought him deeper inside. He propped his body up on his elbows, his face hovering above hers. It felt like he was merging with her. That there was no end and no beginning. That he climbed inside her soul and became a part of her as he thrust.

Mason increased his pace. His thrusts hammered inside her quaking, swollen tissues. She saw herself reflected in his eyes. Deep down, in the dark recesses of her consciousness, she knew that her foundation had altered, that *she* had been altered by saying yes to him tonight.

His control slipped and he buried his face in the crook of her neck. The slap of flesh and the musky scent of their sex filled the room, competing with her moans and his guttural groans. Mason pistoned his hips, his cock pounded her sheath. Between one breath and the next, the climax stole through her system. The ground quaked from the force. Mason jerked, tremors rocking his body as he emptied himself into her.

Mason thrust until he was spent. He collapsed against her, holding her close, his breath heavy against her throat. She rubbed her cheek against his and pressed her lips to his firm shoulder.

At her movements, he stirred against her. Lifting himself up on his elbows, he stared down at her and trailed the backs of his knuckles over her cheek. And the look in his eyes stole her breath. She wasn't the only one who'd been altered by their lovemaking tonight. Then he claimed her lips sweetly, possessively. He kissed her as he released her wrists from their cuffs.

She sighed into him when she was finally able to touch him, running her hands over the muscled lines of his back.

Mason lifted his head and said, "You were beautiful tonight, Em." Then he kissed her on the tip of her nose and withdrew from her body. He undid the cuffs around her ankles before padding into her small bathroom. Her eyelids were drooping. She could hardly keep them open. Multiple orgasms could do that to a person.

But she couldn't believe he was leaving her cabin. That they had finished and he was going to go. After that? It hurt. She was so tired, there was no way she could stop him. And she'd saw her own tongue off before she asked. He should know better, should want to stay with her.

Yet, he waltzed back into her bedroom carrying a washcloth, which confused her. He sat on the bed beside her, spread her thighs and swiped the warm cloth over her pussy. He was cleaning her up. What?

Her eyes at half mast, she watched him toss the washcloth in her hamper, switch out all the lights but the one at her bedside, and then pad back over to the bed. He pulled the sheets and blankets up over her, then climbed in beside her with a bit of a bemused expression.

"I saw your face, Em. Did you honestly think I was leaving after that?" he asked, pulling her into his arms.

"Yes," she murmured against his chest as he cuddled her.

He tilted her face up to his, his gaze direct, and said, "Not going to happen. You're stuck with me now."

Oh goody.

She sighed sleepily against his chest and nodded. Contentment settled over her, wrapped up in his arms as she was with his chest acting as her pillow. When he brushed a soft kiss against her forehead, she felt the reverberations of it clear down to her toes.

Oh yeah, she hadn't just fallen for the land, she'd fallen for the man too. She was too limbless, too brainless after tonight to worry about the implications. She snuggled, inhaling his spicy masculine scent, and slipped off to sleep.

CHAPTER 19

*E*mily and Mason eased into a rhythm over the following week. When they weren't working, they were either at her cabin, but more often than not, at Mason's house. And more importantly, in Mason's bed.

Emily liked his house. She enjoyed cooking in the kitchen. She envisioned herself putting pots with fresh herbs in the window. And Mason and Cole had started joining her for late night dinners. She liked the hominess of it. Loved seeing the delight cross their faces, even from something as simple as chili.

As the days passed, she found herself falling further in love with Mason, the way he took care of her. Just last night she'd come home from a fourteen hour shift on her feet to a hot bubble bath and spectacular foot massage. Mason had incredible thumbs. And he'd not stopped with her feet, either.

Emily spent a day in Jackson, visiting businesses. She had sold twenty booths for the Oktoberfest. Hunt Trail Rides was donating pony rides for the kids. Plus they were going to do riding demonstrations. The Teton Cowboy was donating beer kegs, along with a mechanical bull sans the naughty part. And she had been able to get a discount on tables and chairs for their outdoor event from Garrett. Spencer had put her in touch with Jackson Stone, an officer with the Jackson Hole Police Department—and a member of their club. Jackson was going to help out with parking and make sure that they had crowd control.

Flyers had been put up around town. And tickets were selling—more than she'd thought they would. Enough that they might have to cap the event. She nearly tap danced over it.

But celebrations would have to wait until after it was a rousing success. There was a ton of work to accomplish between now and then. Emily drew up a menu for Oktoberfest, gathered the recipes she wanted to do and did a trial run with each one, adding and subtracting ingredients until she felt they were perfect. She worked tirelessly with Tibby and Faith to ensure that they overstocked on ingredients. She also taught them the recipes because, starting next week, they were going to start making the dough for the pretzels, forming them and then freezing them until the night before.

And then there were the cooking classes. She tinkered with the recipes she wanted to teach and made lists of ingredients and cooking tools they would need to have on hand.

Spencer, bless the man once again, had come through and promised to loan her a few of his line cooks and wait staff to help man the booth and meet the demand on the day of the event.

Emily was beginning to see the benefits of the club. It was like a country club or church, but naughty. It wasn't just a place where the members got their rocks off. They did, and then some. But they also came together to help each other out. They were friends and confidants. Now that she was a member, Tibby and Faith had been a font of information about what it meant to be a submissive. Tibby had even given her some things to try with Mason. Emily smiled at the memory. Those tidbits had been so hot, both she and Mason had been limp noodles afterward.

And she was thrilled at the way Mason showed her something new every night, whether it was a new to her position, some of the different types of bondage—which she had to admit she adored—or some new sex toys he introduced her to. Emily had always thought she was worldly and knew sex. But Mason proved how little she'd known, how sheltered she had been, and how, under his hands, she could experience more pleasure than she had ever thought possible. Her breath caught just thinking about all the wicked ways he loved her. She couldn't get enough of him. She was enjoying every minute of her training, learning to listen to her body, craving the way Mason touched her.

She sighed against the hollow of his neck where she'd buried her face. She was straddling his lap, his shaft still penetrating her. His chest was partially bare, enough that her nipples were abraded by the hair covering his chest. Emily didn't want to move. All she was doing was delaying the inevitable. There was work still to do today. Mounds of it. But she adored the way Mason held her after sex. As hot and as dominatingly alpha as the man acted in every sector of his life, the intimate tenderness from him was unexpected. The way he held her close, his face leaning against hers, a hand splayed over her lower back, holding her in place while the other pressed between her shoulder blades bespoke of softer emotions, of care, and it thrilled her.

Even though Emily knew she needed to move and get up off his lap, figure out where he had tossed her bra in their haste, she couldn't seem to find the energy.

They weren't fooling anyone at the lodge anymore either. Everyone knew their 'meetings' in Mason's office weren't really meetings. Yet she didn't want to move from his lap after their latest bout, even though she knew the registration clerks, along with her sous chef and line cook, were laughing about it.

It was mainly because her legs were still the consistency of tapioca pudding. Mason, for all his gruffness and pure mule-headed stubbornness at times, seemed disinclined to let her up.

On Monday, they'd added the information for the week-long cooking excursion up on the website. It was a beginning.

"Didn't we have some actual work to get to today?" she asked, her words muffled against his chest.

He lifted her face up and gave her a heart-stopping grin. "We'll get around to it eventually."

Her body softened. Need hummed in her veins. How could she want him again? How could she need him again so soon after? She'd thought surely by now one of them would start getting tired of the other. But that hadn't happened. Each day, each time, she fell for him more. As much as she craved the wicked passion when they touched, she loved the way he held her afterward, the way he cared for her. It made her feel important—cherished, even.

When she shifted to try and move off his lap, his hands cupped her rear, holding her in place.

"Not leaving so soon."

"Mason, we have to get some work done today. With Oktoberfest picking up steam, I have final orders to place on supplies and I want to go over the menu again."

"I have complete faith in your abilities. The week-long cooking excursion booked up in forty-eight hours. You're a genius," Mason said, kissing her. Her body stirred as she returned his kiss. She couldn't get enough of him. Always, he kissed her, and she was a goner. Caught up in him.

"About time you realized that," she said, running her hands through his hair. She'd knocked off his hat when he'd first pulled her onto his lap.

"We should go to the club," he said, leveling his caramel gaze at her. At the thought of being naked in front of people other than Mason, she winced and all the air clogged in her throat.

His gaze darkening, his hands kneaded her rear. Tendrils of heat re-ignited within her. He stated, "You're ready, Em. And this is part of my world, part of being my sub. I promise you we will plan our scene beforehand so you will know exactly what to expect. I'd like to claim you here, finally and, I will be there with you every step of the way."

His fingers grazed over her back channel and she moaned. Who knew that she'd enjoy anal play? Certainly not her, but he'd been showing her with butt plugs all week just how incredible it was and how hot it got her.

Although, as much as she was willing to go there, she was worried about having an audience. "I know. I trust you, it's just a little daunting. I mean, I'm going to flash everyone my naughty bits."

"I happen to love your naughty bits," he growled, shifting his hips so she could feel him. She bit her lower lip as desire swamped her. It was heady. It flooded her. She wanted him. Again. So soon.

"We have work to do," she said feebly. Her mild, half-hearted protest sounded weak, even to her ears.

Mason stood with her in his arms and laid her down on top of his desk. His hands caressed her form, whispering over her spread thighs as he leaned over her. Nipping at her chin, he said, "We can work later. Much later. I need you, Em. I always fucking need you."

Consternation and desire warred on his handsome face, like he was just as perplexed by his constant desire for her as she. Emily didn't know why but it made her happy to know she wasn't alone in this quagmire. That what she felt for him, the all-encompassing need that left her flummoxed, was reciprocated. He was right there with her.

"Well, you're the boss." She moaned as he slid deep inside.

Her back arched. Pleasure ricocheted as he thrust. Emily wondered if a body could expire from too much pleasure.

He flashed her a grin suffused with wicked intent. "That I am."

And then he proceeded to show her in, exact detail, just how much he was the boss. Again and again.

CHAPTER 20

*M*ason showered alone that morning. It was the first time that week. But not before Emily had blown his mind, and his dick, before sliding out of his bed. He couldn't get enough of her. She'd fast become an addiction.

And she wasn't having any problems adjusting to the lifestyle. In fact, the more layers he peeled away, the more he began to see that she had the heart of a true submissive. She might be determined, intelligent, and independent, but she also held nothing back from him in the bedroom.

She was eager to please. Open to experiment. She wasn't much for pain. Didn't care for being flogged at all. But she also didn't shy away from experimentation. She'd met each new challenge head on. And she had been honest with him regarding flogging.

He smiled at the memory. She'd indicated with her hand vised around his cock that she would break his thing off if he ever did that again. Mason wasn't a hardcore sadist so it wasn't a loss in his book. He thoroughly enjoyed disciplining a sub. With her aversion to flogging, he'd just have to get creative with her punishments. Although she didn't seem to mind spankings. And there had been quite a few, since her mouth always seemed to fly off the handle at him. He gave her freedom outside the bedroom, because with her personality, she'd never take orders or follow his commands well. In the bedroom, that was another matter entirely.

As he rinsed the suds off his body, he did wonder at times if she mouthed off just to get him to spank her. Their coming together after a spanking always seemed a bit hotter, a bit more out of control, a bit more everything.

They would see how she did that evening at the club. He'd been working with her all week, doing some anal play, stretching her back channel. Tonight, at the club, he planned to take her there. Claim her that way in front of the other Masters.

He knew what it meant, even if she didn't. And he knew she was uncertain about the scene—and, in some respects, about him. That was his fault because of their rocky beginning and the way he had treated her. But after tonight, his claim on her would be rock solid.

He was so fucking possessive where she was concerned. A part of him wanted to keep her completely to himself. Not show her off to the rest of their little club. But he knew, deep down, he needed to. After everything he'd been through these last few months, he felt parts of himself return with her every gasp, her every moan and every silken flutter of her pussy around his dick. Claiming her like this would be a balm to his soul and soothe his battered pride. It was selfish of him.

Emily was unlike any sub he'd been with thus far. Mason wanted her, not just in his bed, but his life. He couldn't seem to go more than a few hours without touching her, without needing her. Even the other night, they had sat on the porch swing and stargazed. Emily had wanted to watch the promised meteor shower and that's what they did, with her curled at his side, her head on his shoulder. There was a comfort and pleasure in just being with her. She'd fallen asleep against him like that. He'd watched her for a bit, snuggled against him, knowing she taken up residence inside him, and he'd begun to hope.

It had scared the shit out of him, if truth be told. Not that he was running away from her, because she was the best damn thing to happen to him in a long time, maybe ever.

He'd been on his own for such a long time, never committing to any one sub. But Emily had fast become the focal point in his world. It was daunting how much she'd come to mean to him in such a short time period.

Mason shuffled down the stairs. He was impressed with the way she was handling the Oktoberfest event for the following Saturday. The woman had been born to organize events. He truly hadn't expected it to be successful. That was on him, mainly because he'd been viewing the world rather negatively. But he admired the way Emily had recruited members of the club to donate time and resources, the booths she'd sold to some of the local businesses, the number of tickets already sold for the event that already covered the cost of hosting it. Anything else they brought in was all surplus toward the lodge. Mason breathed easier seeing returns coming in, both for Oktoberfest and for the cooking classes.

Not that anyone could blame him for his doubt, not after what Claire had done to the lodge. Any time he felt himself almost confessing his feelings for Emily, he remembered the mess his life had become because of Claire and the words stalled on his tongue. He cared for Emily, deeply. She made him smile. And with every throaty moan, she was returning pieces of his soul he'd believed lost back to him.

Every time he loved her, he saw his feelings reflected in Emily's eyes. She cared for him too. He believed that, or he wouldn't be claiming her as his submissive in the club this evening.

It was a first for him. It was a huge step. That should be enough, for now.

The hope she engendered in him of creating a permanent bond chased away the darkness that had settled in his soul these last few months, and he understood claiming her tonight was only the first step.

Cole was at the kitchen table, dressed for the day in his fishing gear, sipping coffee, and munching on one of Emily's biscuits. They were buttery, flaky, melt in your mouth with a hint of honeyed sweetness, yummy goodness. He and Cole had fought over who got the last one a few times this past week.

"Morning," he said to Cole and poured himself a cup of coffee. Again, Emily. Mason didn't know what she did to it, but the way she made coffee... Hell, he was sunk, and falling further every minute where she was concerned.

"You and Emily seem to be getting quite cozy. She was here again last night," Cole murmured.

Guilt assaulted Mason. He glanced at Cole, regretting that he'd made the promise in the first place. He replied, "I know. And I realized I promised that I wouldn't get involved with her, but there's something between us, Cole. Hard to describe, other than I have feelings for her. I'm claiming her at the club this evening."

Cole's eyes widened. "It's that serious then?"

"It is. I didn't expect this, expect her to matter, but she does," Mason admitted.

"I get that. Just be careful. I like Emily, quite a bit, in fact. I think she's great for this place. But you need to be careful, both for your sake and for our business. Jackson messaged me that Claire made bail yesterday," Cole informed him.

"She what?" Mason replied. That bitch got to roam free

while their business limped along because of her. She should rot in prison, not be given a shred of leniency.

"Yeah, apparently her family is loaded," Cole said with a furious shrug.

Her family had money? Mason tried wrapping his brain around that little factoid. It was yet another item she'd hidden from him while she'd been here. What he couldn't understand was why she had done it. Especially if her family was loaded and could afford the substantial amount for bail.

With everything they had on tap to bring this place back from the brink of collapse, this was the last thing they needed. "Shit, we don't need her anywhere near this place. The restraining order is in effect."

"I realize that. But we will need to be vigilant, what with the Oktoberfest event a week away," Cole replied.

"Fuck. What timing!" Mason muttered, pacing, wanting to punch something. He couldn't allow himself to blow a gasket.

"We'll take it as it comes. She can't come here without getting arrested. Jackson's going to try and tail her as much as he can, keep an eye out," Cole added, his demeanor cool, which only infused Mason's anger. How could Cole be so calm? Nothing ever seemed to rattle him, whereas Mason had been knocked off his axis and had yet to regain his balance.

"Jackson can't be everywhere. We should let Alex know to be on the lookout. The rest of the club too. Just in case," Mason said. Even with all the fallout and devastation she'd wrought, there was still more Claire could do. If she let it slip that they were part of a secret lifestyle club, posted it on social media, in the review sections on travel websites, or even here in town, the consequences could be utterly disastrous.

It almost made him want to abort his plans with Emily for that evening. Almost being the proper word. If he caved and acted out of fear of what might happen, that bitch would win.

She'd already taken enough from him that he wouldn't give her the goddamn satisfaction.

"Tell only those who need to know to keep an eye out," Mason said.

"And what about Emily? You going to tell her?" Cole asked, leaning back in his chair.

Mason shook his head. "She doesn't need to know. At least not yet."

Cole raised a brow at him. "You intend on claiming her before all and sundry at the club tonight but haven't told her about Claire yet? That you two were involved?"

"Claire and I weren't serious, little more than fuck buddies. It's none of your business what I do or don't tell my sub. It's for me to decide when I shed light on that relationship. And right now, until the legal case is resolved, she doesn't need to know. It's for her protection," Mason stated.

"You keep telling yourself that." Cole shoved his chair back and stood, giving him a patronizing glare before he left the house.

Mason stood in the kitchen, his mind churning. Claire was free, while the lodge was barely paying its bills and eking out a living. The unfairness of it, that she'd played him for a fool. He wasn't lying when he said they'd been little more than fuck buddies. Had he had tender feelings for her while they were banging each other? Sure. As he did for any submissive. But it hadn't been deep or meant to be long term. Their relationship had been surface variety only. He'd preferred it that way. And so had she, if truth be told.

After scarfing down the breakfast Emily had left for him— biscuits, turkey bacon, which he'd never been a fan of until Emily, and warm cinnamon apples—Mason headed to the lodge. On the walk over, Cole's words burned a hole in his gut. Emily knew that Claire had stolen from the lodge. She didn't need to know that he and Claire had been together. Not yet. Not until he was certain of her feelings.

He would have to come clean eventually. Mason wanted to ensure that their relationship was solid and then he would confess. Until then, it was his job as her Dom to shield her from harm, including his less than stellar past.

CHAPTER 21

*E*mily shivered as they entered the Teton Cowboy. Mason's palm was pressed against her lower back like a possessive brand. It gave her a little thrill.

All day, she'd worried about tonight. Mason had gone into explicit detail about what he planned to do with her tonight in their club. He was going to de-virginize her back channel for everyone to see. Heat flushed up her cheeks. She'd been in a constant state of blushing since she'd woken this morning, enough so that both Tibby and Faith had commented on her state.

Emily's pulse fluttered as Mason guided her through the throngs of people here on a Friday night. The country music was a lively tune, playing over loudspeakers. The myriad conversations and animated voices of people having a good time created a dull roar. At the entrance to Cuffs & Spurs, after a wink from Derrick, who was guarding the private lower level, Mason towed her down the stairs. Her breath caught in her throat.

Emily had never thought she'd be interested in anal sex, let alone consider having it in front of a bunch of people. But since Mason's advent into her life, and into her bed, he had proven all her theories about herself erroneous. Every night for the past week, he'd used a butt plug on her during their bedroom activities. Each night, the plug had been larger, stretching her back channel. The combined sensations of Mason screwing her brains out with the plug in her ass were incredible. The pleasure was nearly indescribable. The Big Bang had nothing on the potency of her climaxes.

Emily trusted Mason. In everything he'd shown her since becoming her Dominant, he'd never faltered. She reveled in the pride in his caramel gaze and preened with pleasure over his praise. Even when there had been instances and certain practices she hadn't cared for, like flogging—because, holy shit, ow! She loved being restrained in bed, or anywhere else, for that matter. She loved giving Mason full control in the bedroom. The way he would look at her once her hands were bound, his gaze infused with salacious intent.

That didn't mean she didn't feel trepidation over the scene they were about to do because she did, in great heaping spoonfuls.

Yet, the way he'd looked at her, with pride and possessiveness, both in the cab of his truck and now, as he escorted her into the club, gave her courage. Made her feel that she could do this, perform a public scene with him. He'd illuminated parts of her that she'd not realized existed.

She'd always enjoyed sex, even though it had always been a bit blasé. Not so with Mason. Sex with him was downright epic and world altering. The way he drew responses out of her, the way she craved his touch, it was like the Earth stood still, and all other life ceased to exist so that only she and Mason were present in time and space. Emily's snack cake addiction had transferred to him. He was the fix she needed every day—sometimes more than once a day.

She couldn't get through a day without him. The

voraciousness of her appetite always surprised her. How minutes after a rowdy, wicked bout, sweat slicking her form, her body still shuddering from her climax, desire would stampede back to life.

They separated briefly into the locker rooms, where Emily stored her purse and knee length pea-coat that she'd worn to hide what she was wearing underneath. Her choice of clothing was not something she'd want to wear on public streets. She had on a black leather mini dress. And it really was mini; it stopped at her upper thighs. The bodice of the dress was a halter style number which left her back bare.

She rejoined Mason outside the locker rooms. He'd stored his coat and shirt. She sighed. Mason shirtless made her ovaries break into song. The chiseled hard planes of his chest made her fingers itch to touch him. But here, now, tonight, she had to restrain her urges and give him what he needed. Her submission.

"Relax," Mason murmured at her temple as he slid his arm around her waist. His fingers grazed the exposed flesh on her lower back and she bit back a moan. She loved his hands on her. The rough callouses never ceased to stir tendrils of heat to life.

"I'm trying to, Sir," she whispered, even as her hands shook.

"You'll do fine tonight," he said, towing her back into the club proper and over toward a table that had another couple sitting at it. The guy had to be one of the biggest men she'd ever seen. All lanky, Jimmy Stewart-ish, he made the table and chairs appear miniature. He was the epitome of tall, dark, and handsome, with his dark chestnut hair that was nearly black. His strong jaw was lined with a few days' growth of stubble. His dark hazel gaze was framed by thick black eyebrows.

The man's arm was curled around the blonde woman at his side. She was stunning in her club gear, in a matching set of red leather bra and panties and nothing else. Her light blue eyes were framed by thick, inky lashes, her lips were curled up in a soft, loving smile at the man at her side.

"Carter," Mason said.

"Mason. Good to see you. And who's this?" the giant said, holding out a hand for him to shake, nodding in Emily's direction. She couldn't help it. She blushed. Her cleavage was nearly popping out of the top of her dress and she was certain that, if she sat, he would get a clear view of her pussy if she wasn't careful.

"This is Emily. Chef out at the Elkhorn and my sub," Mason stated, pride lacing his voice along with a possessive tenderness that curled inside her chest.

Carter eyed him speculatively before he flashed her a kind smile.

"Emily, it's a pleasure to meet you. I'm Carter, and this is my wife, Jenna," he said, indicating the beautiful blonde at his side.

"Hi. It's nice to meet you both," she replied.

"How's Liam doing?" Mason asked as they slid into the empty chairs. Emily fidgeted with the hem of her dress, trying to make it cover more until she finally gave up. If she pulled it down any further, it would expose her tits. So, given the choice between tits or ass, she went with ass. Not that it mattered. Soon enough, everyone would see all there was to see of her wicked bits.

"Teething. Jenna's sister Meghan is watching him for us tonight so we could get away," Carter explained.

"How old is he now?" Mason asked.

"Six months. Hard to believe he's so big already. And growing more into Carter's spitting image every day. You would think after carrying him for nine months that he would look like he came from me, but nope," Jenna said with a small chuckle and glance at her husband.

"Oh, I think he has your ears, love. So Emily, where are you from? I've heard through the grapevine you're not local," Carter said, his gaze inquisitive.

"Los Angeles, Orange County to be exact," Emily replied. Her hands were clutched in her lap.

"And how are you finding life in Wyoming?" Carter asked.

She shot Mason a glance before she replied, "It's different than I thought it would be. There are adjustments, to be certain. I miss my friends but I'm enjoying myself here."

"Is your family in LA?" Carter inquired.

"They are," she said. The last thing she wanted to discuss was her family. Her mom had called that afternoon asking Emily when she was going to get serious and get a real job. They just didn't understand her need to create, her love of working in kitchens. It was an uphill, frustrating battle. Any time she spoke with them, she always regretted it. Emily didn't fit with them, as hard as she'd tried to. There were days when it made her incredibly maudlin. But then she got over it, usually with a snack cake or two, and moved on.

Emily couldn't help but notice that Carter's hand had slid beneath his wife's red leather panties. Or the way Jenna sat with her eyes half closed, her mouth parted in pleasure as Carter said, "And we haven't scared you off yet?"

"Not so far," Emily said, fidgeting at the unanticipated arousal at the sight of Carter pleasuring his wife in front of her. It combined with the scattered moans from couples already engaged in the scene areas. She understood the appeal of the club, now that Mason had awakened her to the lifestyle. How it wasn't just about the scene you did with a partner, but hearing other couples, seeing them lose themselves to ecstasy. It was a potent and heady drug.

Her leather halter abraded her stiff nipples as she shifted.

"Well, we're looking forward to coming to Oktoberfest next weekend. We plan on bringing our son with us."

"He might be a bit young for some of our events, but I'm sure your family will enjoy the festivities," Emily said.

Mason rubbed her back and interjected, "Our scene area just opened up."

Carter said, "Ours too. It was a pleasure to finally meet you, Emily. Mason, good to see you. Enjoy your evening."

"You do the same," Mason said with a nod toward his friend.

He stood and pulled Emily up from her seat. She let him. Her knees shook. Then he slid an arm around her waist and whisked her over to the scene area that contained the sawhorse. Inside the perimeter of the scene area was a small chest of drawers on the right, as well as the wooden sawhorse. The top of the sawhorse was padded and covered with black leather. It stood perpendicular to the wall beyond. There were silver metal loops at various points that Emily knew Mason would use to attach her cuffs to, along with her ankles. Yet it was the full-length mirror on the wall directly beyond that gave her pause. Tremors wracked her frame. She couldn't help being nervous. With the mirror, she'd be able to see all the people looking at her while Mason screwed her back channel.

"Disrobe for me, Em," Mason ordered.

With trembling fingers, she unbuttoned the straps of her halter around her neck and let them fall. Then she unzipped the back of her dress and shoved the material down to her feet, until she stood in nothing but her black lace panties and black heels. She stepped out of her heels, then picked them up along with her dress and stored them on top of the chest of drawers.

She stood in nothing but her panties, her hands clenched at her sides. She glanced at the crowd in the club and panic rose in her breast. She wanted to cover herself and escape. There were men and women staring at her nearly nude body.

Mason stepped in front of her, blocking out the other patrons.

"Eyes on me. Don't pay attention to anyone else but me," he ordered. She focused on his bare chest. That was good. She loved Mason's chest. But she couldn't seem to block out the sounds of the club and the nearby couples in the throes of passion.

"Good, now give me your hands. I'm going to restrain you to the sawhorse now, all right?"

All she could do was nod her head. Her tongue stuck in her suddenly dry mouth. Her heartbeat beat a staccato rhythm. She worried that she was going to start hyperventilating at any moment. She tried to lift her wrists, but her body wouldn't seem to work on her command as fear grabbed hold.

"Sir? I don't know that I can do this," she said, a sob lodged in her throat. She was thoroughly ashamed and bent her head. Typically she had no problem conquering new challenges and didn't allow fear to guide her actions. But it was choking her right now. And she couldn't seem to move past it.

That's when Mason's arms slid around her. There was comfort in them, strength that she leaned into and soaked up like a cat soaking up some sunlight. One of his big hands cupped her cheek and tipped her face up until her gaze met his. Warmth and concern filled his stare as he murmured, "You're doing just fine. Deep breaths for me. I will be with you every step of the way."

She gulped in air, and knew she was likely impersonating a fish out of water. Mason stroked her cheek with his thumb, then lowered his mouth over hers. The moment his firm lips brushed against hers, she moaned. This was what she needed from him. This connection making the rest of the club cease to exist. His tongue stroked over her bottom lip, seeking entrance. Under his coaxing, she opened for him.

His hands caressed the lines of her back while he kissed her brainless. Pleasure slithered in her veins. Her body went fluid at his touch.

He cupped the globes of her breasts in his big hands and rasped a thumb across her nipples. He kissed her and her world boiled down to him. It had never been this way with any other man. And she had the sneaking suspicion he was the only one who would ever command such a response from her body.

When Mason finally lifted his head and ended the kiss, Emily whimpered at the loss. He flashed her a carnal grin, his gaze shrouded with lust.

Then he drew her over to the sawhorse. Gently he positioned her body, bending her at the waist, and settling her torso lengthwise over the padding, where he then fastened her wrist cuffs to loops on the top end. This lifted her chest up and meant she would be looking directly at the mirror. Then he drew her panties down her legs before they were spread over the back V of the sawhorse and Mason placed her ankles into leather restraints.

In this position, her pussy was on display for the entire crowd. She couldn't move, couldn't shield herself from prying eyes, couldn't do anything. Her anxiety rocketed to withering heights. Her hands were clenched into fists. People were looking at her. She didn't know if she could do this. She jerked against her restraints and almost lost her nerve, her safeword on the tip of her tongue.

But Mason knelt before her and kissed her again. His kiss was hungry and erotic, a heady combination of tongue and teeth. His tongue thrust with ardent fervor to initiate a heated duel with hers. Emily felt her body go pliant at his touch.

When he broke the kiss, his breathing was uneven. He ordered, "Eyes on me the whole time. Keep them on me and only me. Understood?"

She nodded. "Yes, Sir."

He kissed the tip of her nose before he stood.

She shivered at the innocuous sweet touch, considering where they were and what they were about to do, it was unexpected, and she felt it clear to her toes. In the mirror's reflection, she watched, her gaze trained on his face. She watched as he touched her. Caressed the lines of her back, stroking over her flesh and stoking her internal forge to life. As he fondled her, the rest of the world dimmed.

His hands, his big, rough hands that she adored, caressed her bum. He drew his fingers through her slit and she gasped. With the pads of his fingers, he teased her clit. Circled the bud, creating jolts of electricity that caused her pussy to quake in eager anticipation. Flicked his digits over the nub and she moaned before he penetrated her sheath with two fingers. She mewled in the back of her throat. Then he lowered his head. At the first touch of his tongue against her anus, she gasped. It was carnal and wicked. She'd never thought he would put his tongue there. Then he rimmed her rosette, laving his tongue over it while his fingers pumped in her pussy.

When his tongue pressed against her back channel and slipped inside the taut ring of muscle, she moaned at the exquisite delight. This was new. With his tongue, he stretched her, much in the same fashion as the butt plugs he'd had her wear this week. Yet it had a different feel. The heat of his tongue as he thrust, the warm puffs of his breath against her skin, created a pleasure so intense it blurred the edges of her vision.

Her lids grew heavy. Mason didn't hold back and the potent nature of their joining flowed between them. It was always present, but this felt like something more. The look of ecstasy on his face. His dark, lust filled gaze stared at hers in the mirror. Emily's body walked a tightrope of pleasure.

The dual sensations were too much for her to hold on for long. Emily came. Hard and unexpectedly.

"Sir," she cried as her pussy spasmed around his digits and her back channel clenched around his tongue.

Mason lifted his face and straightened behind her. She

watched as he withdrew his hand from her pussy and sucked the fingers coated with her juices into his mouth.

Then he shifted and withdrew a small tube from the back pocket of his jeans. He coated her back hole with lube and did the same with two of his fingers, then pressed them against the opening of her channel. She groaned deep in the back of her throat as his fingers pressed inside and penetrated her anus.

She couldn't believe how much she loved the sensation. Mason thrust his two fingers and stretched her, his wicked gaze dark and suffused with lust. Her body trembled. She was hot. Her rear clenched at his fingers as they pumped inside her. It made her feel like she was floating. Like she was resting on charged air, which made every nerve ending come alive and tingle.

Her body coiled in on itself as he added a third finger and then a fourth until they were gliding unimpeded. She kept her gaze on him as pleasure swamped her. In the mirror's reflection, his hand was seesawing in and out.

When he removed his hand from her bottom, she whimpered. Except, in the mirror, she watched as he undid his jeans and freed his cock. Gripping his shaft, he poured lube over his turgid shaft and added another dollop of lubricant to her rosette, then fit the crown at the entrance to her rear.

"Eyes on me," he commanded, holding her gaze in the mirror.

Then his hips rolled, and the head pressed inside. His large cock stretched her almost painfully. She stiffened at the intrusion. But then he withdrew and thrust again, going deeper this time. Stretching her further. With every thrust, his cock drove further inside.

Emily's skin felt stretched. Her rear was on fire. Her pussy throbbed. And through it all, she watched Mason's expression. The way his jaw clenched in concentration as he furrowed his shaft deeper and deeper in her ass until his full length was

ANYA SUMMERS

embedded. Her nerve endings erupted. Lightning flashed and
burned through her core.

The possession in his glance. The way he stared at her, as if
he owned her, as if she belonged to him, as if she was precious
to him. She moaned as he thrust, slowly at first, testing her
body. She shivered and trembled. The butt plugs had been one
thing. But this experience was something else entirely.

She hadn't realized how sensitive these tissues were. Or
how aroused it would make her to have his cock pumping
inside her ass. Or how her pussy would throb in time with his
thrusts. Her mouth hung open on a series of deep, guttural
moans.

She felt herself spiral. She felt herself let go. She gave
herself to Mason in a way she'd never done with anyone. As
his pace increased, his grunts combining with her moans,
Emily understood she'd ceded him her heart and soul
tonight. The importance of their joining this way was not
lost on her. The fierce expression on his face as he gazed at
her. The fury of his hips as he pistoned inside her back
sheath.

He took her up a blinding precipice where nothing else
existed but the two of them. She floated on a sea of intense
pleasure which infused every part of her. She felt like they were
fusing into one being. That they were no longer separate, but
one unit, one heart, one soul. In his touch, in the way he moved
with her, Emily felt his care, his heart—and her own
responded.

It started at the base of her spine and blasted through her
body like a rocket launch.

She screamed as she climaxed. Moaned as she felt him join
her and semen flooded her rear.

Mason pumped inside her as he came, and Emily felt herself
slipping off the precipice. The sound around them dimmed.
She floated in a haze, like she was in a dream. She felt Mason

move around behind her, undoing her restraints. Then he slid a blanket over her body and unlatched her cuffs from the horse.

Emily felt herself slipping. But Mason was there, lifting her up into his arms, wrapping her body more firmly in the blanket. He carried her over to a nearby couch where he settled them both and cuddled her against his chest.

"You did wonderfully tonight, Em. I'm proud of you," he murmured with his lips pressed against her forehead. His hands glided tenderly over her.

"You too," she replied, sleepily.

He chuckled darkly, the sound full of male pride, and then said, "Tell me about your family. When Carter mentioned them earlier it appeared to me that you didn't like talking about them. You tensed when he brought them up."

Still floating, she shrugged and said, "I just don't fit with them. I never really have. I love them and they love me. But in their way."

"And what is their way?"

"They aren't overly affectionate. My parents tend to prize accomplishments—meaning money in the bank—over emotions. My mom's a real estate agent, dad's a heart surgeon. Both of them are in the top of their field. They don't understand what I do, or care for it. My mom still has an office for me at her agency, ready for me the moment I get serious about life," she said, unable to stop the resentment from seeping into her voice.

"I'm sorry," he said, cuddling her close.

"It's okay, really. I tried to be like them for a long time and it was killing my soul. When I applied and got in to Le Cordon Bleu, they acted as if I had decided to join a biker gang and had begun worshiping Satan."

He tilted her face up, his gaze warm, and he said, "I think you're very brave. It takes a lot of courage to go after what you want for your life, to be determined enough to succeed when you don't have the support from those around you. It's their loss, you know. That they can't see your worth or just how amazing you truly are."

She stroked his jaw. His shadow beard prickled over her skin. If she weren't already in love with him, she would have fallen right then and there. Love for him inundated her. "Take me home, Mason."

"Are you okay? I didn't hurt you, did I?" His concern, his care for her almost made her weep.

"I'm fine, really. Better than fine, I just really want to go home and go to bed. Your bed," she said, unable to voice her feelings yet.

His gaze darkened and he cast her a wicked grin. "That can be arranged."

He carted her to the locker rooms, where he helped her dress. Her limbs were heavy, her body sated from their incredible scene. Once they were dressed, her coat fastened against the chill, Mason escorted her from the club.

In the cab of his truck, he pulled her close while he drove. She rested her head upon his shoulder, completely and utterly blissful.

And thoroughly, no holds barred, in love.

CHAPTER 22

*D*uring the week leading up to Oktoberfest, Mason worked nonstop. Everyone at the lodge did the same in preparation for the coming event, most of all, Emily. She was in the thick of it; directing, organizing, cooking up a storm.

Emily amazed him. Her dedication to making the Elkhorn a success. The fact that she was putting in a boatload of overtime between running the Elkhorn daily and pulling off the event this weekend. Mason didn't know how she did it.

But it was the nights he looked forward to the most. By some tacit, unspoken agreement, Emily spent her nights with him, in his home, and his bed. There was a toothbrush for her in his bathroom. And she'd put some of her shampoo and soap in his shower stall. Little by little, she was becoming a solid fixture in his life.

He fucking loved it.

The newfound emotions kept him off-kilter and he wasn't on solid footing yet. Before Emily's advent into his life, he'd been perfectly content living the life of a bachelor, not being beholden to another. Not sharing his bathroom nor his bed.

Claire had never breached the inner sanctuary of his house. All of their intimate relations had occurred either at the club or in her cabin.

But when it came to Emily, having her in his home and bed felt natural. It was like his life had been waiting for her arrival. And he was in this relationship with her for the long haul. Mason didn't want any half measures where she was concerned.

It surprised the hell out of him, and he wasn't necessarily comfortable with that knowledge. Nor was he ready to voice the turbulent sea of his emotions just yet. They would get there, in time. Mason had contacted their lawyer, Kent, and already had a new contract for Emily in the works. He planned to solidify her presence here. Ensure that she was here long term.

By Friday morning, the event had sold out. Mason and the rest of the Doms had spent the day erecting the tables, tents and booths. It was backbreaking work but, seeing the way it was all coming together, he knew it was going to be a success.

They'd closed the Elkhorn today, offering boxed lunches for meals to current guests. Emily had been in the kitchens all day long with Tibby, Faith, and a few of the line cooks from the Teton Cowboy. He could tell because the scents wafting on the breeze as they'd erected tents and tables made his mouth water.

The sun had set by the time he located her, up to her elbows in kitchen prep.

"Emily. That's enough for today. Everyone's exhausted. You need a good night's sleep," he said, noticing the way she was dragging. The lines of fatigue around her eyes.

"Can't right now. Way too much to do," she said, ignoring him.

And this was where he would draw the line in the sand with her. As her Dom, it was his job to ensure she took care of herself, even when she was being stubborn and mule-headed.

Not giving her a chance to tell him no, he scooped her up over his shoulder, then said, "Tibby, Faith, why don't you two finish up whatever it is you're doing in the next fifteen minutes and go home so you both can get a good night's sleep?"

"Put me down, you overgrown jerk!" Emily screeched.

He banded an arm across her thighs and whacked her butt with his free hand. "Enough, Em. Tibby, Faith, I meant what I said. Please follow my orders," Mason ordered.

They both replied, "Yes, Sir," like the good little submissives they were.

The wildcat in his arms, however, was another story entirely. Emily sputtered and strained.

"Dammit, Mason, put me the fuck down," she screeched.

He paid her little heed as he carted her out the back door and took the path up to his house. "Emily, it's for your own good. We can't have you so tired you're falling on your ass tomorrow."

"You don't get to tell me what to do! Fucking Neanderthal!" she snapped, flailing her arms.

He should have cuffed her first before hauling her out of the kitchen. But that was an oversight he would soon rectify. He smacked her bottom again. "Enough, Em. Settle the fuck down."

"You settle down, you big jerk."

Mason entered his house, heading back toward the stairs— at least, until he heard the distinct rumble in her belly. "When was the last time you had anything to eat?"

"It doesn't matter. Set me down," she snarled, gouging his back with her nails.

He course corrected, with Emily still struggling against him, and headed into the kitchen. Before he set her on her feet, he grabbed his cuffs off the table. He'd planned on presenting her with them, all ceremonial like, but she'd forced his hand. Mason lowered her feet to the floor but managed to hold on to her wrists. Emily tried yanking them out of his grasp but he was stronger.

"Mason, stop. Let me go." She struggled against him.

"I wish I could. But you blatantly disobeyed me," he growled.

"Disobeyed? Are you kidding me? You're the one who came into my kitchen and started ordering me and my staff about. You crossed a line back there and you fucking know it. I'm so mad at you right now. You had no right," she snapped.

Once her cuffs were fastened and her hands restrained together, he tilted her face up with his free hand until their gazes clashed. Her hazel eyes flashed, anger seething in her glare. He didn't know why, but it aroused him like nothing else. She aroused him like no one else.

"Let's get one thing straight. I'm your Dom. And as such, when I ask you to do something, I expect you to follow my command without question."

"Screw you, asshole. No one comes into my kitchen and orders me about. You were out of line. I don't care if we're screwing each other, you had no right."

"That does it. I have the only right, Em," he said.

Mason maneuvered her over to the kitchen table, turned her around and bent her over it. He drew her arms behind her back and fastened the cuffs together. Then he held her down with one hand while the other unfastened her jeans, yanking them down with her panties. He shoved her chef's jacket up so that it was bunched above her waist and left her bare bottom exposed.

"What the hell do you think you are doing? Unhand me, you—"

Thwack! His hand cracked against her bottom. At her screech, he growled.

"It's my job to ensure you take care of yourself. You're dead on your feet. And when I asked you to stop, you gave me lip in front of other submissives. That will not go unpunished. You earned this fucking spanking."

He smacked her bottom and the sharp crack filled the kitchen. As did her muffled cries.

"I hate you," she sniffled, making his heart ache.

"Lie. You enjoy provoking me. This wasn't the first time and, with that mouth of yours, it certainly won't be the last. Now take your punishment like a good submissive."

He swatted her behind, enjoying the way the milky globes reddened beneath his palm. He didn't miss the moisture now slicking her crease, or the fact that her yelps of startled pain had shifted into breathy mewls. Nor the fact that she tilted her hips up slightly, begging for his forceful stroke.

Christ, it made him so fucking hard. He loved watching this fierce woman bend to his command.

His woman.

He issued thirty whacks until her pretty heart-shaped ass was glowing ruby red. He stroked his fingers through her drenched folds, pleasure filling him at her startled, passion-infused gasp.

"Mason, please."

"What did you call me?" he murmured, teasing her flesh. His fingers caressed the outer rim of her folds, enjoying the way she tried to squirm and direct his hand.

"Sir, please, I need you."

"That's my girl," he growled and knelt behind her. He shoved her jeans down to her ankles and spread her thighs, then did what he'd been waiting to do all damn day. He tasted her. Swiped his tongue through her slick heat, reveling in the taste of her honeyed nectar.

At her startled moan, he grinned before sucking her little nub into his mouth. Curling his tongue around the bud, he swished his tongue in circles around her clit. He licked her. Her scent invaded his nostrils and taste flooded his mouth. Then he ate at her pussy like a man starved. He wasn't gentle. He feasted. Flicking his tongue repeatedly over her clit, loving the way it swelled and engorged for him.

His hands gripped her hips, not letting her wriggle or move as he commanded a response from her body. She was more malleable after a few good orgasms. Thrusting his tongue inside her sheath, he penetrated her and relished the way her tissues clamped around his tongue as if trying to draw his appendage deeper.

Emily's sweet, throaty moans were music to his ears. His dick throbbed in his jeans, aching to feel her the hot clasp of her pussy.

"Come for me," he growled against her cunt. He pinched her clit between his thumb and forefinger as he plunged his tongue inside her.

Her body jerked, her hips bucked, and moisture flooded his tongue.

"Mason, Sir. Oh God!" she cried.

Then he stood, ready to take her. He unzipped his jeans and then said, "Shit. Em, I'll be right back. I need a condom."

"No, you don't. Please, Mason. I'm on the pill. Just please fuck me," she whimpered.

He stilled, his body vibrating with desire. His voice low, he asked, "You sure?"

"Yes, just please do me."

He shoved his jeans and boxers down, freeing his dick. He gripped his cock and ran the head through her swollen folds, groaning at the sensation. At the contact, feeling her unhindered by a thin rubber membrane, he gritted his teeth at the wave of pleasure bombarding him. He guided his length into her welcoming heat and his eyes all but rolled into the back of his head. Emily, bareback, was the most exquisite sensation, the way her hot cunt clutched and squeezed him.

Fuck. He nearly blew his load right then and there.

Gripping her hips, he flexed his hips and shuttled his length in and out. Christ, it had never been this good before Emily. Had never been this good with anyone else. Need grabbed him by the throat. He pumped his dick in hard brutal strokes. Emotions swamped him. He wanted this, wanted her, always.

Dreams he'd always considered out of his reach, he saw actualized with perfect clarity with the woman writhing and canting her hips beneath him. Pleasure unlike anything he'd ever known took hold. He lengthened his strokes, making each one count. Her cries of ecstasy drove him to withering heights of passion.

With his touch, he didn't just fuck her, he tried to imprint himself on her. Show her with his body that she was precious to him, that she was the only woman for him. He knew in the recesses of his soul that there would never be another for him. That she and only she held the keys to his heart and, he feared, his soul.

The vulnerability of that truth, his heart fully engaged by Emily, for her, rocketed through him. Emily had opened him up in ways he hadn't thought possible, and she called to him in a way no other woman ever had. Enthralled by her, Mason held her tight, increasing the tempo of his hammered thrusts. Her mewls of passion drove him wild and tested the boundaries of his control.

He wanted her not just for a night, but for always. He wanted her warming his bed from here to eternity.

Overcome with the rising tide of his feelings for her, Mason gave her all of him as his control snapped. He fucked her like a man possessed. Groaned as her sweet cunt spasmed around his pistoning cock. Roared as he spilled himself inside, her pussy quaking around his dick, drawing out his climax.

His torso lay against her back, her hands trapped between them as he fought to regain his senses. He kissed the back of her neck as he straightened and got a throaty moan from her.

He undid her cuffs and massaged her arms before sitting on one of the chairs and pulling her onto his lap.

He caressed her cheek with his knuckles. Emily looked up at him, her eyes clouded with emotions. "Well, that's one way to stop an argument," she murmured.

"I meant what I said, Em, it's my job to take care of you. Even when you're too stubborn to take care of yourself," he said.

She softened against him. "Mason," she sighed, "I know you mean well. But maybe we need to talk about some boundaries. How would you like it if I came into your office and started ordering you about?"

He would hate it. He understood her point. Not that he was in the wrong here. She'd been working herself into the ground all week long—for him, for the lodge. "I'm still going to put my foot down if I think you're pushing too hard. You've been working around the clock this past week. And while I know the event tomorrow is a huge deal, you were dead on your feet in the kitchen. I won't have you making yourself sick. So, for tonight, just let me take care of you. I'm going to feed you and then tuck you into bed."

She shook her head but her gaze was soft and inviting. "What am I going to do with you?"

"I can think of a couple things off the top of my head," he said, wagging his eyebrows at her.

She snuggled against him and murmured, "Me too."

And his heart tumbled over in his chest. He cuddled her close, enjoying the way she felt in his arms. She fit him perfectly. She sighed against him as he stroked a hand over her back.

Mason wasn't certain how long they sat there, but it was long enough that Emily fell asleep against him. Her soft snores filled the kitchen and clutched at his heart. She belonged to him now, in every way imaginable. She called forth every protective instinct he had inside him. Emily was easily the most affectionate woman of his acquaintance.

He loved it. Loved her need of him, to be close to him. That she didn't push him away after sex but clung to him. Even in the dead of night, he craved having her near. Moving gently, he stood with her in his arms and carried her up to his bed.

Once they made it past the Oktoberfest event tomorrow, they needed to talk. He wanted her with him, here in his home. He knew it was a big step. And he'd have to make sure Cole was fine with it too. But his bed and his arms each night was where she belonged.

CHAPTER 23

Saturday morning dawned bright and early. The first rays of gauzy sunlight filtered in through the curtains. The weatherman had called for sunshine and crisp fall temperatures. And, seeing the sunlight, Emily smiled. That was one worry off her back. When you hosted an outdoor event, you were beholden to Mother Nature's whims.

She didn't even remember coming up to Mason's bedroom last night. He'd been correct. She had been tired. But they were still going to need to work on their communication. Although, thinking about last night and the way he'd so easily tossed her over his shoulder all caveman-like and brought her here, was it any wonder that her entire system just seemed to sigh at the memory of it?

Mason lay on his back beside her, sleeping peacefully. She yearned to touch him, caress his jaw, run her fingers over the broad expanse of his chest, down the happy trail bisecting the six pack of his stomach, and then dip her hand beneath the blankets to his shaft.

But if she did that, she would never get up and conquer the million or so items on her to do list for today. Regretfully,

Emily shifted, tossing the blankets back to slip from Mason's bed.

"Just where do you think you're going?" he mumbled, his voice gruff and sleep laden. Just at the sound of his voice, which always reminded her of dark rum and cigars, warmth pooled in her belly.

"Mason, as much as I would love to stay in bed and while the day away with you, I have to get to work. People will be here in a few short hours, demanding food."

He tugged her into his arms and she didn't resist, much. She had to at least save face and not show him that, where he was concerned, she had no willpower. It was like if she were left alone in the Ding Dong factory. Mason murmured and his hands—God, she loved his hands, those big, working man hands—slid over her back and cupped her bottom. "That sounds like fun. I think we should do that tomorrow. Spend the day here. You've earned it."

"But the Elkhorn..." she protested, albeit rather feebly, because at the thought of staying in this big comfy four-poster bed with Mason all day, her entire system electrified.

"I already decided to keep the restaurant closed tomorrow. There will be some clean up we'll need to do. But all the club members will be here in force to help with that. So other than that, it's the plan for Sunday."

She melted against him. "I like the sound of that."

He chuckled. "I thought you might. And we can move your stuff in here tomorrow too."

"Move my stuff here? You want me to live with you?" she asked with a breathy whisper as Mason rolled her beneath him and nestled his big body between her thighs.

"You're already here most nights. It would make it easier— on both of us, but you especially—if you had more than just a toothbrush here, don't you think?"

She cupped his cheek. His stubble prickled over her skin. And she held his gaze. "Are you sure?"

"Yeah. I am. I like you in my bed every night."

She sighed. There were times she wanted to strangle the pig-headed man and there were others, like now, when he made her insides melt faster than butter in a microwave. "Me too."

"Is that a yes?" he asked, flexing his hips in a gentle rhythm, his shaft rubbing against her sex. The delicious feel of him against her was making her so hot. She wanted to forget everything else but him and the way he loved her.

"It's an: I will think about it and let you know after Oktoberfest is done today," she replied with a guttural moan at the intensity of passion he evoked within her body.

"I bet I can convince you," he murmured, his gaze infused with desire.

"Oh yeah, how?" she asked with a catch in her voice as his hands cupped her rear and the head of his shaft pressed against her core.

He leaned in and whispered a suggestion in her ear. Her breath expelled in a rush of desire.

"But the event?" she said.

"I need ten minutes, tops," he said, rolling his hips and plunging inside her quivering sheath.

"Well, if you're sure it won't take longer than that," she said, arching her back as he thrust.

"It won't," he promised with a groan as his lips claimed hers.

And then every last thought fled as he proved just how skilled he was at making her forget everything but the wicked delights of his body moving against hers. And it only took him five minutes before she was screaming his name.

$\sim$

OKTOBERFEST ROLLED out and opened with only a few minor hitches. Nothing to worry about. There was always a problem that needed to be addressed at these types of affairs. By noon, the lodge grounds were crowded with families and throngs of people.

The food was going out as fast as their fingers could make it but everyone was enjoying themselves. Spencer was working the beer booth, along with Matt from the club. They had another beer station set up on the opposite end, with the lodge bartenders working it.

Emily could hear the loudspeaker down at the stables announcing the next smattering of events down there. Alex was giving different demonstrations and had even called in a few favors with some of his rodeo buddies.

She had spied Jackson, along with a few other officers from the Jackson Police Department he'd roped into working the event today, helping keep the peace and keeping an eye on anyone who had one too many beers. Even though they'd placed a cap on the number of beers a person could have, that didn't mean some knucklehead wouldn't get around it.

Cole was over at a booth, giving demonstrations on outdoor survival skills. A few of the subs were handling the face painting, which was a huge hit with the kids. Sexy Garrett was holding a raffle over in the tent area for a chance to win a luxury weekend getaway at his ski resort.

Carter and Jenna had shown up with their son. Meghan was with them and Emily couldn't help but notice the way she and Spencer glared at one another.

And then there was Mason, moving from booth to booth, helping her oversee the event.

Butterflies flapped their wings in her belly every time she caught his heated gaze. She carted another pan of freshly baked pretzels and couldn't stop herself from looking for him. She was a moth to his flame. And now he'd asked her to move in with him. It was all happening so fast.

Did she want to live with him? God, yes. She loved sleeping beside him every night. Loved feeling his strong arms around her. Loved... him.

And wasn't that just her problem? She'd fallen so far, so fast that she felt like she was trying to keep her sense of self, worried that she would lose herself in Mason.

Then again, hadn't she already?

It was the question that plagued her throughout the day. Her heart was already on board. It was Emily's head that needed convincing. She took over for Tibby at the booth in the afternoon so that she and her daughter could experience some of the fun. She handed out pretzels with nacho cheese sauce. There were the bratwursts stewed with sauerkraut, caramelized onion pretzel rolls with caraway salt, jumbo pretzels with beer cheese sauce, wiener schnitzel, beer braised brisket, traditional Sauerbraten, potato salad by the gallons, meat pastries, and more. And those were only the main dishes. They didn't include the hot dogs, burgers, grilled chicken, French fries or the myriad number of desserts.

The event ran until seven thirty. But by six, the hordes were beginning to diminish. That was fine by Emily, however, because they were leaving with smiles on their faces. She didn't stop running all day, until the final guests climbed into their cars and pulled away.

She smiled as they began cleaning up, everyone working in concert to take down stations. She wrapped up doggy bags of the leftovers for club members and volunteers. Both Alex and Garrett professed their undying love for her food.

She was in the kitchen, overseeing the last of the clean-up, when warm hands slid around her midsection.

"Come with me. We can finish the rest in the morning," Mason murmured. His voice carried a hint of sexy gruffness that always stirred her, even when she was ready to drop from sheer exhaustion.

"You're right. I already sent everyone else home," she said, turning in his arms.

"And we should do the same." He nuzzled her neck.

"I like the sound of that," she replied and let him tow her away from the kitchen and out the back door.

The moon was full and bright overhead. Nearby, an owl hooted. And Emily felt more satisfied and happier than she'd been in a long time. It had a lot to do with the man at her side. Maybe, just maybe, she'd give this cohabitation bid a try.

MASON GUIDED EMILY up the path to his house, pleased that she hadn't fought him about leaving the rest of the clean-up until tomorrow. She was dead on her feet. He was, too, but his first priority was seeing to her. As they neared the house, he noticed a car he didn't recognize in the driveway.

Tension entered his system. In the darkness, he couldn't tell who was sitting on his stoop. But he didn't like it. His arm around Emily's waist, they headed toward his front porch.

When he spied the all too familiar face, anger riddled his frame.

"Hello, lover," Claire purred as she stood. Even after a stint in jail, she looked good. Granted, the boobs were fake, just like the rest of her, but that didn't diminish the fact that she was a looker from the top of her bleach blonde hair to the tips of her toes. And yet, it was ironic because seeing her now, in the moonlight, with everything fake, she didn't hold a candle to Emily.

"You are not allowed to be anywhere near the lodge and you know it. Get the fuck off my property now and I might think about not calling the cops," Mason snarled. Emily was ramrod straight beside him.

"Oh, pooh, I love it when you get all dominant like that. How would you like me?" she purred again, posing like a cover model on his front steps.

"Leave. Now," Mason commanded. He wanted to throttle the bitch for all the trouble she'd caused him. And for having the balls to come here, to his house.

Claire's gaze drifted over to Emily. "So this is who you replaced me with, who you put in my kitchen? And apparently, in my bed, too."

Emily flinched against him and looked like she'd been struck. "Your kitchen?" she asked, glancing between them.

He hated the horrified expression on her face. The disbelief. The hurt he noticed in the lines of tension in her form. It was his fault. He should have told her about Claire.

"I'm the previous chef, sweetie. Most of the dishes you're making were my creations. And Mason wasn't just my lover but my Master," Claire replied, giving Emily a patronizing and rather condescending glare.

Emily glanced accusingly up at him. "Is what she said true?" she asked, extricating herself from his arm about her waist. Her hands were clenched into fists. And in the moonlight and low half-light from the front porch, he saw her lips tremble.

Fuck.

"Yes," Mason growled. He wouldn't lie to her. Not with the proof standing a few feet from them.

Emily withdrew from him entirely. She wrapped her arms around her torso, her chin jutting out, and said, "I see. You two apparently have some catching up to do."

"Em," Mason said, reaching for her.

Emily shook her head and backed away from him, but not before he caught the sheen of moisture glinting in her eyes. She raced down the path, heading toward her cabin. Mason would catch up with her as soon as he evicted Claire from his property.

He rounded on Claire.

"Why the fuck are you here?" he seethed. Anger vibrated through him. He couldn't believe he'd ever thought she was attractive. Looking at her now, knowing the destruction she'd wrought, his hands clenched into fists. Mainly to keep himself from wringing her damn fool neck.

"Because I missed you. I missed us," she simpered and stepped closer.

"Try again," he snarled, crossing his arms in front of his chest.

"Oh, all right. As a condition of getting probation along with house arrest and not going to prison, I have to pay off everything I took," she explained with a shrug, as if what she'd done to him—done to the lodge—was no skin off her back. It infuriated him. He'd never cared for her, not really. What they'd had together had been nothing more than physical chemistry. And now he couldn't even see how he'd once found her attractive. Hot, even.

"And how do you plan to do that?" Mason asked, refraining from touching her. If he did, he would throttle her to within an inch of her life.

"Daddy doesn't like his princess to have to worry about things like that. This," she said, holding out a white envelope, "should be everything. You'll have to sign some documents too, stating you've been paid, yada, yada, and then you never have to see me again."

"Your father? But you took over two million!" Cole had mentioned something about her being loaded. Mason snatched the envelope from her hands. Opening it, he stared at the check with all the zeroes on it, along with the attached documents.

"What can I say, my family's rich. Dad owns a conglomerate, a few sports teams. I'm not really even sure what he does half the time. And this is coming out of a small portion of my inheritance."

How nice for her. Mason's head spun. She was paying him back every cent she'd taken. "I need my attorney to look at this, verify it with the courts."

"Certainly. Now how would you like me, for old time's sake?" she simpered and fluttered her fake lashes at him.

"Leave now or I won't sign shit, and you can rot in prison for all I fucking care," Mason said, not hiding his anger or the disdain he felt for her.

"Fine. I'm going. Sheesh, what the hell happened to your sense of humor?" Claire said, walking down the stairs and heading past him toward her car.

"You did," he snapped, not hiding an ounce of his disgust.

Claire swiveled and leveled a glance at him. "I'm sorry, Mason. I know I can be a real bitch." She slid into the car. Mason watched until her car had left the lodge property before he headed down the path.

Once he'd explained everything to Emily, it would be fine. They'd crossed a lot of boundaries in the time they'd been together. He'd claimed her as his submissive. They would get past Claire's intervention and interruption, then be stronger for it.

It was time he told her everything.

CHAPTER 24

*E*mily moved around the cabin in a whirlwind. She fought back the tears which threatened and leaked out as she tossed clothing into her suitcases. She was leaving. There was no way she could stay.

How could she have been so stupid? Not that she'd expected Mason to be a monk or assumed he hadn't had a past. After all, she did, and he hadn't held that against her. But the problem was he seemed to like to dally with the chef. And she had been stupid enough, needy enough, naïve enough not to see that she'd merely been a placeholder in his bed.

She bit back the sob as she dumped her clothes into her suitcases, not worried about order.

She could practically hear her mother rolling her eyes in disdain at her stupidity. That she'd been too stupid to see the signs. Why hadn't anyone told her about Claire? Beautiful, stacked, blonde bombshell Claire. And okay, so some of her insecurity came from the fact that she'd always been viewed as lacking by her family, by the society and culture of Los Angeles. She had hips and an ass. She had a small swell of belly —from her snack cake addiction, no doubt.

But she'd given Mason all of herself, every nook and cranny, and had thought it meant something. That she meant something to him… when she was really just the latest to occupy space in his bed.

She wondered, if Claire hadn't appeared, how long she would have lasted in his bed. Heaven help her, she'd begun seeing a permanence with him, had seen herself living in his home, maybe even a little boy with grubby fingers, with his smile and her eyes.

Pain lacerated her form and she gripped the dresser. She couldn't fall apart just yet. She needed to leave first, find a place to stay tonight, even a temporary one, and then she could decide her next move from a place of strength.

"Emily, open up," Mason said, pounding on the front door.

"Go away, Mason. I don't want to talk to you." *Or see you. Or allow you to see that you broke my heart.*

The lock flicked. The door wrenched open. Mason strode in. His gaze narrowed when he spied her suitcases.

"You're leaving," he said accusingly, his gaze incensed.

"There's no point in me staying," she said, defeat clouding her voice as she grabbed the items from the top of the dresser and dropped them into the nearby suitcase.

"Actually, I have a contract with your signature on it. You can't leave without a breach of contract. Not to mention your stake in the restaurant, the cooking classes? Those were your ideas and I expect you to see them through to completion," Mason said with a tick in his clenched jaw. Fury vibrated in his big body.

Like he had a right to that anger. It ignited her own.

"So sue me for breach of contract. I don't give a damn. Tibby can run the cooking classes. She's more than competent enough and has the recipes I had planned. As for my stake in the Elkhorn, you can shove it up your ass," she spat and closed the overfull suitcase on the bed.

Mason stood frozen, his face hard as granite, not giving anything away. He snarled, "You can't leave. I'm your Dom, dammit, and I forbid it."

"You forbid it? Fuck you, Mason. And if you even think to lay a finger on me right now, I will scream bloody murder until every guest on the property hears me. Don't worry, seems to me like you're able to find replacements easily enough. I'm sure you will land on your feet." She gestured with a wave toward the door. "Get out. I don't want to see you. If I meant anything to you, you will do as I ask you for once and leave me be."

"Em," he said, approaching her.

She backed up a step and held up her hand to stop him. If he touched her, she would cave. She shook her head. "We're done, Mason. I don't want your excuses or your apologies. I want you out of my life. Understood?"

His face shuttered and closed down. "Why won't you hear me out? Tell me that, at least. You owe me that," he said.

"I don't owe you a thing. You want to know why? Because I'm tired of being used. I'm tired of being lied to."

"But I—"

"Do you know why I left La Vida? Why I flipped out on Chef Ormond in public? I showed you the video of me cursing him out in the dining room. But you never stopped to ask yourself why. Chef Ormond pretended to be my family. Pretended that the ideas I had for La Vida were valid. Discussed them with me, let me develop new dishes and revolutionize La Vida. I helped turn it back into a premiere establishment. The night we had critics come to test out the new menu, he never even mentioned me. I slaved to bring that restaurant back from the brink, to bring Ormond back from mediocrity, and he stole my work. Lied to the press that those were his latest creations.

"So you'll forgive me if I don't buy what it is you're selling here, Mason. You should have told me, should have been

213

honest with me from the start. Your silence, that you could omit something that big, especially once I let you in, let you touch me..." She wrapped her arms around her torso. Tears fell unheeded.

"Emily, I'm your Dom. You belong to me," he said, gripping her biceps.

"You lied to me. And then there's the fact that you can't see we're supposed to belong to each other. That's what a real relationship is—where we tell each other things, like 'oh, hey, so funny story, the chef that embezzled those funds I told you about, we were an item and she stole money from my business right beneath my nose.' I've been nothing but open and honest with you, but I cannot abide liars."

"I never lied."

"You omitted the truth. Same difference. You never let me in. Now, take your hands off me. You lost the right to touch me when you couldn't respect me enough to tell me the truth."

"Emily, I'm sorry, I'm—"

"You were right. We don't belong in each other's worlds," she said. "Just go, Mason. If you have any feelings for me at all, please respect me enough to leave me be. I don't want to see anymore. You're not my Dom. I don't belong to you."

He flinched at her words. They stood like two wary boxers in a ring, awaiting the bell for the final knock out round. Then he nodded. His expression, which had held such tenderness not an hour ago, was hard as stone.

"Where will you go?" he asked.

"That's no longer your concern now, is it?"

Then Mason strode out of her cabin without a backward glance. He slammed the door behind him. It shuddered on its hinges. Emily's knees finally gave out and she slid into a heap on the floor. She'd finish packing in just a minute. When she could breathe again.

CHAPTER 25

*A*fter a sleepless night at the hotel she'd found in downtown Jackson last night, Emily had reached some conclusions. She loved it here in Jackson and didn't want to leave. Just because it hadn't worked out with Mason and the lodge didn't mean there weren't other restaurants in the area that could use her expertise. Although that may take some time. So what she needed was a job in the meantime.

Emily didn't want to involve Tibby or Faith, as much as she adored them. Cole was out because of his allegiance to his brother and the lodge. But there was one person she'd met since she'd moved here whom she knew she could count on.

After a brief shower and room service breakfast, she headed out with a destination in mind. The double doors with the cowboy on the bucking bronco actually brought a smile to her lips. It was familiar.

Emily stepped inside the Teton Cowboy and approached the hostess, Paige.

"Is he in?" Emily asked, her hands clenched at her sides. If this didn't work, she'd have to rethink her game plan.

Paige nodded and said, "Yes, let me get him for you."

Emily said, "You're busy and I know the way to his office. It's urgent and private." She blinked back the sudden onslaught of moisture.

Paige looked at her with sympathy in her chocolate gaze. She waved her along and said, "Okay, go on back."

Emily walked through the Teton Cowboy, ignoring the entrance to Cuffs & Spurs. It made her heart ache just thinking about it. But it would get better, given time. Maybe, eventually, she could go back there and not feel like her heart was being ripped from inside her chest.

At the closed door to Spencer's office, she inhaled a deep breath and knocked.

"Come in," Spencer said.

Emily pushed the door open. He was reclining in his leather chair, studying a folder in his hand. He wasn't dressed in business attire today but jeans and a black tee that was molded to his broad chest.

He raised a dark brow when he spied her and smiled. "Emily, didn't expect to see you here. I figured you still be in bed after yesterday. Great job, by the way. Have a seat."

She closed the door behind her and did as he asked. Her stomach was clenched in knots.

"What can I do for you?"

"I was wondering if you had any positions for a cook. The temporary run with the Elkhorn isn't going to work after all, and I just need something, anything will do, until another job opens up," she said, fighting back tears.

"Why isn't the lodge going to work out?" Spencer asked, his gaze holding hers like he was attempting to divine all of her secrets. The problem was, if she gave him full disclosure, she'd turn into a weeping mess again.

She shook her head, trying to clear the moisture entering her field of vision, and glanced down at her lap. "It's just not the right fit. But I'd like to stay in Jackson and to do that, I need a job. And a place to live. If you know of any short-term rentals that aren't too pricey, I'd appreciate the referral, as well."

"Well, this is rather unexpected," Spencer replied.

Emily steeled herself, then lifted her head to see Spencer's black gaze studying her.

He continued, "I thought you and Mason were an item. He claimed you as his submissive the other night in the club. I'm surprised he let you leave."

"We aren't anything to each other. He doesn't own me," she said, fighting the sudden onslaught of tears.

"But you love him," Spencer stated. The kindness in his eyes was almost too much. Emily winced. Were her feelings for Mason that obvious? Because it was true. She did love him, with everything she had. Which was why she felt like her heart had been ripped from her chest.

She replied, "It doesn't matter the way I feel. It's done. Do you have a job for me in your kitchens or not? Because if not, I need to find something, anything will do at this point. I can't go back to Los Angeles."

"If it's money you need, I can get you a loan."

She shook her head. "No, I don't do loans. I earn my way or not at all."

Spencer's gaze never wavered, his eyes seemed to catch every flicker of emotion. Then he said, "I could use an extra line cook. It's nothing fancy. Not what you're used to, of course, but it should help until you can find another position as head chef. Here in Jackson that shouldn't be hard if you're intending to stay."

Her shoulders relaxed and the knot of worry unclenched in her chest. "Thank you, Spencer. I appreciate it."

"You don't have any idea where you plan to stay? Where are you staying now?" he asked.

"At the Rotunda Inn, for now. That's the next thing on my agenda. If you know of a place that's not sleazy and relatively reasonable price-wise, I'd be in your debt," she said. She wanted something quaint that didn't cost more than she wanted to spend.

"Come with me," Spencer ordered, standing up from his desk.

"Where are we going?" she asked.

"You'll see. Just come with me," he repeated, brooking no room for argument. As he would be her new boss, she didn't argue. She didn't have the heart or the energy. If she pissed him off, her situation could become precarious. No job, no money, no place to live and she'd have to crawl back to Los Angeles where her parents would say *I told you so*.

Her stomach churned in dread at the thought.

She followed him past the kitchen and storage areas to a set of stairs that led to a second floor. She followed him up, curious where he was taking her. At the entrance, there was a keypad lock that he punched a code into and then opened the heavy wooden door.

Her jaw dropped as she stepped inside. It was elegant and modern, all sleek lines. Not much to the color scheme, shades of gray and ivory. She turned in a circle in the entryway. The hardwood floors were nearly black in color, with slate-colored walls and white trim. "What is this place?"

"My home. It's where I live." He shrugged, heading down the hall. She stood stock still. He didn't expect her to sleep with him, did he?

He shot a bemused glance at her over his shoulder, like he knew precisely what she was thinking, and said, "Relax. I don't ever sleep with the help."

Curious at what he wanted to show her, she trailed after him. He stopped at a closed door. Gripping the handle, he shoved it open and walked inside. Emily had no choice but to follow him. It was a richly furnished bedroom in neutral colors. It was roughly the size of the one she had at the cabin.

More than enough space. He said, "It's not overly large, but you would have your own bathroom, access to the kitchen, and living room. But my private suite of rooms are off-limits."

"Is that where you hide the bodies?" she asked.

Spencer chuckled. "Among other things. I'll program a code for you at the door, that way you don't need a key and you can stay here, temporarily, until you figure something out."

"Why are you doing this?" she asked, amazed at his generosity and kind offer. He was going to let her stay here until she got back on her feet.

"You're one of us, a member of our club—and we take care of our own," he said with a shrug, as if that should explain everything.

"Thank you. You don't have to do this, but I will take it."

"Good. Now, let me go program that code and then I have a million things to do. You start on Monday. That should give you the day to pack your stuff from the Rotunda Inn and get yourself moved in here," Spencer said. "Oh, and one more thing, here's my number, program it in your phone and I will text you the code. Don't share it with anyone. I'll get it to you within the hour. There's parking around the back of the building for employees where you can park your car. The key code I'm programming for you will let you into the parking lot as well."

"Yes, Sir. I will," she said. After thanking Spencer again, Emily left the Teton Cowboy. This was good. A positive development. She didn't have to go slinking back to California a failure.

Emily just had to survive. Pretend like her heart wasn't slowly bleeding out.

CHAPTER 26

*M*ason spent the following week leading extra guided walking tours booked last minute that Cole wasn't able to cover since he was on an overnight fishing excursion. He was glad for the chance to get away from the lodge. It gave him the chance to mull over the fight he and Emily had had on Saturday night.

There was no way around it. He'd fucked up. Big time.

Only he had no idea how to go back and fix it. How could he explain that Claire hadn't meant anything to him? Not in the way Emily did. Claire had been fun. She'd revved his engines and he couldn't deny that when they'd been an item, he'd enjoyed her charms. He was a guy and had been unattached. He shouldn't be lambasted because he had a past.

And while he admitted he hadn't told Emily that he and Claire had been an item, there had never been a chance.

Although that wasn't true. He'd had chances aplenty. But any time he'd considered telling her, Emily would smile at him —or, in her case, snap at him—and he'd been a goner, more concerned with feeling her beneath him, feeling her unravel, watching her startled shock as he pushed her boundaries.

The first group he led was a family of five who were overzealous hikers. Brian and Mary Shannon with their kids; Joe, Katie, and Charlie—all teenagers who were not necessarily happy at the forced activity. They got along well enough, but by the time the hike was finished for the day, their Subaru putting the lodge in its rearview mirror, Mason had been exhausted.

Instead of calling Emily, he'd trudged home, showered, and cooked a frozen pizza for dinner. While normally he would have been more than satisfied with the pizza, it couldn't hold a damn candle to Emily's handmade confections. In the weeks she'd been around, he'd begun to look forward to and count on her buttermilk biscuits for breakfast and having that day's special for dinner.

The following day he had an all-day trail hike with a group of ten. Five couples in their late thirties to early forties who had all been friends since college and liked to meet for a reunion every other year. It was a simple excursion on a moderately difficult trail.

Again, by the time he'd made it home after the hike, he'd simply poured himself into bed and not moved until the next morning.

So the week had sped by and he'd yet to speak to Emily. He'd tried calling her a dozen times but she was avoiding his calls. Fuck, he'd missed her in his bed, which was a new sensation. He'd never missed a woman before. Never thought he would want a woman in his bed permanently.

But there you had it. Mason wanted Emily back. Had realized too damn late that he loved her.

And he had no experience in trying to win a woman back. He'd never lacked for a bed partner at the club. Usually the subs were lined up and he could take his pick. He had enjoyed the submissives at the club—and they him.

In the past, if things had gotten too serious or taken on a

hefty weight of responsibility, he'd been the one to cut ties. Cole had been correct when he'd said that Mason didn't do permanence. But that was before Emily.

She made him want things, stuff he had never considered until now. Like building a family, longevity and, yes, permanence. And, for the first time, his balls didn't shrivel up at the thought.

Even though he was swamped with paperwork that he'd not been able to tackle this week because of his tours, Emily was never far from his mind.

He contacted his lawyer, Kent O'Brien, to check and see if the plea deal Claire had mentioned was accurate. Considering the way that bitch had deceived him, Mason wouldn't be able to celebrate until he was certain it was official.

"Mason, I'm glad you called. I just finished speaking with the prosecuting attorney's office. Claire was correct in that her attorney did work out a plea bargain agreement where she will get six months of house arrest, then five years' probation to be served out of the State of New York, and will not see the inside of a prison cell if the restitution is paid in full. Her attorney, a Dan Fogler out of Manhattan—real asshole, too, if you want my opinion—confirmed that the check is real and legitimate."

Mason relaxed. There was an unclenching in his gut and he took a deep breath. "What are the steps we need to take to get this resolved? I'm fine with her plea deal if all the money she stole is repaid in a lump sum."

"Well, there are a few stipulations we should add. Her attorney has an addendum he wants you and Cole to sign that basically states you aren't going to try and sue her for civil damages."

"It would serve her right if we did," Mason muttered.

"If you want to go that route, I don't blame you. Personally, I would. But working in this business, I'm a bit more vindictive than you. However, if we do, it could take you longer to get the restitution money."

He grimaced. While everything they had done to save the lodge had worked and would keep this place chugging along through the end of the year, the thought of not being able to give Christmas bonuses to their employees who tended to count on those at the end of the year rubbed Mason the wrong way. Had Claire dinged his pride and hurt him with her actions? Absolutely. Was he going to be a dick about it and go after her for more? No.

It wasn't worth it. Wasn't worth continuing this saga. He wanted her out of his life for good.

"No, Kent. I think, at the end of the day, Cole and I would just like it done as quickly as possible. I do want a stipulation that she is prohibited from setting foot on any and all lodge property. I don't want her within five hundred feet of it at the minimum. She is not to engage in any contact with myself or Cole. I also want an NDA that states she cannot talk about the lodge, its inner workings, or the people here—or even mention this place, or we will sue the fucking pants off her."

"Finally, a client with some goddamn sense. I can have those drawn up by the start of next week and will contact her attorney to hammer out the last of the details," Kent said.

"Thanks for that."

"You and Cole owe me a day out on the lake," Kent said.

"We'll set up a day soon, before winter sets in. Take the boat out and see what we can catch."

"Good deal. I'll be in touch as soon as everything is finalized for you to sign," Kent murmured and disconnected the call.

That was something at least.

Cole strode in, slamming the door behind him, obviously incensed.

"Really, Mason? Did you have to go and fuck things up with

Emily? And fail to tell me about it before my three-night fishing trip? For fuck's sake, what did you do?" he snapped, taking a seat across from him.

"I'm working on it. We had a fight. Couples do it all the time. It's no cause for concern," Mason said, although he was still working on locating her and she wasn't answering her phone when he called. He had no idea where to even look for her, or whether she had even stayed in Jackson. For all he knew, she'd high-tailed it back to Los Angeles. If that was the case, he would hunt her down and haul her ass back here. Now that the legalities with Claire were wrapping up, he could take the time off to fetch her back.

"Oh, really? You think there's nothing to get upset about? I just had lunch with Spencer. Apparently, Emily went to see him this past Sunday about a job and place to live. She's working at the Teton Cowboy as a line cook. And moved in with Spencer until she can find a place."

"What?" Mason asked. At least she was here. Why hadn't Spencer contacted him and let him know?

"You didn't know?" Cole asked.

"No. We had a fight. Claire was here after the Oktoberfest, sitting on our front porch like she'd owned the damn place. Emily found out about Claire and me before I had a chance to explain."

Cole cocked his head. "You hadn't told her about Claire yet? You're a fucking idiot, you know that?"

"That's beside the point. The point is, we had a fight and I will fix it. We've been a little busy this week, what with the extra tours, and then this shit with Claire coming to a close."

"So it's finished then, with Claire?"

"More or less. I just spoke to Kent. Her attorney made a deal where she doesn't serve more than house arrest as long as the restitution is paid in full at the time of sentencing in one lump sum. I agreed that we were fine with that. Kent's going to add a few things to the agreement they want us to sign which will basically say we won't go after her for monetary civil damages and the like. I want to make sure she never sets another foot on our property and can't talk about the lodge, its inhabitants, or even the club. I realize that the club has an NDA clause, and will get Spencer up to speed once this is all finalized."

"I agree on the legal aspect. It will be nice to have that money back in the business accounts," Cole replied thoughtfully.

"It will. Especially since we changed everything over to new accounts, with new logins and passwords, so she can't get her grubby fingers on another cent."

"As for Emily, you're a fucking idiot," Cole said.

"Say that one more time and you can sleep in the fucking stables," Mason said.

"Mason, you've always had it easy where women are concerned. And until she came along, you never were serious about one. I've seen the way you two are together. Don't throw it all away because you're stupid. You should have told her about Claire. I don't know why you would have kept what she did to you a secret."

Mason rubbed a hand over his face and looked at his brother. "I messed up. It's not been easy knowing I let you down, let our parents down by my actions. All the people who work for us count on me to do the right thing by them, and because I thought with my dick instead of my head, I failed them."

Cole rolled his eyes. "You always were one for theatrics. So Claire screwed you over, boo-freaking-hoo. You're fucking up the best thing to ever happen to you because of her. I may not have been on board with you and Emily being an item at the beginning, but I watched you with her. You forget, I know you better than anyone. I've never seen you that way with another woman. So fix it."

"You're one to talk. You haven't been serious about anyone since Lana," Mason snapped, even though his brother was one hundred percent correct. He'd managed to screw up the best thing that had ever happened to him.

Cole's gaze narrowed and his face turned to stone. Then he bit out, "At least I had the courage to put my neck on the line and loved her. I've had the love of my life. There won't be another. And you're changing the subject. Stop deflecting, this isn't about me, but you and Emily. No matter what, you need to convince her to come back and be our chef. She's fucking brilliant in the kitchen."

"I don't know how," Mason replied, feeling more than a little defeated.

Cole rolled his eyes. "You're a fucking Master. Start acting like one. And you might want to, I don't know, apologize for being a moron. I know it chafes the pride a bit, but when you look into the future, do you want one with her in it, or not?"

Mason leaned back in his seat. Cole was right. As usual. On every account, except one. Cole was wrong about Lana being his one and only—but he'd leave that alone for now.

"I will take care of it. Even if I can't fix my personal relationship with her, I will see that she comes back as chef of the Elkhorn."

"Give her a higher stake in the restaurant," Cole offered with a casual shrug.

"What?" Mason replied, certain he hadn't heard right.

"She originally asked for a partnership, split fifty-fifty with us. I say give her that. I know we'd want to do it all legally so she can't sell her shares back to anyone but us. Kent is already fixing up the Claire thing. May as well have him draw up a partnership agreement too."

Rubbing his chin, Mason turned it over in his mind. With

resolution of the legal woes from Claire in sight, they would be back in the black again and they could take the hit to their finances. And, knowing Emily as he did now, if she was given free rein, she'd make the place sparkle. She was intelligent and had a sound head for the business side of things, to boot.

"If you're on board with that, I'll call Kent back and get the arrangements made," Mason said, still wondering how he was going to approach Emily.

Cole was correct. He was a Master and he'd not been acting like it.

After Cole left the office, Mason contacted Kent about the partnership agreement with Emily. It was a move in the right direction. He had a few other things he needed to put into place if he was going to win her back. She still wasn't answering his calls so he did the next best thing. He called Spencer.

"I was wondering when I was going to hear from you," Spencer said.

"You should have called me the moment she came to you," Mason growled.

"She asked me not to. She's cried over you, a lot. Just thought you should know."

"And is she crying on your shoulder?"

Sounding more than a little exasperated, Spencer replied, "Dude, she's not with me. I'd never touch her and you know it, so get your fucking panties out of the twist they're in. She came to me, asked for a job and help finding a place to live. I did both. It's what I would do for any sub in need."

Mason rubbed a hand over his face. Spencer was a good guy. He never should have blasted him. But where Emily was concerned, he was downright possessive. He said, "Tell her to go to the club tonight."

"That I can do." Spencer chuckled.

"Thanks for looking out for her, Spencer."

"It's what I'm here for."

Mason disconnected the call, then went to work on the rest of the preparations for tonight. Before the night was over, Emily would be back at the lodge. The only question that remained was whether he could convince her to forgive him.

CHAPTER 27

*T*hat afternoon, Spencer had stopped in the kitchens at the Teton Cowboy and requested that Emily attend the club that evening. He said it would be good for her and he wouldn't take no for an answer.

In deference to him, for all the help he'd provided her in her time of need, she couldn't refuse him. Even if Cuffs & Spurs was the last place she wanted to go. And she realized the irony of the fact that she lived two stories above the club. That little tidbit wasn't lost on her.

And going to the club would probably be better than what she'd originally had planned, which was gorging herself on Ho Hos until the pain in her chest subsided or she ran out, whichever happened first.

So, to be a good little club member, Emily went. She even adorned herself in the black leather mini-dress that Spencer had procured and left out for her in his kitchen with a note that she was to wear it.

She didn't want to be here. Had avoided coming to the club because everywhere she looked, she saw Mason. It was like a knife through her chest. And dealing with the pain, with the loss, was the last thing she wanted. Emily was avoiding her feelings like a dieter avoiding the scales.

She sat at the bar, sipping on a Mai Tai and contemplating the dismal state of her life. Her mother had called, again. It was like she could sniff out when Emily's life imploded upon itself. She'd offered Emily a Mercedes this time if she finally gave up her 'silly little quest' to cook for other people.

She sensed movement as someone slid into the seat beside her. Emily grimaced. She wasn't fit company. As much as she didn't want to disregard Spencer's request, she wasn't in the mood for this place.

It hurt to be here. She was adrift in a sea of devastating agony, holding on with all her might to keep from drowning.

She glanced over. Her heart tumbled over in her chest.

Mason.

She drank in the sight of him, still so devastatingly handsome that he took her breath away. He'd not shaved in a few days and dark stubble lined his jaw. His lips, the ones that had brought her such pleasure, were drawn in a compressed line. But it was the heat in his gaze as he studied her that made her tremble.

"Emily. We need to talk," he said, his eyes searching hers.

She wondered what he saw. That she loved him. That her heart felt like it had been wrenched from her chest. That she hadn't been able to breathe without him near. She hated being so weak. Despised that she wanted to cave in and turn to him. But to what end? She didn't know if she could trust him, not after the secret he'd kept from her.

"I don't think it's a good idea. Please go away, Mason," she begged him quietly, proud of herself that her voice didn't waver.

"No. You owe me the chance to explain," he demanded, reaching for her.

She flinched. Anger clawed at her chest. Owed him? That was how he was going to play it? "I don't owe you shit." She slid off her saddle seat. "Just stay away from me, Mason."

Spencer was at the end of the bar as she passed. She said, "I just can't, Spencer. I'm sorry."

She strode past him and took a right down the hall, hurried past the locker rooms to the elevator and rode it up to Spencer's place. The only way you could ride up the elevator was with a code to get in, which meant the only person who could follow her up and gain entrance was Spencer.

She entered the living room and paced, unsure what she should do. The sob that had been lodged in her chest finally broke free. She'd had everything she had ever wanted within her grasp and then lost it all before she knew what happened. Emily slid to the floor in the center of the living room, overcome with her grief.

She was startled when arms lifted her up. She raised her head, expecting Spencer. Instead of Spencer's black gaze, she stared into Mason's molten caramel depths. His scent surrounded her and, if anything, that made the pain more fierce.

"Mason? Go away. Please." She tried to hide her face from him.

But he didn't listen to her pleas. He carried her over to the nearby black leather couch and sat with her on his lap. His hands gently stroked over her back. Her body rejoiced at the feel of him.

"Em, look at me, please. You're breaking my heart, love. Look at me," he commanded softly.

Knowing she didn't have a choice, humiliation filled her. She lifted her face.

"I love you, Em. I'm so sorry I didn't tell you that Claire and I had been an item. It was nothing serious. She meant nothing to me. It was my pride more than anything that kept me from

231

telling you about us. And I didn't want you to think you were taking her place in my affections."

Emily's heart stuttered in her chest. Tears clouded her vision. "You love me?"

He gently cupped her face between both his hands. "More than life itself. My world doesn't work without you in it. And I'm not talking about the lodge or the restaurant. It's having you there at home in the evening when we're both done with work, having you sleep beside me each night and waking up with you in the morning, the way you aren't afraid to challenge me, and are right more often than not. I love you so fucking much. I don't just want a night, or a temporary term as your Dom. I want forever with you. Marry me, Em. I can't promise you that life will always be easy and smooth, but I can promise I will love you until my last breath."

Any resistance she had evaporated. He caught her tears with his thumbs. And his love was there, blazing in his tender gaze.

"I love you, Mason. So much, it terrified me. That, when I heard the full story, I freaked. No one has ever gotten me the way you do. And it hurt to think I was nothing more than a placeholder," she murmured, her hands on his chest.

"I'm so fucking sorry. I never meant to hurt you that way. You're not a damn placeholder for anyone."

Warmth suffused her and she smiled. "I know that now. Yes. Yes, I'll marry you."

"Yeah? You sure? Because once it's official, I'm never letting you go again," Mason said.

"I am," she replied.

"Thank God," Mason growled and closed the short distance between them. Claiming her mouth with his, he kissed her brainless in under ten seconds flat, showing her with more than words that he loved her. She moaned into him. It had only been a week since she'd tasted him and had his lips on hers, but it had felt like eons.

She was greedy for him. She needed him. Emily shifted on his lap until she straddled him. She kissed him back with all the pent-up emotions that she'd bottled in her heart. Her hands slid up his chest to his neck and she knocked his hat off, threading her fingers into his hair to keep his mouth on hers. She loved his mouth.

He caressed her back and gripped her butt. Then his hand snaked up under her skirt. At the feel of his palm against her flesh, she mewled into his mouth.

And then someone cleared their throat. Rather loudly.

Emily lifted her head. She and Mason glanced over to find Spencer, consternation stamped across his features. "I'm just here to get something for the club. Remember my rules: keep it to your bedroom."

"He's right. Sorry, Spencer. We can move it down the hall," Mason said, stroking a gentle hand over her back.

"Actually, take me home, Mason," Emily said.

A smile spread over his face. "I thought you'd never ask. Let's pack your things."

"I never unpacked them," she confessed and heat rushed into her cheeks at the admission.

"Is that right?" Mason gave her a lopsided grin, his eyes glimmering with amusement and love. So much love, it humbled her.

She shrugged and climbed off his lap, shooting Spencer a glance. The man was hiding his grin, but she could tell by the gleam in his gaze that he was pleased with the development. "Thank you, Spencer, for everything. But I quit."

"I'm here if you need anything," Spencer said. "Mason, I'll see you at poker on Sunday."

"Thanks, Spencer," Mason replied.

Spencer nodded and strode past them. Then Emily went to her room with Mason on her heels. She hadn't lied about not unpacking. It had been silly of her, but then again, in her heart of hearts, she had believed they were destined—fated, even. Because no one had ever touched her, moved her the way Mason did. Other than needing to grab her toiletry items from the bathroom, she was ready.

He grabbed her suitcases as she hefted her small leather satchel. "You have your knives?"

"Of course I do."

"Good. Let's get you home."

"I like the sound of that." And oh, did she ever. Mason helped her cart her suitcases down to her car, then had her follow him in his truck back to the lodge and his house. He helped her carry her things inside. But before she could take them upstairs, he stopped her.

"I have something for you. Couple of things, actually," he said, towing her into the kitchen.

On the table was a manila file that he picked up and handed to her. She took it from him, wondering what he was up to. "What is this?"

"Just open it," he said, a small smile playing over his lips.

She flipped the file open and began reading the contents. Her heart thumped. Tears pricked her eyes. She lifted her gaze to his. "Are you sure about this?"

"One hundred percent. There are stipulations, like your percentage can only be sold back to the lodge, that type of thing. But yes, that will make us full partners in the restaurant."

"And Cole's okay with this? When I said fifty percent, that was during negotiations. I never thought or intended to get it."

He shrugged. "I promised you full autonomy, didn't I? This just makes it official. Without you, this place wouldn't have survived. Just like I won't survive without you in my life and in my bed."

"Mason," she sniffled as he tugged her close.

He removed the file from her hand. His palm caressed over her back. "I had to sweeten the pot... if you didn't say yes of your own accord."

And then he surprised her further. He released her and lowered himself onto one knee. "I know you said yes already, but I want to do this properly with you. So, Emily Fox, love me, build a life with me, have children with me."

When he withdrew a ring from his pocket, her sniffles increased. It was a simple, elegant platinum band with a solitary diamond in the center that sparkled up at her. She looked into Mason's eyes, saw his emotions, the love he held for her, and the promise of their future. With her heart in her throat, Emily said, "Yes."

He slid the ring over her finger and it fit perfectly. Just like he fit her so perfectly. Then he stood and swung her up into his arms, carrying her up the stairs.

"I have plans for you tonight, Em. Be as loud as you need to be," he said, shutting the bedroom door behind them.

"But Cole…"

"Is on a weekend fishing trip with clients," he assured her.

"So we have the house to ourselves?"

"Umhmm." He backed her over to the bed. Their hands made quick work of their clothing as they tumbled onto the mattress.

And when Mason slid home inside her, holding nothing back, the love apparent in his eyes, Emily surrendered to the need, to the desire, to his wicked love that she could never live without.

The road she'd driven to get here might have been paved with coffee, Ho Hos, and a love she never expected to find. But it had been worth every mile, because she finally found her way home.

~The End~

ANYA SUMMERS

Born in St. Louis, Missouri, Anya grew up listening to Cardinals baseball and reading anything she could get her hands on. She remembers her mother saying if only she would read the right type of books instead binging her way through the romance aisles at the bookstore, she'd have been a doctor. While Anya never did get that doctorate, she graduated cum laude from the University of Missouri-St. Louis with an M.A. in History.

Anya is a bestselling and award-winning author published in multiple fiction genres. She also writes urban fantasy and paranormal romance under the name Maggie Mae Gallagher. A total geek at her core, when she is not writing, she adores attending the latest comic con or spending time with her family. She currently lives in the Midwest with her two furry felines.

Don't miss these exciting titles by Anya Summers and Blushing Books!

Visit her on social media here:
http//www.facebook.com/AnyaSummersAuthor
Twitter: @AnyaBSummers
Goodreads:
https://www.goodreads.com/author/show/15183606.Anya_S
ummers
Sign-up for Anya Summers Newsletter

Connect with Anya Summers:
www.anyasummers.com